I0764660

Convincing Lou

Jodie Wolfe

This is a work of fiction. Names, characters, places, and incidents either are the product of the author's imagination or are used fictitiously, and any resemblance to actual persons living or dead, business establishments, events, or locales, is entirely coincidental.

Convincing Lou

Cover Art by *Nicola Martinez*
White Rose Publishing, a division of Pelican Ventures, LLC
www.pelicanbookgroup.com PO Box 1738 *Aztec, NM * 87410
White Rose Publishing Circle and Rosebud logo is a trademark of Pelican Ventures, LLC

Publishing History
First White Rose Edition, 2024
Electronic Edition ISBN 978-1-5223-0477-7
Hardcover Edition: 978-1-5223-0486-9
Published in the United States of America

Dedication

To my Lord and Savior. When I set out to write this book, I thought I had an understanding of what it meant to trust. But You took me on a different, deeper journey. Even in the midst of heartbreak, You showed me the importance of trusting You through the waters, through the rivers, and through the fires. Even then, You are there.

To Ruth Gunnett – Thank you for answering all my horse questions and helping me write hopefully believable horse scenes. Any mistakes are on my part.

To my dear friend Peggy Grove – Thank you for taking the time to read through and help spot my errors. I'm thankful for you.

To my brother, Gregory Kramer – Your support, prayers, and encouragement through the writing process for this book have meant more than you'll ever know.

To my beloved, David. God gave me a treasure when He brought you into my life. Thank you for sticking with me as we pass through the waters, rivers, and fires. Thank you for your faithful love and support. Your encouragement means the world to me. I love you, sweetheart.

1

When thou passest through the waters, I will be with thee; and through the rivers, they shall not overflow thee: when thou walkest through the fire, thou shalt not be burned; neither shall the flame kindle upon thee. Behold, I will do a new thing; now it shall spring forth; shall ye not know it? I will even make a way in the wilderness, and rivers in the desert. ~ Isaiah 43:2, 19

Burrton Springs, Kansas
December 3, 1877

Four weeks. Four weeks until Ellie Lou Williams lost everything her late husband had worked so hard to achieve. Her chest constricted, and a sharp pain shot the length of her left arm. Where was her deep faith in God when she needed it the most? Dried up and crumpled like a dull, brown leaf separated from the tree in fall. Useless. Ground under a shoe until it became pulverized. No good to anyone. Where was the elusive peace she'd talked about with others, pointing them to Scripture? Why did she feel like the Israelites during the years in the Bible where God was silent in between the Old and New Testament?

Her words from a few months ago rose to haunt her. "My life is in His hands to do with how He sees fit. I will do whatever I can to keep this ranch because it's what Charles would've wanted, but if it somehow gets taken away, I still must trust God has a plan even when I can't see it." She snorted. That was easy to say until she had to actually live it. *I feel as if I've lived a lifetime since I said those words, God. If I lose the ranch, I have nowhere to go. Nobody alive to rely on*. She toed her boot in the thick dust along the street. *Are you listening, God?*

"Hi, Ellie Lou." Mary Scott waved. "I haven't seen you in town since all that excitement at your ranch a few months back."

She wouldn't call being held at gun point 'excitement.' Too bad there hadn't been any reward money for the capture of the outlaws who'd held her. If there had been she wouldn't be in this mess.

"Were you planning to stop by Betty's shop?" The elderly woman slipped her arm through Ellie Lou's. "Or perhaps you were going to see Gertrude at her place instead."

Ellie Lou glanced at the shop. The sign said Ruffles And Stitches. She hadn't seen much of her newly wedded friend, Gertrude Valentine, but a visit could wait until another time. "I can come in for a few moments to see Betty."

"Oh, good. She's been in such a dither." Mary tugged her in the direction of her niece's shop.

Ellie Lou held back a sigh. Best to focus on someone else's troubles instead of her own for a bit. "What's got her upset?"

The bell above the door chimed as they entered the dress shop.

"There you are, Aunt Mary." Betty Hadler fanned her flushed cheeks. "We've got to do something."

Mary released Ellie Lou's arm and patted her niece's hand. "Now, dear, I'm sure your fiancé will show soon."

"But he was supposed to be here weeks ago. He said he only had to make a short stop in Topeka. I'm afraid something's happened to him." Betty withdrew a handkerchief from the pocket in her skirt and dabbed her moist eyes. "The stagecoach has been coming regularly, so he couldn't have been delayed because of that."

"Now, now. Don't you fret."

Ellie Lou cleared her throat, unsure whether to step away from the private conversation or to remain. She took a step backward

"I'm thinking of hiring someone to go after him." Betty sniffed and wiped her nose.

Ellie Lou's ears perked. Could this be an answer to her prayers? *Please, Lord.*

"I'm sure that's not needed." Mary squeezed her niece's shoulders.

Betty shook her head, her carefully pinned brown curls bouncing with each motion. "No. I'll see if I can pay someone seventy-five dollars to bring Jeffrey here. Our wedding is less than a month away.

Something's happened to him. I feel it in my bones." A tear trickled down her pale cheeks.

Ellie Lou gasped at the extravagant amount. She swallowed. The sum would more than cover the money she owed the bank. She could pay off the loan and not have to worry about her home being taken away. Surely this was God intervening in her situation.

"That's way too much, Betty." Mary's lips pinched together.

"He's worth it. I'm sure he would do the same if I was the one missing." Betty glanced out the window.

"If you tell me more about him, perhaps I can go and find your fiancé and bring him back to Burrton Springs." Ellie Lou's words escaped before she had time to fully weigh the decision. "I don't have anything going on right now and can easily get away." She could take her two remaining horses with her, which would enable her to leave the ranch for a bit. It wasn't as if she had fields to tend.

"Truly?" Betty's eyes filled with additional tears.

Ellie Lou quickly calculated the mileage to Topeka. It was doable to get there and back, allow time for the search, return to collect the compensation, and deposit it in the bank to pay off her loan before the end of the year. It had to be the Lord finally speaking to her. Finally, He was breaking His silence.

Betty withdrew something from her pocket. "I have a tintype of my fiancé. It should help you find him." She handed it to Ellie Lou.

Ellie Lou studied the serious looking young man. "Do you mind if I take it along? I promise to take good care of it."

Betty nodded. "You can't tell it from the tintype, but he has light brown hair and blue eyes. He's well-to-do. We've known each other since childhood." She twisted her hands. "I just don't understand what could be keeping him so long. I'm afraid…"

Ellie Lou touched Betty's arm. "I'm sure he's fine. Just hasn't been able to get a message to you. Don't you worry. I'll find him for you. In fact, I'll head home now so I can get an early start in the morning." She tucked the tintype into her reticule.

"Are you sure it's safe, dear?" Mary frowned. "I've never heard of a woman riding that far on horse by herself."

Her heart stalled a beat. She'd learned the hard way trouble had a way of happening when you least expected it. Ellie Lou stood a little taller. If she took extra precautions, no harm would come her way. But it wouldn't work to go dressed as a woman. She'd have to don her husband's clothes and pose as a man. If she could perform this one job, her problems would be solved.

~*~

As soon as Caleb Dawson performed this last job, his problems would be solved. He'd only agreed to the assignment because it was on his way to Burrton Springs. At least he hoped he'd find his old friend, Joshua Walker, there. Last Caleb had heard, Josh had settled in the small town. Rumors had circulated that the former Deputy U.S. Marshal had moved to where his sister lived. Caleb had worked with the man on and off through the years and never knew Josh had a sister.

"G'dyup, Chestnut. The sooner we find this varmint, the sooner we can start a new life." One where he didn't have constant reminders of the darker side of the law. He'd had his fill. He was more than ready to start a life where trouble didn't come his way. Maybe he'd learn to relax and let down his defenses.

His horse surged into motion.

Caleb withdrew the wanted poster from his vest pocket. A drawing of the criminal stared back at him. The man had last robbed a stagecoach and killed three passengers. A young man and a couple. The description also stated the outlaw had robbed the bank in Topeka. Caleb had stumbled across the stagecoach shortly after the theft. He'd hoped to save the passengers, but they were already dead when he'd arrived on the scene. Lined up and shot in the back. All three had fallen with their faces on the ground. He shook his head to rid himself of the memory.

Don't rightly know what causes a man to go bad, Lord. He chomped down on the inside of his cheek. He'd seen enough pain during the war to know it changed a man. Made him hollow inside.

~*~

Three days later

Ellie Lou was beginning to regret her decision to chase down a delinquent groom. What did she know about tracking? Apparently, nothing. Her muscles complained as she knelt and studied the dirt. A myriad of tracks covered the path. How was she supposed to determine who left them? She hated to admit it, but she was out of her element. She studied the sky. The purple clouds tinged with green that had dotted the horizon at dawn were long gone. The day had started unseasonably warm but now there was a chill in the air. A drop of rain splashed on her face.

She bit back a groan as she stood. Rain would wash away what little of a trail she'd found. Ellie Lou couldn't hold back a yawn. Sleeping on the ground had been harder than she'd anticipated. She ran a hand along the tight muscles in her neck. Her head throbbed with each beat of her heart. Using a saddle as a pillow hadn't helped matters.

Ellie Lou dropped down and went to the pack horse. She dug into the pack on Honey's back. She found her husband's rubber coat and pulled it on over her own. Gathering the reins, she boosted up into the saddle. She glanced at the sky. It would be dark soon, especially since the rain was increasing. Best find a decent place to make camp. Somewhere off the trail where she'd be safe. Away from any onlookers stumbling upon her. The only trouble was, the flat Kansas prairie didn't have many places to conceal her.

The saddle creaked as she kneed Storm, her horse, into motion. The stallion tossed his head. Ellie Lou patted his sleek, dark neck. She clicked her tongue so Honey would follow them. Light from a campfire glimmered ahead. Best to find somewhere to hide the horses before she crept for a closer look.

A slight dip in the land appeared on her left. A small cluster of cottonwood trees nestled in the middle of the gully. She urged Storm towards it. Seconds later she dismounted, tying both horses to a branch of one of the trees.

Ellie Lou patted both of her horses and whispered, "Keep quiet, you two. I'll be back in a bit." She slung a length of rope over her left shoulder and slipped her husband's pistol from his gun belt. Her hand shook at the weight of the gun. She should've spent some time getting familiar with it before she took off on this adventure.

Her husband, Charles, had always talked about teaching her to shoot, yet she'd been too busy to find time for those lessons. But he was gone, and she'd never learned. She regretted that now.

Direct me, Lord. Keep me safe. She took a deep breath. *And help me find Jeffrey.* Her breath hitched in her chest, and she pinched the bridge of her nose. She'd been in such a hurry to start her quest and find the overdue groom, she'd forgotten to ask what his last name was. Great. What kind of bounty hunter was she? Well, not exactly a bounty hunter, but still. She knew better than to rush off without a thorough plan. Or at least she thought she did. Apparently, desperation caused her to do crazy things and not think straight.

She scrunched her toes in her husband's boots. The sock stuffed into the toe of each boot helped to keep them in place. She adjusted her Stetson. There was more room in it since she cut off a good portion of her hair before she set on her journey. She had planned to crop it close to her head, but at the last minute she opted to leave it just below her shoulders. Long enough she could pin it up and not be discovered to be a woman providing her hat stayed in place.

The bindings on her chest dug into her skin. How she longed to loosen the strips of cloth. She tugged the vest, making sure it helped to disguise her bosom. She hadn't washed her face since she started her journey, so she'd hopefully looked more like a man instead of a woman. While she felt more exposed wearing Charles's britches, it had been a necessary part of her disguise.

Time to stop thinking about her attire and concentrate on the matter at hand. Ellie Lou crouched closer to the campfire, thankful for the prairie grass, and the whispering wind which helped to disguise her footfalls. At least she prayed it did.

A man sat by a blazing fire.

Her stomach rumbled as the scent of rabbit and beans filled the air.

Darkness descended as she continued to watch the man.

She crept a step closer and hunkered close to the ground.

The man turned and stared in her direction.

Her heart pounded in her ears. Could he hear it? She willed herself not to move.

He stayed seated. Didn't reach for the rifle propped beside him.

Her pulse thrummed.

He looked like the tintype in her saddle bag.

She slipped her pistol into the gun belt and swung the rope in a loop. It swirled through the air.

2

While Ellie Lou hadn't had lessons on shooting a gun, she was an expert when it came to swinging a lariat and capturing her target. The loop sailed through the night air, circling around the man. She tugged with all her weight.

The man struggled and tried to turn towards her.

She yanked again, tugging him off balance and knocking him to the ground.

His body stilled. Was he playing possum?

Her stomach clenched. Not allowing herself to consider the consequences, she ran towards him, keeping resistance on the rope.

He hadn't moved a muscle. His eyes were closed. His white Stetson had slipped off when he fell backward. Dark red stained the ground.

Dear God, please let him be alive. Her fingers shook as she pressed them against the side of his neck. A steady beat pumped against her fingertips. *Thank You, Lord.* She slipped the rope off his torso and quickly checked his pockets. A paper crinkled as she withdrew it from his left side. She also found a set of steel bracelets. Why would Jeffrey have handcuffs? She shrugged. They would come in handy. She pocketed the paper and slapped the handcuffs on one wrist, shifting his body so she could clip both of his hands behind him.

Grunting as she adjusted him to a seated position, Ellie Lou bound his calves with her rope. Best to keep him off guard until she had the chance to talk to him. She unbuckled his gun belt, relieving him of his pistols and ammunition, and scooped up his rifle.

Ellie Lou glanced at him.

He still hadn't moved.

Should she check his boots and make sure he didn't have a knife stowed somewhere? Best to be cautious. She removed the man's boots and discovered a blade in each one. Tucking them under her gun belt, she shifted his footwear out of reach.

The rain continued as Ellie Lou gently nudged his foot with the tip of her boot. Still no movement. Maybe she had time to run and collect her horses. She scurried into the night, stumbling over a patch of prairie grass, but she managed to keep a hold of the man's weapons.

Back at the horses, she untied the reins. "Come on." She clicked and the pair followed her. "Doesn't make sense. Why would a city fella who's supposed to get married soon be rambling the countryside as if he had nowhere special to be?"

Storm snorted and tossed his head.

"Maybe he doesn't trust travel on the stagecoach and wanted to make his way to Burrton Springs on his own." She chuckled. "Bet he's been lost the past couple weeks."

She ground-tied her horses beside his magnificent mare. Maybe he'd be interested in striking a deal and swapping a stud fee in exchange for the offspring his horse and Storm could produce. It would help in the long run to build up her herd but wouldn't solve her current problems.

One thing at a time. One day at a time.

The man was in the same position.

Ellie Lou strapped his gun belt to her waist. She tucked the knives into her saddle bag and his rifle in the pack of supplies she'd removed from Honey. After a good rub down of her horses, she slipped the tintype from her pack and studied it in the dim light from the fire. Sure looked like the man on the ground. What a relief to have found him so soon. If all went well, she could collect her pay from Betty, and have it in the bank by early next week. *Forgive me for doubting Your care of me, Lord.*

Her stomach growled, and she glanced at the pot hovering above the fire. Wouldn't hurt to help herself to some food, would it? She could always share some of her supplies with him once he woke up.

Decision made, she dug in her supplies and found a plate and spoon. Back at the fire, she moved the pot away from the heat and lifted the lid, breathing deep. It smelled like the best meal she'd ever had. Scooping a hefty serving onto her plate, she dipped her head and said a quick prayer.

Her tongue exploded with flavors as she chewed the rabbit and beans. She couldn't identify the spice he'd added to the dish, but she liked it. Maybe he'd share his recipe once he woke up.

Ellie Lou studied him.

Not a muscle flitted.

Maybe she should take another gander at his head. It hadn't bled much, but maybe there was something else going on. She set her empty plate aside and stood.

Dusting off her backside, she crept closer to him. Her fingers hesitated over his neck before she got up enough nerve to check his pulse again.

Strong and steady.

She tiptoed to the back of him and studied his head.

His hair was wet from the rain, but the blood had stopped flowing and was already crusting.

Guess there's nothing I can do except wait for him to wake up. As she sat down across from him, the paper in her pocket crinkled. Ellie Lou withdrew it and studied it. A man's face stared back at her. Why would Betty's fiancé have a wanted poster in his pocket? It didn't make any sense. Maybe there was more to the man than Betty realized. That must be it. After all, look at her friend, Gertrude. When her fiancé came to town to marry her, he ended up being a criminal and was arrested as soon as he stepped off the stagecoach. Good thing she hadn't ended up with the scoundrel.

Best to be on guard. One never knew if someone wasn't who they said they were. Just look at the trouble she'd had at the ranch a few months ago.

Decision made, she'd do whatever it took to stay awake until the man woke up and she could question him. She'd better get some coffee started. She had a feeling she would need the extra boost to get her through whatever lay ahead.

Help me stay awake, Lord. Keep me safe so I can get the money from Betty for this delinquent groom. Could You make him agreeable to go with me when he wakes up? You know how much I need this.

~*~

Caleb woke to a throbbing head and cold, wet feet. His body trembled with the frigid rain pelting him. The wind had picked up. He'd been awake for a while but had stayed quiet so he could learn more about his captor. He couldn't believe someone had gotten a jump on him. Caleb prided himself on his abilities especially after being one of Sheridan's scouts in the war. Guess it proved he shouldn't be a U.S. Marshal anymore. Good thing he'd hung up his badge in Topeka. Once he found this last outlaw, he'd settle down to the quiet life.

There hadn't been a sound from his captor for a while. Should he chance opening his eyes to better access the situation?

He took a quick peek.

A small gasp escaped his imprisoner's lips. Small, flat lips. Big brown eyes widened. There was no way those eyes belonged to a man.

Caleb cleared his throat. "What's your name?"

"Name's…" the word came out in a squeak. The captor cleared her throat and coughed. "Name's Lou." This time the words were said in a deeper tone.

"Lou, huh?"

Lou's hands shook as she adjusted her brown Stetson, pulling the brim to cover more of her face. She stood and Caleb bit the inside of his cheek to keep from making a sound. There was one thing he knew about his captor. 'Lou' was a woman posing as a man. The question was, why? And how had he allowed a woman to get the drop on him? "What do you want with me?" Best to get her talking.

She didn't answer right away, but paced back and forth, her hand resting on her gun belt.

No. Wait. *His* gun belt. Embers flared in his chest. She had no right. He glanced at his stocking feet. If she'd removed his boots, she'd likely found the two knives he'd hid there.

"Plan to take you where you're supposed to be."

What did that mean?

Lou had a gift for giving answers that were as clear as mud, just like every other woman he'd encountered over the years.

His head pulsed as he strained to make sense of the situation. The handcuffs chaffed his wrists, and his shoulders complained. Just how long had he been in this position? His stomach rumbled.

Caleb's thoughts fuzzed as he tried to remember what had happened before the captor had come upon him. What had he been doing? The pieces fell into place. He'd stopped to make camp. His supper was just about ready. He'd been on the trail of the outlaw. "You're making a big mistake."

Lou stopped short, tripping over a tuft of grass. Almost as though her boots were too big for her feet.

He filed the information to examine later.

Even though dirt lined her face, there was no disguising her fine cheek bones and chin. She shook her head. "I don't think so. You look exactly like your tintype."

Tintype? Had she retrieved the wanted poster from his pocket and somehow thought the outlaw was him? His head hurt. What exactly had he hit his head on? She did know the difference between a tintype and a wanted poster, didn't she?

"Shame on you for not letting Betty know what delayed you." A frown marred her face.

"Betty? Who's Betty?"

Her mouth gaped open. She swallowed. "Just how hard did you hit your head on the rock when you fell?"

A rock? He growled. "I wouldn't have hit it at all if you hadn't lassoed me." This discussion wasn't getting anywhere, and it was making his head throb more and more. He closed his eyes against the sudden, searing pain.

~*~

Caleb's body slumped over.

Ellie Lou scurried to check him.

His heart still beat steadily. So, what had caused him to pass out again?

She caught her lip between her teeth. If it wasn't the middle of the night, she'd get them back on the trail towards home, but she'd never been great when it came to directions. There was no way she'd find her way in the dark, especially with the rain wiping out her tracks. Too bad she didn't have enough strength to get him on the back of his horse and have him do the trail finding. She'd find a way come daylight. The question was, at what point should she take off the handcuffs and unbind his feet?

Ellie Lou halted. In her search of the man's pockets, she hadn't come across a key for the handcuffs. That meant he had to have them somewhere in his pack, or she'd somehow missed them when she'd gone through his pockets. Best to search them again.

She crept closer.

He appeared to be sleeping. But was he faking, hoping to catch her unawares?

Settle down. He doesn't know you're a woman.

Her fingers trembled as she patted his pockets one more time. Didn't seem to be anything there. She dug into his vest pocket and found a slip of paper. His coat didn't have anything hiding in it either.

Ellie Lou breathed a little easier when she moved towards his pack of supplies. She glanced back at Jeffrey, but he hadn't budged. Should she go through his pack? Somehow it didn't seem right to do so. It wasn't as if he was a criminal. He was just late and hadn't told his fiancée about the delay. If she were in his position, she wouldn't want someone rifling through her things. Was it wrong to keep him tied up?

The paper and wanted poster she'd removed from him felt as if they were on fire in her pocket.

Forgive me, Lord. I shouldn't have taken his things. I'm not here to judge the man, just to get him back to his intended, whether he wants to be there or not is on him, not me. If he's having second thoughts about his wedding, he can take it up with Betty. All I know is You provided an opportunity for me to save my ranch by rounding him up and taking him back to Burrton Springs, and I aim to do so. There's nothing stopping me from collecting the wage Betty offered. Thank You for providing, Lord. Forgive me for doubting You.

She settled against her saddle and tried to get comfortable. She'd better get some sleep, so she'd be rested for whatever she had to face tomorrow.

The wind picked up and snowflakes started swirling around her. Ellie Lou shivered. *Can You hold off the snow, Lord? I sure don't need another complication.*

3

Caleb couldn't stop his body from quaking. Why was he so cold? He struggled to remember. His feet were like ice blocks. Almost as if his boots had somehow come off in the middle of the night. Not that he could tell what time it was.

He shivered and bunched his shoulders.

In a flash, it all came back to him.

His head throbbing. Handcuffs. No boots. *Lou*. The rain now turned to snow.

He bit back a groan as he stretched his cold legs, drawing them closer to his torso.

The wetness of his legs told him it had been snowing for a while. If he didn't find a way to get his boots on, he'd be dealing with frostbite. The wind blew snow down his neck. "Lou."

Had the sidewinder left him or was she still nearby?

Nothing.

He cleared his throat. "Lou!"

His horse whinnied, followed by a shuffling sound.

"W-who's there?" The words came out pure female and not the tone she'd used to disguise her voice earlier.

He'd likely awakened her, and she hadn't gotten her bearings yet. Too bad he couldn't get the drop on her. If he could see her…and if he wasn't tied up.

"You need to put my boots on my feet, or I won't be any good to you." There was no way he was telling her his name yet.

She gasped. Almost as if she'd forgotten all about him.

A minute later, he heard snow being brushed off something. Hopefully she'd empty his boots of snow before she shoved them on his feet.

He stretched his legs.

Lou was patting the ground nearby.

"Over here."

She crept closer, her fingers grazing his toes.

He bit back a groan.

"I'm sorry." The words were whispered. "I tried to put your boots on earlier but couldn't get them on when you were sleeping."

He sucked in a sharp breath as she started massaging his feet. The sensation of pins and needles stabbing almost caused him to cry out again.

She didn't speak anymore and rubbed his feet vigorously. She had the good sense to not be rough in her handling.

He grunted a few minutes later. "Think you got them warmed up enough to put the boots on." He flexed his foot as she put the right boot on followed by the left. "Thank you." The image of Jesus washing His disciples' feet flashed. Caleb swallowed. He'd never had such an intimate act performed on him before. Especially being done by a woman. He didn't know how to respond, let alone what to think about it.

"Is that any better?" Her words were lower again.

He nodded, unsure whether he had a voice after her ministrations.

"Sir?" Her fingers fumbled at his neck.

His pulse ratcheted up a notch or twenty. He was thankful for the darkness, not trusting what his expression would show her at the moment.

"Once it stops snowing, we'll head out." Snow crunched as she crept away from him. "I tried to keep the fire going, but with this wind and snow, I couldn't."

He heard her rifling through something. His pack? Or could it be hers?

A moment later, she draped a blanket around his shoulders, tucking it in around his chest. "Hope it helps to keep you warm. Can't have you catching your death of cold. I need you to stay healthy."

What did she mean? Just what exactly did she plan to do with him?

~*~

Ellie Lou huddled into her coat, flipping up the collar to ward off the blowing wind and snow. It did little to keep the wetness off her. She shivered. What a miserable night. Usually she loved snow, but that was when she enjoyed it from inside her warm home, and not in the middle of who knew where in a blinding snowstorm.

I'd appreciate it if You cause the snow to move on, Lord. She glanced at the night sky. Snow continued to fall. Ellie Lou couldn't see it, but she could feel it. She shivered again as she searched for the blanket she'd shoved aside when Jeffrey had called and awakened her. She hadn't thought she'd be able to fall asleep with the weather conditions, but exhaustion had overtaken her.

She stooped. Her fingers grazed the woolen blanket. She shook the snow off before wrapping it around her shoulders.

The temperature had dropped since she'd fallen asleep. The constant wind made it feel even colder.

Jeffrey hadn't said anything since she'd rubbed his feet. Was he bothered by it? She hadn't meant anything by it other than to warm them.

Ellie Lou swallowed. She hadn't touched a man since her husband, Charles, died over a year ago. A tear pricked the corner of each eye. She sniffed. Thinking about him right now wouldn't help matters. Giving in to her grief wouldn't do anything to get her out of this mess. Besides, until she learned more about Jeffrey, she'd be safer if he continued to believe she was a man. Even though he was committed to Betty, that didn't mean it was entirely proper for him and Ellie Lou to be on the trail together without a chaperone. Something she hadn't considered before she'd agreed to find and bring him back to Burrton Springs. She massaged the tight muscles in her neck. Should've known better than to go off half-cocked.

She turned toward the handcuffed man. He hadn't moved. At least not that she could tell. Not that she could see much with the darkness of the sky and the whipping snow. With no fire, she needed to come up with another way to keep them warm. If the man died, Betty wouldn't likely want to pay her.

Ellie Lou sighed and moved closer to Jeffrey. Like it or not, the best way for them both to stay warm throughout the night was to spend it side by side, where hopefully their combined body warmth would ward off frostbite or worse.

She sucked in a breath, drawing the blanket closer. The quicker she got it over with, the better. Surely Charles would have understood her decision.

~*~

Caleb jumped as Lou settled down beside him. She kept a few inches between them as she wrapped another blanket around both of them. Heat radiated from her body.

"Figured there's no sense in us facing the elements on our own." Her words were breathy and deep. Almost as if it cost her a lot to say what she was thinking.

She didn't say anything else, and only shifted from time to time before her body finally relaxed and she drifted off.

He could hear soft puffs as she slept.

Her frame settled against his.

He'd wrap an arm around her if she hadn't handcuffed them behind his back. Not because he cared a lick about her other than to make sure they both survived the night. He'd be hard pressed to find the key to his handcuffs in his pack without her help, especially when he was trussed up like a steer ready for branding.

Lord, help me here. I don't have time for these shenanigans.

You know all I want is to find Klaude Kidman, collect the reward money, and have enough cash to start a new life. But with this snow, his tracks are long gone. I want to get the man behind bars before he hurts someone else, Lord. Is that too much to ask?

He shifted. Lou murmured something in her sleep and nestled closer to him, her gloved hand resting on his chest.

His heart rate spiked. He couldn't help but wonder what it would be like to have a wife. A family. He'd given up on the idea ever since he'd lost his parents in the middle of the war with the South. Caleb had seen enough pain through the years to know he didn't want to live through more if he didn't have to. And the last thing he wanted was to open himself up to caring about someone and potentially losing them. If anything, the war had taught him to keep his feelings in check. To not get too close to anyone.

He glanced at the woman beside him. The blinding snow prevented him from seeing her clearly. Best to steer himself from getting involved with whatever scheme she had going on.

~*~

Ellie Lou shivered. Had she left a window open? Drowsiness lifted as she opened her eyes. The world was covered in white. Snow and wind continued to blow. A good foot or more was on the ground with no signs of stopping anytime soon. She shifted and sucked in a breath when she realized she had been practically sprawled across Jeffrey's side. What must he think of her? Good thing he thought she was a man, just sitting close to keep warm during a miserable night.

He hadn't moved. Hopefully, he was still sleeping. Best to take care of the horses and her morning needs before he awakened.

She brushed the snow off the blanket and stood. Wind whipped snow into her eyes, stinging her face. Her feet complained as she trudged a few feet away. She stamped them, trying to get some feeling back. Glancing backward, she could barely see the horses and Jeffrey. They needed to find somewhere to get warm until the storm died down. She shifted a few steps farther until she could no longer observe the campsite. Unbuckling her husband's pants, she quickly took care of her needs, and adjusted her clothing. Her stomach growled.

Turning back toward camp, or at least where she thought camp was, she shielded her eyes from the blowing wind. If they weren't careful, they'd be wandering around in the storm. Her gut clenched. There was no way around it. She would have to untie Jeffrey so he could help them get to safety.

"Lou?" His voice carried above the wind.

Which direction had it come from?

"Here." She yelled back, forgetting to deepen her voice.

"Come this way."

"Keep calling so I can find you." She plodded through a snowdrift.

The wind picked up, howling as the snow blew sideways. She couldn't see a foot in front of her and wasn't sure if she was going the right way.

"Jeffrey? You there?" Her words were sucked from her.

"Lou?"

Ellie Lou stumbled ahead. Her foot sank deeper than she anticipated. Pain seared through her leg as she went down. She cried out in pain. "Help me, Jeffrey."

~*~

"Lou?" Caleb groaned as he used a big rock to heft his body upward. He wobbled as feeling rushed back to his bound feet. Pins and needles pierced with each hop.

Wind whipped.

Which direction had Lou taken? He'd been half awake when she'd left him. "Answer me, Lou."

"Help me." Her words sounded full of pain and distant. Just how far had she meandered?

"I'm coming, Lou." He hopped a few steps and listened again. "Keep talking, so I know where you are."

"H-here."

He hopped another step. And another.

Help me find her, Lord. "Lou?"

"I c-can't s-see where you are."

He could hear her teeth chattering, so he must be close.

Please, Lord.

He squinted, shifting his head so the snow wasn't blowing directly into his eyes.

There. Ahead. She lay in a mound.

He hopped, stumbled, and fell face first into a snow drift. Groaning as he struggled, it took a minute before Caleb managed to get back on his feet. Two hops had him beside her. "What happened?

Where are you hurt?"

"M-my ankle." Tears filled her eyes. "Must have stepped in a prairie dog hole." Her chin wobbled. "C-couldn't see it with the snow."

What a predicament. He couldn't check her ankle with his hands secured behind his back. "You'll have to untie my feet, so I can get back to my pack quickly and find the key to my handcuffs. Unless you already have the key on you."

Her chin wobbled. A trail of tears streamed down her face. "I d-don't have it. Didn't want to invade your privacy."

He snorted. The least they had to worry about now was his privacy.

4

Ellie Lou blinked back her tears. A fella wouldn't be crying over a tumble. *You need to stop fussing.* She bit her lip and struggled to a sitting position.

The man collapsed on the snowy ground beside her, shifting his feet near her hands. "If you untie my feet, we'll find a way to get back to camp together."

She struggled for a few minutes with her gloved hands, but the knots wouldn't budge. Slipping off her gloves, she concentrated on one of the knots to no avail. Her fingers shook with the cold. "I c-can't get it."

He grunted. "They're too iced up with the snow. We'll have to cut them. Where did you put my knives?"

"I don't want you cutting my rope."

He sighed. "You'll have to trust me if we're to live through this storm."

Trust? Could she trust a man who didn't let his fiancée know he was delayed and didn't seem in any hurry to show up when he was supposed to? Seemed a mighty tall order.

"Look, we can't stay outside in these conditions much longer. We need to find cover for us and for the horses. Where are my knives or do you have one?"

The wind picked up, blasting them with snow.

Ellie Lou shivered. She glanced at the man on the ground beside her. His blue eyes were scrunched against the wind. She lifted her coat and removed her husband's knife from a small sheath strapped to her waist.

He shifted his feet towards her. Watching. Waiting.

She pulled the knife back. "Promise me you won't cause me any harm."

His gaze found hers. "I promise, ma'am, no harm will come to you."

She dropped the blade in the snow. He knew. How had he discovered she wasn't a man? She swallowed and dug into the pile of snow until her fingers grazed the handle. "Stay still."

"No need to worry about me. I won't be moving a muscle."

It took a few seconds to hack through the rope.

He flexed his feet once the bindings were free. "We need to work together to get back to camp, especially before conditions get worse and we can't see to find it. I can't help you with your ankle until I'm free."

"How do I know you won't run off?"

He chuckled. "There's no need to fret about my taking off when we're both in the same predicament. Let me get up first, and we'll somehow get you up. No, tell you what. I'll squat and you can use me to pull yourself up." He quickly got into position. "Be careful now, that's it."

She grunted as she used his broad shoulders to pull herself to standing. A misstep had her sucking in her breath at the flash of pain surging up her leg.

"You all right?" He shifted his shoulder to steady her.

She nodded, not trusting herself to cry out again.

"Together, now. Hold on while I stand."

They managed to both stay upright.

"Wrap your arm around my shoulder and lean on me so you don't put any pressure on your foot until we can take a look at it."

She nodded. "Which way is camp?"

He studied the ground. "That way. Need to hurry before our tracks are covered."

She hopped. Pain seared through her body with each jolt.

"Do you think you'll make it?" He stopped for a few seconds.

Ellie Lou gave a quick nod.

"Hang in there. I think we're almost there."

One of the horses snorted. The horses had to be close.

They continued until the horses came into view. Their backs were covered in snow. The several snow-covered lumps had to be their packs. The man steered them toward his.

"Ease down to the ground there." He stooped and aided her as she sat on the snowy ground.

A sheen of sweat trailed down her spine despite the cold temperatures.

"You'll need to dig through my supplies. The key is wrapped in a strip of leather toward the bottom of the pack."

She shifted a little closer, brushing off the snow and pulling the pack onto her lap. Moving clothes and some papers, she dug deeper into the leather sack. She felt a small bundle. Ellie Lou tugged it out. "Is this it?"

He nodded.

She untied the strip of leather and grasped the key. "You won't leave me, will you?"

"No, ma'am. I would never leave a lady in distress."

Her brow pulled as she considered his words. Could she believe him when he hadn't followed through with his promise to Betty?

What should I do, Lord? How do I know if I can trust him? What if he leaves me and takes off with all my supplies and horses? What will I do then? I thought You were aiding me in my search, but I'm beginning to wonder.

The man's deep blue eyes studied her. He wasn't pressing her to unclasp the handcuffs. Just patiently waiting for her to make her decision.

She swallowed and licked her chapped lips. Taking a deep breath, she motioned for him to turn around.

He did so and stooped a little so she could easily access the handcuffs.

The metal clicked as the steel bracelets came off.

She grabbed them and pocketed it along with the key. Best to be prepared in case a situation arose in the future.

His face flinched as he hunched his shoulders and rubbed his wrists.

She imagined they were hurting quite a bit after being in one position for so long. "Now what?"

He glanced at her boot. "I can tell your foot's swelling already. We need to find cover before we deal with it. I came across an abandoned soddy and small outbuilding a mile or so back towards Topeka."

"How will we find it in this kind of weather?"

"Are you a praying woman, Lou?"

She nodded.

"Then you better be praying."

~*~

Caleb didn't like how pale Lou's face had grown in the past few minutes. As much as he wanted to take time to stretch his stiff arms and shoulder muscles, he needed to find shelter for them and fast. If the weather wasn't so awful, he'd take her boot off, but he couldn't risk her getting frostbite in the process. He shook the two blankets and settled them around her shoulders. He needed to find shelter so he could get his feet warmed up too. They hurt with each step.

"T-thank you." Her teeth chattered as she held tight to the fabric to keep the wind from blowing it away.

Guide me, Lord. We need to find the abandoned place I saw yesterday. But with this weather, I can't tell which way to go. You'll need to direct our steps, Lord. He continued to pray as he dusted off the snow on the horses, the saddles, and their packs. Caleb glanced around their camp. He found his Stetson. Brushing it off, he plucked it on his head and pulled his bandana up to help keep the snow from blowing in his face. He made quick work of saddling their horses. Caleb squinted through the blowing snow. He didn't see any other snow-covered objects.

He stooped and swung Lou into his arms.

She yelped.

As careful as he could, he settled her in his saddle and swung up behind her being careful not to bump her foot.

Lou sucked in a breath. "W-what're you doing? I can ride my own horse."

He nudged Chestnut's side, and his mare started a slow pace through a snowdrift. "Take us to shelter, girl." He tugged on the reins for her horses to follow him. "Don't want you falling off your horse and not being able to find you. Best if we stay together."

She sat rigid for a few minutes.

"You can relax against me. I won't bite."

She moaned when the horse stumbled.

The wind picked up. Snow blasted their sides. Caleb couldn't see beyond Chestnut's ears. His gut clenched. He'd heard many a story of folks wandering around in a snowstorm only to be found frozen to death after the snow stopped. *Don't let that be us, Lord. Show Chestnut where to go.*

He kept praying, begging the Lord to guide them to shelter.

Lou sagged against him. He tightened his arms around her so she wouldn't slip to the ground. She likely had passed out from the pain.

Caleb had no sense of how much time had passed as they continued through the blizzard. His fingers grew numb as he struggled to hold on to her horses. He'd long since given Chestnut her head, trusting his mare to lead them to somewhere away from the elements. She'd saved his life more than one time along the trail over the years.

The wind shifted and something large took shape just ahead of them. Chestnut whinnied when they reached it and came to a halt.

He held onto the reins as he swung down. "Whoa." He glanced back at her two horses. They'd come to a stop and stood with their heads down. They weren't likely to roam in this weather.

Stumbling through the snow, he pounded on the wooden door. "Hello! We need your help!"

He strained to hear a sound over the wind. Nobody came. He knocked again as he pulled the latch and shoved the door open. "Hello in the house."

Nobody responded. He squinted, trying to see into the dark room. It took a minute for his eyes to adjust, and he could make out a small table with a lantern half-filled with kerosene and a small tin of matches from the look of it. A bed stood in the corner beside a stone fireplace. A small stack of wood sat in the opposite corner. The place looked as though it had been abandoned for a while. It smelled like something had died inside. He wrinkled his nose and struck a match. Lifting the globe, the wick sparked to life. Replacing the glass, he hurried outside.

Lou hadn't moved.

He shook her awake. "Come on, Lou. Found us some shelter." He didn't wait for her to answer but swung her into his arms.

She sucked in a breath and rested her gloved hand on his chest.

His breathing hitched as he carried her across the threshold and settled her gently on the bed. "I'll be back as soon as I can. Need to get the supplies in and see if there's somewhere to put up the horses."

She nodded.

Outside, he made quick work of stripping the horses of their burdens and placed everything under the table in the small building. Caleb closed the door snuggly behind him and went back into the blowing wind. He shielded his eyes, trying to see through the snow. There ahead was another soddy type structure. This one was bigger than the house. He shoved the door open and glanced inside. The scent of old hay filled his nostrils. At least the horses could be protected from the elements too.

Caleb left the door open and crossed to the horses. He tugged the reins and the trio plodded after him. There weren't separate stalls. He removed their tack and set them on some old crates in a corner. He fumbled in his pack, and pulled out a rag and grain sack. He quickly rubbed the horses down and gave each a handful of grain. A metal bucket sat near the crates. He went outside, filled it with snow, and hoped it'd melt enough for the horses to drink, although they didn't seem to be enthused about drinking right now. He set it aside and patted each horse. "I'll be back to check on you when I can."

He stumbled back to the soddy.

Lou gasped when he opened the door.

He crossed the room and knelt beside her. "Now, let's see about your ankle."

Her lips pursed together as she shifted so he could examine it.

"I'm afraid we'll have to cut off your boot."

"No. Please don't." She sucked in a breath. "I don't have anything else to wear…and these were my husband's." A tear rolled down her pale cheek.

He ran a hand along the scruff on his face. "Let me get some snow. Maybe I can place it inside your boot, and it will bring the swelling down enough to slip the boot off."

"Please." Her big brown eyes implored him.

He swept off his Stetson and opened the door. Stooping, he scooped a couple handfuls of snow into his hat and closed the door. Crossing the room, he tucked snow into the top of her boot, shoving it down as far as he could.

Her eyes widened, but she didn't complain.

"Sorry about the cold." Best to try and distract her from it. "You said the boots were your husband's? What happened to him?"

5

Tears welled and flowed down Ellie Lou's cheeks. "He was poisoned. Died a little over a year ago."

"I'm sorry." Jeffrey knelt and wiggled her boot.

She sucked in a noisy breath.

He glanced at her and scooped some more snow into the top of the boot. "This will hurt. I'll apologize up front. I'm afraid there's no way around it."

She nodded and braced herself. "Just do it. The quicker it's off, the better."

"What was your husband like?"

Ellie Lou closed her eyes as she pictured her late husband. She smiled, remembering all the times he teased her through the years.

Pain seared through her ankle and leg as Jeffrey worked the boot from her foot.

She sucked air in through her teeth to keep from crying in pain. Moisture pricked her eyes.

"We'll need to remove the stocking too."

"Let me do it." She shoved his hands away.

"You sure?"

"Yes."

He averted his gaze.

She struggled to roll up her ice encrusted pant leg. Ellie Lou made quick work of carefully removing the stocking. "You can look now."

His fingers hovered above her ankle. "I don't like the way it's swelling so much. It's got some ugly bruising and already has doubled in size. Did you hear it snap when you stepped in the hole?"

She struggled to remember. "I wouldn't say snap, but there was a popping sound."

"Can you move it at all?"

A sharp cry escaped as she tried to flex the joint.

Jeffrey's brow furrowed. "Does it hurt to touch it, ma'am?"

It took her a moment to work up enough nerve to examine the bruised skin. She winced at even the lightest of touches.

He knelt before her and gripped her upper calf. Twisting her leg right, then left. "I don't see any bones poking through the surface. Hopefully, you didn't break anything. More than likely, you tore a tendon."

She narrowed her gaze. "You a doctor or something?"

His expression fell, and he glanced away. "No. Just have had some medical know how."

"I'm sure it will be helpful once you're married."

His light brown brows quirked. He gently set her leg back on the mattress. "Best get a fire started. I have a feeling this snow will last a while."

Within a few minutes he had a blaze burning in the fireplace.

"I'll be back in a bit. Want to set up a rope between the house and the barn of sorts."

"You think it'll get that bad?" Ellie Lou shifted on the bed trying to get more comfortable.

"Good chance. While I'm outdoors, I'll see if there's any more firewood stacked up near the house." He knocked the remainder of the snow from his Stetson and set it on his light brown hair. "If I'm not back in a half hour or so, shoot off a round so I can hear it."

Her chest constricted. What would she do if he got lost in the storm, and she couldn't get around because of her ankle? Her breathing accelerated.

Relax. Worrying won't help. Best to get my mind on something else.

She wrinkled her nose. Where was the dead animal? With the room starting to warm, it made the smell even worse. She shifted to the edge of the bed. Squinting as her eyes adjusted to the dim light in the soddy, she scanned the living quarters. There, by the table leg was a small scrap of fur.

Ellie Lou shivered. If they were to be held up indoors until the storm abated, she refused to share the space with dead vermin. She shifted to the edge of the bed, careful not to put pressure on her foot.

She hopped the short distance to the table and stooped, holding on to the edge. The odiferous scent of decay almost bowled her over. Balancing on one leg, she withdrew a handkerchief from her pocket and wrapped it around her mouth and nose. Ellie Lou untied her saddlebag and found the garden trowel she'd packed. Her head started to swim with the continued bending over.

"Need to take care of this right away." She scooped up the remains of the mouse onto the trowel, praying it would stay in place as she hobbled to the door. With each pain-filled hop, the carcass shifted. Two more steps and she'd be at the door.

Hop.

Hop.

Her heart and head pounded as she gripped the latch, taking a second for the room to stop spinning. She tugged on the door.

Wind and snow immediately blew inside, chilling her to the bone. She shivered and gripped the door frame with one hand and flung the mouse remains outside with the other.

Just then, the man stepped into the path of the small dead body, and it bounced against his broad chest before dropping to the ground.

She sucked in a sharp breath. An apology formed on her lips.

~*~

Caleb halted mid-step as something furry and foul smelling was flung at his chest. Snow swirled around him. His gaze drifted upward.

Lou's eyes widened, and she gasped. "I'm so sorry. I didn't mean for it to hit you." She wobbled as she gripped the wooden door frame.

He frowned and swept her into his arms.

She yelped.

"Told you to stay put." He carried her to the bed, depositing her on the lumpy mattress. Turning, he walked two paces and secured the door. A chill filled the room. "We don't have much fuel for the fire. What made you do such a fool thing as leaving the door open?"

She removed her bandana and tucked it in a pocket. Her mouth gaped open for an instant before she snapped it shut, and she felt the flush rise in her cheeks. "You have no right."

He swept off his snow-covered Stetson and clapped it against his gloved hand, knocking the snow onto the floor. Caleb stared at it for a moment. He hefted a sigh as he removed his coat, bandana, and gloves, and draped them over his saddlebags to dry. Shoving a hand through his hair, he bit back a groan. Instead, he sent a prayer heavenward. He crossed the room and knelt, adding another log to the fire. "If we're to be trapped together for a few days, we'd best start being civil with each other."

"You're the one who hasn't been civil."

He crossed his arms. "And you think knocking a man unconscious, handcuffing, and trussing his feet like a calf is respectful behavior?"

She had the decency to look remorseful. "Sorry. I probably should've talked to you first about why you were taking so long to get to Burrton Springs."

Caleb scratched his head. How did she know about his plans to look up Josh Walker? He didn't remember mentioning it to her.

"You think you would have let Betty know the reason for your delay." She shifted so her back rested against the dirt wall.

"That's the second time you've mentioned her name. Who is she?"

"So, you've gotten cold feet and will just leave your bride hanging?"

Had she said bride? He rubbed his temple. His head was starting to ache. The knot on the back of his head probably didn't help matters. "I don't know what you're talking about, ma'am. I've never known a Betty."

"Why would you say such a thing? Are you refusing to marry her?" She crossed her arms.

"Marry who?"

"Betty, of course." She winced as she shifted her foot and sucked in a quick breath.

Caleb settled on the floor. "I think we'd better start at the beginning. Who are you really and where are you from?"

She bit her lip and didn't answer him right away. "As I said, my name's…Lou. I have a horse ranch in between Burrton Springs and Hutchinson."

He doubted Lou was her real name, but he'd let it go for now. The question was, had she told the truth about where she lived? Best to try and find some more information about her. "Why were you alone?"

Her teeth scraped across her bottom lip again.

He'd seen enough outlaws through the years to know when a person was stalling for time. What did the young widow have to hide?

~*~

This conversation wasn't going at all the way Ellie Lou anticipated. Why was the man being so cagey about knowing Betty? What was he hiding? She racked her brain trying to remember what all Betty and Mary had said about the man, but all she could remember was Jeffrey had been a childhood friend. Ellie Lou closed one eye as she tried to recall the few conversations she'd had with Betty and her aunt over the past few months. They'd come from New York City. Betty's father had died. They wanted a fresh start. Was there anything else?

"You planning on answering my question?" Jeffrey extended his lower limbs and leaned against the table leg.

She glanced at him. What had he asked?

Silence stretched between them.

He cleared his throat. "What were you doing on the trail alone and posing as a man?"

"I don't know why that would be of interest to you."

His brows rose. "Considering you're the reason we're stuck in this hovel together; I think I have a right to know what's going on."

"It's not my fault I stepped in a prairie dog hole." She shifted her ankle to find a comfortable position. "If it weren't for this snowstorm, we'd be on the trail back home, and I'd soon be getting my pay for bringing you in."

"So that's what this is all about? Reward money?" He scowled. "I wouldn't have figured on you being a bounty hunter."

She couldn't meet his gaze. "I. That is…I'm not. Usually."

"What makes you think I'm the person you're hunting for?"

Of course, he was Betty's fiancé. Who else would he be? "Now, Jeffrey, this conversation isn't going anywhere."

"Jeffrey? Why did you call me that?"

"Because it's who you are. Betty's been worried sick over your delay in coming, especially with the wedding only a few weeks away." She glared at him. "How dare you galivant around the countryside and not let her know the reason for you not arriving on time? Obviously, you don't know the first thing about how to be a good husband. I'm tempted to let Betty know the kind of man you really are."

He held up a hand. "Hold up there. I don't know who this Jeffrey is, but lady, you've got the wrong person. My name's Caleb Dawson."

Was it a trick? Why would the man lie about his name? It made no sense.

6

Caleb's head throbbed. The volley of words from Lou had gotten him no closer to learning who she really was and why she thought he was Jeffrey. He rubbed the back of his head, wincing when he connected with the bump he'd somehow gotten when Lou had lassoed him. "Let's start at the beginning. Who's this Jeffrey you're trying to find, and why is there a reward for him?"

Her long fingers traced a small mark on the knee of her britches. Although they almost looked too big to be hers. Her husband's, maybe?

"I'm waiting." He crossed his arms.

Her gaze darted to meet his before falling back to stare at her pant leg again. "I'm not exactly sure of his last name—"

"Are you joking? You're searching for a man, and you don't even know his last name?" He chuckled. "Obviously you haven't done any tracking before, have you? Thought you said you were a bounty hunter. Just how many lies have you told me?"

Her head came up, and her chin jutted. "I didn't say I was a bounty hunter. You said it. I mean…that is…you make me uncomfortable."

"Will you tell me, or not?"

She hefted a sigh. "How do I know I can trust you?"

He rubbed his hand along his jaw. Stubble scraped against his palm. He needed a shave.

"Are you sure you aren't Jeffrey? You look a lot like him."

"Are you talking about the wanted poster you swiped from my pocket?"

Her cheeks flamed with color. She at least had the decency to dip her head and appear chagrined. "I planned to give it back to you."

Although he noticed she didn't. Maybe it was in her saddlebag, and she didn't want to get up with her injured ankle. What was it about this woman that rubbed him like sandpaper on an open wound? He cleared his throat. "Back to this Jeffrey. What's your connection to him?"

She studied him, running a hand across her forehead. She puffed out a breath.

Caleb forced himself to relax, to convey he wasn't a threat to her. Although he wasn't exactly sure how to do that since he hadn't been around womenfolk very often through the years.

"Betty has a lady's dress shop in Burrton Springs. Jeffrey, her fiancé, was expected a few weeks ago. The last word she had from him said he had to make a brief stop in Topeka. She's heard nothing since." She nibbled on her lip again.

Was she debating about continuing?

"Their wedding is in a couple weeks. She said she wanted to hire someone to find him." Her cheeks flushed with color.

"And you volunteered? Do you have any experience with tracking or bounty hunting?"

Her gaze darted to his before flitting away. "No."

Her answer was so soft he barely heard it.

The fire crackled, as a log shifted in the fireplace.

"What made you think you'd be able to find him?"

Lou glared at him.

Definitely got her feathers ruffled.

He bit back a smile.

"I had to." She shifted on the bed. "Failure to do so isn't an option."

Caleb cocked his head as he studied her. "Why is it so important to you to get the pay this Betty woman has promised you?"

Moisture dotted the corner of her eyes.

He flinched. He had no idea what to do with a weeping woman.

"It's not any of your business." Her coffee-colored eyes flashed.

"I think it is when I'm the one who was mistaken for this Jeffrey. Least you can do is let me know what he looks like so I can keep an eye out for him."

She shook her head. "No way. I need this money. I'm not letting you sweep in and find him. Besides, Betty is counting on me, and I plan to be a woman of my word."

"What made you believe I was Jeffrey?"

"Because you look similar." She went back to rubbing the mark on her pant leg.

He ran a hand along his jaw again. "Maybe Jeffrey got cold feet and decided not to get hitched."

"Then why would he say he was on his way but had to make a stop in Topeka?" Her brow furrowed. "Besides, if he'd already proposed and planned to be married by the end of the month, it makes no sense he would delay making his way to Betty. What groom wouldn't be eager to see his bride-to-be?"

"What more do you know about him?" He shifted his weight and the table leg creaked. Best not put too much pressure against it.

Lou licked her lips. Why did she seem nervous? What wasn't she telling him? She glanced down and the fingers on the side of her leg trembled.

"Your ankle bothering you? Want me to get some more snow to help with the swelling?" He glanced around for something to hold snow other than his Stetson again.

She gave a brief nod. "We can hold off a bit yet."

"You sure?" He studied her. "Don't want the swelling to get too bad."

"I'm positive."

A gust of wind rattled the door.

They both stared at it.

She hadn't answered his question. Should he press her more?

"I got the feeling he's a city fella. Betty came from New York City."

Sounded like she knew very little about the man she was stalking. Well, not exactly stalking. But he couldn't call her a bounty hunter either. What did that make her? An overzealous woman in need of making money fast? Why was she so desperate to need the pay promised? What was she avoiding telling him? Why did her vague description of Jeffrey seem familiar?

~*~

Ellie Lou tried to gauge Caleb's reaction without giving him full eye contact. He said he wasn't Jeffrey. Would he have a reason to lie to her? He hadn't mentioned anything more about himself other than his name. Should she be suspicious about it? She didn't feel comfortable being stuck with a man during a storm when nobody she knew had an idea where to find her. Although with this weather, it wasn't likely someone would come looking for her either. She'd left so quickly, there hadn't been time to let anyone know her plans other than Betty and her aunt. Surely, they'd send someone to come find her if she didn't return within a week or two. Right?

I thought You'd answered my prayers, Lord. With this ankle, how am I supposed to find Jeffrey now? I don't want to let Betty down, and I desperately need the money. What will I do if You don't provide for me? Where will I go? What will I do?

No answer came. But then, God had been silent lately other than when she thought He'd provided this opportunity for her. Maybe it hadn't been. Maybe this was a test.

Moisture sprang to her eyes, and her throat tightened. *Oh, Charles. As time goes on, I miss you more and more. Miss your wisdom. Your...* She put a halt to her train of thought. Going down that trail would only make things worse. Ellie Lou squared her shoulders and sat up a little taller. Feeling sorry for herself wouldn't help to solve her current problems.

If the man before her wasn't Jeffrey, she needed to either find the delinquent groom-to-be or come up with another idea to get the money in time to pay off her bank loan. She shifted and the paper in her pocket crinkled. The wanted poster. Maybe she'd find an answer to her situation there.

One of Caleb's eyebrows quirked.

Could he tell what she was thinking?

She cleared her throat. Best to get his direction elsewhere. "I think I could use some of that snow, if you wouldn't mind."

"Not at all." He stood, shrugged into his coat, and placed his Stetson on his brow. Digging in his pack, he retrieved a small pan before he slipped on his gloves. "Be back in a minute. Stay put."

She nodded.

As soon as he closed the door behind him, she slipped the paper from her pocket. It crackled as she unfolded it. Her heart hitched as she stared at the man.

It only took a minute to read all the pertinent information on the poster. The outlaw was wanted dead or alive. A reward of $500 was offered.

A lump formed in her throat as she read about the crimes the man had committed – robbing a stagecoach of a mail pouch, shooting all three of the passengers in the back, holding up the bank in Topeka, and getting away with thousands of dollars.

Should she continue the search for Jeffrey or try her hand at finding this Klaude instead? Ellie Lou tugged on her lower lip as she weighed the pros and cons. She'd promised Betty to find her beau, but if she found the outlaw while looking for Jeffrey, she'd wind up with enough money to pay off her debt and increase her herd. Something she'd had to cull over the past year when the military had cancelled the contract they'd made with Charles. It had done little good. She still had to take a note out on the property, praying she'd somehow be able to find a way to pay it off.

The door to the soddy swung open, snow billowed inside. Ellie Lou shivered.

Caleb stamped his boots. His coat was covered in snow. His white Stetson had accumulated a bit of precipitation in the short time he'd been gone. "What you got there?"

She shoved the paper back in her pocket. Her conscience pricked. She'd been taught to return things that didn't belong to her. The problem was, if she did, she wouldn't have the information about the outlaw. And if she said something to Caleb about going along with his search, he'd find a way to prevent her. He already thought she didn't know what she was doing. Well, he might be right, but there was no way she'd agree with him on the subject. "Thanks for getting the snow. I appreciate it." Best to change the topic.

He studied her for a few seconds before handing her the pan of snow. He unwound his neckerchief from his neck. "You might want to wrap some of it in here before you put it on your ankle."

She accepted the slip of fabric.

"Here, let me. No use you getting your hands cold since I have my gloves on." He stepped forward and wrapped a huge chunk of snow in the fabric, winding it a few times before kneeling and placing it on her swollen ankle.

Ellie Lou swallowed. The simple act of kindness made her miss her husband even more.

Caleb stood. "By the way, don't get any ideas."

She shifted her position. "What do you mean? What are you talking about? I told you I'd stay put and I did."

He shook his head. "I don't mean just now." He motioned toward her pocket. "That outlaw will take a professional to round him up. Something you aren't. You'd only get yourself hurt in the process. Or worse."

She narrowed her gaze. "I may not have a lot of experience, but it doesn't mean I couldn't capture him."

He didn't answer right away. Instead, he took off his coat and draped it over the edge of the table. He swept off his Stetson. His light brown hair had a crease mark from where the hat had rested on his head. Caleb smiled, a dimple flashing in his cheek. "You and I both know you have no business trying to find anyone, let alone a dangerous man like Klaude."

She wanted to smack the grin from his face. "Just because I haven't done this before doesn't mean I can't be good at it."

He snorted. "Lady, I doubt you can find the way back to Burrton Springs on your own."

Ellie Lou shifted forward, thrusting her hands on her hips. "You have no right to talk to me like that."

His brow quirked again.

"I'll prove you wrong."

7

Caleb didn't know what it was about Lou that got under his skin. Like a bad case of poison ivy. Constantly irritating and rubbing when you least expected it. Under any other circumstances, he would've thought to protect her. He'd get there. Eventually. Once the embarrassment of being caught unawares wore off. He just wasn't there yet. Caleb could imagine what his ma would've said if she was still alive. But she and Pa had died before he took off to fight in the war. It'd been a number of years since Caleb had heard her admonitions. Oh, how he missed them.

He shoved the thoughts aside. His stomach rumbled. "Guess we never had any breakfast, and it's long past. And I never had any supper last night either. Are you hungry?"

She blushed and murmured, "Sorry." Her stomach rumbled loud enough he could hear it.

Caleb chuckled. "I'll take that as a yes."

She shifted on the bed. "I can help."

He put a hand on her good ankle. "Stay put. Keep icing your leg."

Her mouth snapped shut.

He rummaged through his saddlebag until he found a small sack of dried beans. He withdrew them along with the wrapped cloth of the leftover rabbit he'd shot last evening. It had been cold enough overnight to keep the meat from spoiling. He also took out a small packet of seasonings. "Hope you don't mind beans and rabbit again." He dug deeper in the pack and pulled out his bake oven and lid.

"If it's as good as what you made last night, I welcome it." Lou's face relaxed. "I've been meaning to ask what spices you added to it."

"Paprika, cayenne pepper, salt, and a little bit of wild onion and garlic I dried a while back." Caleb dumped the beans and spices in the pan along with the leftover snow. He crossed the room and hung the pan over the fire on an iron hook, placing the lid on top. "That'll take a few minutes to soak before I add the rabbit."

"It's not often I see a man cooking. In fact, I've never seen it." Lou shifted on the bed, wincing as she adjusted her foot in a different position.

"You learn to do a lot of things when you're on your own." It took Caleb three strides to cross the room.

"There isn't someone special in your life?"

His gaze flickered to hers. Was she back to thinking he was this Jeffrey again?

She puffed out a breath. "Look, I'm not trying to be contrary. Just trying to make conversation since the weather appears to have us stuck together for a while."

He sighed. "Sorry. No, there's nobody special." One day maybe. "How's the ankle doing?"

Pain flickered across her face. "Bearable."

Caleb nodded. "As long as you don't put pressure on it. It'll take longer to heal if you don't stay off it."

A frown marred her dirt-covered face. "Don't figure that's an option. As soon as the snow lets up, I need to get on the trail again."

He leaned against the dirt wall. "Oh, what plans do you have?"

She squirmed before she answered. "I promised to find Jeffrey."

Caleb nodded. "Wouldn't hurt for you to describe him. Maybe I saw him when I was in Topeka."

Lou rubbed the side of her face. She glanced at him and then at the fire crackling.

The scent of the beans and spices permeated the air, causing his stomach to rumble. He crossed the short distance. Using his glove, he lifted the lid and dropped the hunk of rabbit meat into the pan. He turned back toward her.

She nibbled on her lower lip again.

He waited, refusing to rush her decision.

"I suppose it won't hurt provided you promise me something." Her eyes darkened.

"What's that?" No way would he agree without knowing the

particulars.

"You let me bring him in."

He chuckled. "Lady, I have no desire to round up a fella who decided he didn't want to get married."

Her nostrils flared.

Caleb bit back a laugh. Sure didn't take much to get her riled.

She huffed. "That's not exactly a promise but," she motioned at her pack, "if you fetch that for me, I can show you what Jeffrey looks like."

He handed it to her.

Lou untied the leather strap and flipped the pack open. She searched for a few seconds before removing something and offered it to him.

He stared at the tintype of a man.

She really did have a tintype.

His gaze fell back to the likeness. His gut clenched. Caleb had seen the fella before. He swallowed as he handed it back to her.

"So have you seen him?" She gripped the photo, glancing at it.

He waited until her gaze met his. Taking a breath, he nodded.

"How long ago? Did you talk to him? Did he say where he was going next? Was he injured?"

Her questions came in rapid fire succession.

He moved closer to the bed but didn't touch her. "I hate to be the one to tell you this, but if this is Jeffrey." He tapped the tintype. "He's no longer living."

She gasped. Her hand trembled. "H-how do you know?"

Caleb sat on the edge of the bed. Close enough to hopefully provide some comfort without touching her and making her uncomfortable in the process.

Lou blinked back tears.

He gripped his hand in a fist to keep from brushing the moisture from her cheek. The uncharacteristic desire startled him.

"Caleb?"

Right. Back to their discussion. "I came across him and two other stagecoach passengers a couple weeks back." He hesitated. Could she handle hearing the rest of the story?

"What did he say?"

He leaned closer. "He uh, didn't say anything."

She was quiet for a moment. "Wait, the wanted poster said something about a stagecoach robbery."

The tears came faster.

"Said something about three people being shot in the back." She stopped, rubbing her finger across the tintype. "You aren't saying…"

He gripped her hand.

Her gaze flew to his.

"I'm afraid he's dead. Shot in the back."

~*~

This could not be happening. Ellie Lou flicked the tears away. *How will I tell Betty, Lord? And what am I supposed to do now?* "Are you sure you aren't mistaken? Maybe the man you saw only looked like Jeffrey."

Caleb shook his head. "I'm sorry. I know it's not what you wanted to hear. The only identification I found on the coach was on his bags. They had 'J. Murphy' stamped into the leather. The U.S. Marshal was trying to determine which of the three had a last name of Murphy. I guess now we know. The marshal sent a wire to the stagecoach company to learn more information. They confirmed the man was from New York City. They weren't sure who the couple was or where they came from."

"New York?" Her chest tightened. It surely was Jeffrey then. "Do you think it was this Klaude Kidman who killed them?" She didn't need to withdraw the wanted poster. The man's name was already emblazoned into her memory.

"I don't have any doubt."

Her gaze met his before dropping to his hand resting on top of hers. When had that happened? She withdrew her hand, tucking it beneath her leg, trying to ignore the comfort he'd provided through the small gesture. Ellie Lou didn't want to think about finding physical consolation from anyone other than her husband. And he was no longer there to provide it. "Do you have any idea where

Klaude is?"

Caleb shifted and settled farther away from her. "I was tracking him before the storm hit."

He didn't mention she'd caused his delay in searching for the outlaw.

Best if she didn't say anything about it either. "Any thoughts on where he'd head next?"

"My guess is he'll lay low for a bit. He'll expect the law to be after him. Up until this point he hadn't killed anyone, but he's in a different class now with shooting people in the back."

Embers sparked as a log shifted in the stone fireplace. Ellie Lou watched the flame flicker and dance as the wood burned. Her stomach gurgled as the scent of rabbit, beans, and spices filled the small area.

"Figured I'd head to Burrton Springs to touch base with Josh Walker. He used to be a deputy with the Marshals, so he might have heard some news about Klaude."

"Joshua Walker?" Ellie Lou's gaze swung back to Caleb's. "He's not likely to know about it since he isn't the sheriff in Burrton Springs any longer."

"I hadn't realized he took the job as sheriff." Caleb rubbed his hand along his jawline.

It was something he'd done a few times now. Was he lying when he did it, thinking about shaving, or was he nervous about something?

Ellie Lou dragged her gaze away from the man's strong jawline. "Josh took over for the doctor in Burrton Springs."

"Really?" Caleb's hand stilled. "Wouldn't have ever figured on him becoming a doctor. He never liked being in a town, let alone wanting anything to do with a medical person. I wonder what changed?"

Ellie Lou shrugged. She'd never heard why the man had altered his profession only that he had. "He's married and has a baby girl."

"You're sure we're talking about the same Joshua Walker?" Caleb scratched his head.

She edged further away, trying to put some more distance

between them. "His sister is Jules. I think someone in town said it's short for Julia. Although I've never heard anyone call her that. So how do you know Jules and Josh?" Maybe she'd learn more if she got him to do some of the talking.

"Knew Josh years ago. I was a U.S. Marshal, and he was one of my deputies. Never heard about a sister when I knew him. Josh didn't come to town often and kept mostly to himself. Good tracker though. He rounded up many outlaws over the years. Surprised he got out of the profession." Caleb, walked to the pot, pulled on his glove, and lifted the lid. "Looks as if it'll be ready soon. Do you have a tin plate? I only have one. If not, I suppose we can share." He dropped the lid back in place, crossed the room, and rummaged in his saddlebag, withdrawing a plate and silverware.

"Wait, you're a U.S. Marshal?" Her throat tightened. Just how much trouble was she in for capturing a lawman?

"Was one." He peered at her.

Ellie Lou wanted to lick her lips, but she couldn't produce enough moisture in her mouth to do so. She coughed. "You, uh, aren't a lawman anymore?" *Please, Lord, let his answer be no.*

He shook his head. "No, otherwise you'd be in a lot of trouble." He waggled his eyebrows.

Her heart quickened.

A smile flashed. "I promised a friend I'd help with one more capture."

Thank you, Lord.

"Now, how about we get some grub going?"

She shifted her pack onto her lap, and dug deep until she found her plate and utensils. Ellie Lou handed the platter to him. "Maybe Sheriff Valentine will have heard about Klaude and what he's been up to."

His head came up. "Valentine, you say? His name's not familiar."

"Used to be one of my employees until I had to let him go."

One dark eyebrow quirked as he studied her. "Why's that?"

How much should she tell him? She took a deep breath. "Things were slow at the ranch. I had to sell off a lot of my herd. I guess Enoch knew I might have to let him go at some point. He decided to work part-time as a deputy in Burrton Springs. Eventually it led to his taking over as sheriff when Josh stepped down and became the town doctor. I think Josh trained for a while with the old doc before the man retired." No use sharing about the military contract Charles had and how it fell through, or all of her other troubles. It wasn't as if Caleb could help her in any way. And now her only hope of saving her home evaporated with the knowledge she wouldn't be getting the payment from Betty.

Betty. How would she tell her the sad news of her fiancé?

Caleb dished the food onto their plates. "Grub's ready. I'm sure you're hungry." He handed it to her. "Careful there, it's hot."

She gripped the edge of the plate. "Thank you. Didn't realize how empty my belly was getting."

He grinned. "Figured we both feel the same way." He dug the toe of his boot into the dirt floor.

Was he nervous about something?

"I hope you don't mind." He dipped his head, not meeting her gaze. "I always pray before meals."

Before she could respond, he started praying.

"Thank You for the grub, Lord. Let it nourish our bodies. Help Lou's ankle to heal. Thank You for the protection from the storm. Keep the horses safe. In Jesus's Name, amen."

She snapped her gaping mouth shut. Maybe he wasn't such a bad guy after all.

8

Caleb sneaked a peek at Lou before he dug into his meal. She hadn't said anything about his prayer. It wasn't clear what her thoughts on faith were. Although she'd been mighty uncomfortable when he'd mentioned being a U.S. Marshal. He bit back a chuckle and settled on the floor, taking a bite of rabbit. Flavors exploded in his mouth. He'd been a little heavy handed on the cayenne pepper. Hopefully she wasn't bothered by it. Caleb had always been partial to having a lot of flavoring in his food.

"Mmm. This is wonderful." Lou took another bite of her meal. She swallowed. "Thank you. Sure appreciate it."

He nodded.

Something thudded against the wooden door.

Her gaze shot toward his.

He set his plate on the table and pressed his ear against the door.

No sounds came for a few seconds.

Another thud and a scratch.

"What do you think it is?" Her words were whispered.

He put his fingers to his lips and withdrew his Colt revolver.

Her eyes widened. She set aside her plate and withdrew a knife.

Odd. She hadn't chosen to use one of the guns strapped to her waist. And why hadn't she removed her gun belt when he'd set her on the bed?

Another scratch.

"Might be a critter," he whispered.

"You should check." She kept her tone low. "Maybe someone needs help." She shifted to the edge of the bed.

"Stay put."

He reached for the latch and tugged open the door only a crack.

A small dark nose pressed in the gap followed by a whimper.

"It looks like it could be a dog." Lou hopped the short distance and stood beside him. "Let it in. I think she's hurt."

How could she determine that by only seeing a nose?

He shook his head and opened the door a little farther.

The critter shoved through the crack. Snow covered its coat making it impossible to tell what color it was.

"Get back on the bed." He glared at her.

She ignored him, instead stooping down and extending her hand. "It's all right, girl. Nobody will hurt you."

The dog glanced at Caleb and growled.

"I think this is a bad idea."

"Don't let him bother you, girl. You're welcome here." She crooned at the critter as if it were a small child.

The dog shook and snow went flying across the dirt floor.

"You're not thinking, woman. Get back. For all we know the dog might be rabid." He moved to get between her and the dog.

Her eyes flashed at him.

The mutt whimpered and snuggled against Lou's side.

"Why are you being so mean?" She glared at him as she petted the dog. "Can't you see she's harmless. The only one who's dangerous is you."

The dog yipped, lowered her head, and tucked her tail between her legs.

Caleb scrubbed a hand across his face. "At least let me check the critter first." He motioned toward the bed. "Best you get your foot elevated again."

"We can check her over together." Lou wobbled precariously before sitting hard on the floor.

She didn't say anything, but he imagined she hurt from sitting down quicker than she intended. Probably hadn't done any favors to her ankle either.

Women.

Who needed them?

Lord, help me.

Caleb sighed and stooped beside the dog.

The animal didn't growl this time but studied him warily.

He slowly reached his hand towards the mutt.

It hesitated for a moment before sniffing Caleb's outstretched hand.

A small tongue licked it. The dog shook its body again, clearing itself of enough snow to reveal a black, furry body with a white spot on its chest. No way of telling what breed it was though. The mutt whimpered and licked its front right paw.

"Aww, I think she's hurt." Lou reached her hand toward the injured limb.

"Wait!"

The dog growled at Caleb's raised voice.

He sat on the floor to hopefully appear less threatening to the mongrel.

The dog watched him warily.

"I won't hurt you." He kept his fingers extended for the dog to sniff. "Just want to see what's ailing you."

The dog must have finally decided he wasn't a threat because it licked his hand a few more times.

"Let's check you over." He gently lifted the dog's paw and examined it.

The dog whimpered but stayed still.

A huge chunk of ice was wedged between the pads.

Caleb untied his handkerchief and gently worked at the ice, using his hand to help melt it.

The dog shivered but didn't pull away.

Lou shifted closer, petting the dog's head. "Shh, it'll be all right, girl. We won't hurt you."

The lump of ice broke free and dropped to the dirt floor.

"Is it bleeding?" Lou bent closer.

A waft of dirt and rosewater mixed in Caleb's nostrils.

No matter how much she tried to disguise her gender with dirt and men's clothing, it didn't work when she'd used rosewater to either wash her hair or as a perfume. Either way, the scent was distracting.

Caleb shook his head. Best to get his thoughts back where they belonged. He gently lifted the dog, running a hand over each limb and along the mutt's back. He studied each paw but couldn't see any other issues. "I think it's the only problem." He ruffled the dog's ears. "And by the way, it's a boy, not a girl."

Lou's cheeks flamed with color. She dipped her head, and her Stetson blocked him from seeing her face.

How long was her hair? What color could it be? He hadn't seen her without the hat since they met last night. If you could call it meeting, when he'd been knocked to the ground. Not much of a how-do-you-do.

The dog squirmed, enjoying the attention they were giving it.

"I bet it's hungry." He stood. "Let me get you back on the bed, and then I'll get some of the rabbit for him."

He stooped and lifted Lou in his arms.

She let out a yelp.

Her face was close to his as she clung to his shoulder.

Maybe having a gal in his arms wasn't a bad thing.

Just not something he could afford to think about until after he found Klaude and got him behind bars. Best to remember that.

~*~

For a few seconds, Ellie Lou experienced safety. Security. Something she hadn't known since Charles died. All while being in Caleb's arms. She shook her head to clear her thoughts. The pain must be getting to her. No way she'd develop an interest in a man who had a profession of chasing outlaws. Well, make that a past profession. But still. He planned to go after Klaude. It wasn't as if Caleb had been clear on what he would do after he rounded up the fugitive. For all she knew the man would leave the area, and she'd never see him again.

Goodness. What is my problem, Lord? You'd think I was a young schoolgirl again swooning over the first fella who showed me kindness. Guard my heart, Lord. The last thing I need is to fall for a man. That's not on the agenda. Saving the ranch is. Are You listening, Lord? I don't see any answer to my problems other than going after this Klaude. It's doubtful

Caleb would be willing to share the reward and have us work together. Likely not even worth mentioning.

"Something wrong, Lou?"

Caleb's words drew her from her prayer.

How long had it been since he sat her on the bed?

She cleared her throat, refusing to glance his way. "Just fine. Come here, boy."

The dog limped over to her. A second later the mutt snuggled down beside her.

"He'll make the bed all wet." Caleb shoveled the last bit of his meal into his mouth before crossing the room and scooping out a hunk of rabbit meat. "Besides, he's probably hungry." He snapped his fingers. The dog jumped down and trotted over to Caleb, his tail wagging in anticipation.

Ellie Lou picked up her plate and took a bite of her now cooled meal. Her stomach gurgled as she watched the dog devour the food "Wonder how long he's been wandering around. Do you think he belongs to someone?"

Caleb picked up the plate when the dog finished. "More than likely, although we'll have a hard time finding them after the storm lets up."

We. Did that mean he planned to stay with her a while longer and not leave her stranded? Dare she ask him?

She ate in silence for a bit. Best to work up to getting an answer from him. "You been in Kansas long?"

"A number of years." He petted the dog.

The mutt wagged his tail before sitting down in front of the fire. A moment later he was curled into a ball. At least the dog had a full belly and would be able to warm up.

"You mentioned you were a U.S. Marshal. What're your plans now?" She settled against the sod wall.

"I already told you about going to see Josh. Was there something else I should be doing?" His brow quirked.

Ellie Lou struggled to control the heat creeping up her neck. "You said about finding Klaude. What about after he's in jail? What're you planning then?" Was it too personal of a question?

Caleb paced the small enclosure.

Did she make him uncomfortable? There wasn't any way she'd get him to agree to work together if she didn't try to make amends for her treatment of him so far. "I'm uh, sorry about last night. Didn't mean to mistake you for Jeffrey." Hopefully he'd accept her olive branch of peace.

"Well, I guess as long as you don't spread a rumor about how you caught me, there's no hard feelings." He winked at her. "Can't have it getting around I was bested by a woman."

Maybe she wasn't too bad at hunting a man. Ellie Lou sat up a little taller. After all, she'd managed to get the drop on a professional lawman. It had to count for something, right? "Have you, uh, ever had assistance rounding up a fugitive? Not a deputy, but someone else…" Couldn't hurt to at least test how warm the waters were. She wouldn't come outright and ask him.

"Why you asking?"

Ellie Lou made a point of not making eye contact, instead readjusting the quickly melting bundle of snow on her ankle. She shrugged. "Just making conversation."

She refused to glance his way as silence stretched between them like a tangible wedge. She'd wait him out, even if it meant biting her lip to refrain from speaking.

"Had a couple deputies I recruited through the years, but they've been experienced men. Not someone who goes off half-cocked. Some local sheriffs have helped from time to time too."

She wouldn't rise to his bait.

"Most of the fugitives we're searching for are dangerous. Not someone to fool around with just to collect reward money. Definitely not like a bride-to-be recruiting you to search for a delinquent groom. So don't get any ideas in your head." He strolled across the room and jiggled the latch to the door, making sure it was secure.

In other words, he didn't think she could handle tracking, finding, and bringing in a wanted man. He only thought she could manage to find someone who wasn't dangerous. Ellie Lou hitched her chin. She had no business thinking she'd be up for the task, especially when she didn't know the first thing about completing such a project.

But God help her, she wanted to prove the man was wrong. That she was capable of doing the impossible.

I'll show him he's wrong about me. I may be injured, but it doesn't mean I can't do something once I set my mind to it. Just wait and see, Caleb Dawson.

9

December 19, 1877

Nearly two weeks trapped in a soddy with a widow and a dog was enough to drive any man to distraction, and Caleb was no exception. The blizzard had raged for three days of snow and frigid temperatures followed by a deceptively warm day. Lou had chomped at the bit, wanting to be on their way, but he'd insisted the drifts needed time to melt. Truth be told, he didn't want to be caught along the trail if another storm cropped up. Especially since the first storm was unlike any he'd ever seen before.

Good thing he'd followed his intuition, since two days after the first blizzard a second one raged, even worse than the first one. It had been five long days since the last of the snow fell. Drifts had piled up close to ten feet beside the barn and soddy. He kept waiting it out, praying each day the sun would melt the snow enough so they could get on the trail to Burrton Springs.

Fortunately, the sod barn had a wooden barrel of leftover feed, so the horses had had enough to tide them over. Good thing he'd found some critters frozen to death by the barn that had provided food for Lou, the mutt, and him. Along with the provisions in their packs they'd had just enough, but they were out of food now. The faster they got to civilization, the better.

With Lou's ankle still swelling, he didn't dare have them camp outside overnight. No, they'd have to push hard and make the trip in one long day. Having her leg hanging down was sure to complicate the healing process.

The sun would soon be breaking the horizon. He checked the embers in the fireplace one more time. They were cold. He glanced up as Lou opened the door. She'd been taking care of her business outside. It had been embarrassing enough sharing the space with a member of the opposite gender. He'd be glad to return her to town where someone else could help watch over her. "You about ready?"

The dog danced around Lou's legs as she hobbled to the bed and sat.

Sweat dotted her forehead. As much as she kept insisting her ankle barely bothered her anymore, she wasn't being completely honest with him.

"Yes. Saddled Honey."

He smacked his forehead with the palm of his hand. So that was why she'd been gone so long. Crazy woman. Why was she so insistent on refusing his help?

Her chin came up. "Ready whenever you are. Just need to get my packs on Storm." She shifted to the edge of the bed. "Come on, boy." Lou snapped her fingers and the dog's tail wagged.

"You planning on taking him along to Burrton Springs?" Caleb hefted Lou's saddle bags.

She started to protest, and he narrowed his gaze at her. She at least had the good sense not to argue with him.

"Unless he decides to go off on his own. Figured it couldn't hurt to take him with us. Maybe we'll come upon someone along the trail who will have heard something about him." She shrugged her shoulders. "You never know."

"Best put a hand on my shoulder so you can keep as much pressure as possible off your ankle." He shifted the packs he carried so she could easily grip him. He had planned to carry her to her horse once he saddled it but from the look on her face, she'd refuse him.

The faster they got on the trail, the better.

She secured the door behind them and hopped the short path to the barn where the horses were stamping their feet and snorting in the cold, predawn air. It had lightened enough to see a few patches of prairie grass peeking through the snow.

He set the packs down and lifted her onto the saddle before she could protest. The leather squeaked as she shifted her weight.

Caleb made quick work of securing the packs, tightening the leather straps. Swinging up in the saddle, he glanced at the horizon. Looked to be a clear day which would make it easier to navigate in the general direction of Burrton Springs. Snow still covered any trail there might have been. "You figure out which way to go?"

Color filled her cheeks, and she shifted her Stetson lower on her face as she studied the ground. "I, uh." She swung her gaze to the north, east, and west.

He bit back a chuckle.

No denying it. The widow was a greenhorn. If only he could get her to admit it.

"Well, you tell me. You're the one who wanted to head to Burrton Springs. I haven't exactly decided where's best for me to travel next." Her eyes twinkled as she brought her head up and stared at him.

Caleb shook his head. Whoever married this woman would be driven to distraction. He just knew it wouldn't be him. "We're actually heading south."

Her cheeks flamed even brighter. Almost like a prairie rose.

"Besides, we talked about you seeing the doctor. I mean, Josh. He can best tell you what else you should be doing for that ankle of yours." And while they were there, he'd learn if his prior partner had heard anything about Klaude. Although he'd be sure to ask for information when the widow wasn't present. He didn't need her trailing after him, thinking she could take the outlaw captive on her own. She'd be sure to get in serious trouble, if not harmed or killed. He'd do whatever it took to keep her safe and away from the fugitive.

No matter how much he'd pestered her over the past couple weeks, she'd refused to tell him why she needed the money. After sharing about her deceased husband and his horse ranch, Caleb didn't figure Lou was a woman to go off without some sort of plan. Something had driven her to go on the trail alone to find a delinquent groom. Something other than money from the bride-to-be. Lou didn't strike him as a woman who did things flippantly. Desperate maybe, but definitely not a woman who did something without serious thought behind it. Question was, what drove Lou? What had befallen her since her husband died that had her needing money? So much so she'd struck out on her own on a dangerous trail? And why did he care so much about what happened to the young widow? To the extent he was willing to go out of his way to see her safely home.

~*~

Sheer determination and grit were what held Ellie Lou's weary, trembling limbs in the saddle. She couldn't imagine how she'd be doing if she'd had to hold the dog for the entire journey. The poor mutt would've been on his own if it weren't for Caleb keeping an eye on him and holding the pup as needed.

Throughout the day, the former lawman had offered to slow down their pace, but she'd refused. She had to prove herself capable of keeping up with him, or he'd never agree to take her along to find Klaude. Her eyes drifted closed, and she caught herself for the third time from slumping over in the saddle.

Bright moonlight reflected off the banks of snow. Days of sunlight had melted a path of sorts, or at least from what Caleb called it. They'd be thoroughly lost if she were leading the way home. She yawned.

"We're almost there from the look of it." Caleb's voice rang through the cold night air. "Hang on a little longer."

She didn't have the energy to respond.

Storm jiggled his head.

She loosened the reins and patted his sweaty neck. Midday Caleb encouraged her to switch steeds, especially when he mentioned her mare, Honey, was pregnant. Ellie Lou could kick herself for not recognizing the mare was carrying a foal. What kind of horse rancher was she? Clearly an inexperienced one. Charles would've been disappointed in her. She prayed they hadn't pushed Honey too hard on the journey.

Caleb had made a point of taking breaks several times. Even still, many hours had passed since they started before dawn.

Ellie Lou hated to think about how sore she'd be once they finally reached their destination. She didn't have the energy to direct him to her ranch. Hopefully someone in Burrton Springs would take pity on them and put them up for the night. She'd be willing to sleep almost anywhere at this point.

Her thoughts blurred, her brain feeling like mush. She shifted in the saddle. Her backside told her she'd been in the saddle for a long time. Ellie Lou's foot throbbed with each beat of her heart. She had the feeling she wouldn't be able to remove her boot without stuffing snow in it again.

Why, Lord? Why did You have this happen to me? I thought You were helping me to pay off the loan on the ranch. How come every time I think You're directing me, the bottom drops out? Are You even listening to me, Lord?

"Whoa." Caleb's murmur interrupted her prayer.

"Where are we?" Her voice came out in a croak. *Dear, God. Help me not to catch an illness as well. Isn't it enough I injured my ankle?*

The Lord apparently wasn't joining in on her conversation. Was He back to being silent as He'd been in the past few months?

"I reckon it's Burrton Springs." Caleb glanced at the darkened street. Not many lanterns shone in windows. "Any idea where Josh lives?"

She shook her head. "Only know where his sister and her family reside."

"Well, I guess that's the best place to start. Are we close to their place?"

It took her a few seconds to get her bearings in the darkened town. A moment later the moon broke free of a cloud. "Over there." She motioned. "They're the house beside the church."

Caleb clicked and all three of the horses plodded along, their heads down.

Ellie Lou gripped the saddle horn to keep herself from falling.

"Whoa." Caleb swung from the saddle.

How could he be as fresh as when they'd started hours ago?

She jumped when his hand rested on her knee. Had she dozed off again?

"Stay here while I get directions."

She didn't have the energy to nod in agreement.

A door creaked open.

"Howdy. Sorry to bother you at such a late hour." Caleb's words drifted her way.

"How can I help? I'm Pastor Drew."

"I'm trying to find Joshua Walker. I understand he's a doctor now?" Caleb glanced back at her. "My companion's been injured."

"Oh, my." Light shone as the pastor opened the door farther. "Josh, we got someone here in need of your services."

A few seconds later a man poked his head out of the doorway. He pulled on a coat as he stepped outside. "What seems to be the trouble?" He glanced at Caleb, and then towards her.

The scene from when she'd been held captive at her ranch a few months prior flashed across her mind. How could she have forgotten Josh had been a part of rounding up the outlaws after it was all over?

"Mrs. Williams? Is that you?" The doctor hurried toward her. "Are you injured?"

Caleb's gaze swung her way. The light from inside the house lit his face enough to see his raised eyebrows.

Whether she liked it or not, he now knew her real name. Well, at least part of it. She'd never told Caleb her last name either. Despite spending time with him the past few weeks, she'd withheld sharing it until now. She hadn't told him her real reason for needing the money either. There were some things a woman wanted to keep private from having just anyone knowing. After all, the only other person in town who knew about her financial concerns was the bank owner and her dear friend Gertrude. She'd do what she could to keep it that way if at all possible.

"Ellie Lou?" The doctor's words interrupted her scattered musings. He stepped closer.

Her thoughts blurred as everything went black.

10

Caleb sprinted as Lou started to fall off her horse. He caught her before she hit the ground. *Probably shouldn't have pushed her so hard today. Although it was either that or starve in the soddy. God, help her to be fine. I don't want anyone to suffer on account of me and my decisions.*

"Best bring her to my office." Josh glanced at him. "Caleb, is that you? Leave your dog here and my brother-in-law will put him up in his barn." A smile stretched across his face. "Haven't seen you in a few years. You're looking good."

Caleb nodded, keeping his gaze on the snowy walkway. He didn't want to slip and fall when he had Lou in his arms. Make that Ellie Lou. He studied her pale face. No. She'd always be Lou to him.

A few minutes later, Josh unlocked the door to a building in the middle of town. "Give me a second." His friend fumbled with something before he struck a match and lit a lantern. "This way." He headed down a hallway.

Caleb followed, careful not to bump Lou's head or ankle against the walls.

Josh motioned to a table. "Place her there. What seems to be the problem?"

As gently as he could, Caleb laid Lou on the examination table. "She hurt her ankle a couple weeks ago." He removed his gloves and placed them in his coat pocket.

Lou's eyes fluttered, and she moaned. "W-where am I?"

"In my office." Josh put his hand on her leg. "We need to cut off your boot. There's no way we'll get it off otherwise."

"No, please no." She bit her lip as tears rolled down her pale cheeks. "Put snow down my boot to bring down the swelling. The pain isn't too bad." Her voice had a rasp to it.

Josh shook his head. "That may have been an option before, but it won't work this time. I'm guessing you've had your leg hanging all day while being in the saddle. It will take too long to get the swelling down with snow. I'm sorry, Ellie Lou."

"Are you sure there's not another way?" Caleb glanced at Lou and then his friend. "She's kind of partial to those boots."

"Sorry. Too much danger of her circulation being cut off considering how long the blood's been pumping into her foot." Josh pulled a stethoscope from a shelf. "Thought you would've known better, Caleb."

Heat burned up his neck and into his face. "Didn't have much of a choice."

Josh's brows rose, but he didn't say anything more as he listened to Lou's heart.

A set of coughs racked her body.

Caleb's friend frowned and reached for a set of shears.

With the first cut into the leather, Lou's soft sobs nearly broke Caleb's heart. It was as if she was losing a part of her deceased husband in the process. Somehow, he'd find a way to make it up to her. Even though it hadn't been his fault she'd stepped in the prairie dog hole, he should've come up with some other way to get them food. Should've waited until the swelling had gone down more before they made the trip. He rubbed his hand along his jawline. He needed a shave again.

Lou grasped his hand. Her gloved fingers rested in his palm.

Without thinking, he laced his fingers through hers wishing he could somehow take her pain away–both physical and emotional. One thing he learned over the past weeks was the young widow had tenacity. Maybe not always the best common sense, but at heart, she wanted to do the right thing. Couldn't fault her for it. She hadn't ever shared why she needed the cash, but it had to be significant enough she'd left the safety of her home to round up a missing groom. Too bad the fella had been shot. Maybe Caleb could help Lou by breaking the news to the waiting bride, who no longer would be a bride. How did you tell a woman something like that?

"There." Josh's voice interrupted Caleb's musings.

Lou swiped tears with the back of her glove. Her Stetson toppled to the floor in the process. Blonde hair sprawled around her shoulders.

Funny. He thought it would've been longer.

Josh shifted her foot up and down.

With each motion, Lou gasped.

The doctor shook his head. "You've got a really bad sprain here, Ellie Lou. You'll need to stay off it for a few weeks if you want it to heal properly."

She propped herself on her elbows. "I can't do that." She coughed.

"Let me see your throat." Josh brought the lantern closer.

Lou opened her mouth and stuck out her tongue.

"Doesn't look great. I'm guessing you caught something as well. Best to rest your voice." He set the lantern down. "Are you hurting anywhere else?"

She shifted on the bed but didn't answer.

Probably hurt everywhere after their long ride. Caleb doubted she'd admit it though.

"At least you don't have a fever. Still, I don't want you staying alone at your ranch." Josh set the lantern down. "In fact, I think it's best if you stay in town for a few days so I can keep an eye on that ankle and your cough."

Lou shook her head. "I won't impose on anyone."

Josh frowned. "I'm sure we can figure something out. You can spend the night here. I have a bed in the other room. I use it sometimes when I have a patient who needs to be closely monitored. You're welcome to use it." He glanced at Caleb. "You can bed down in my barn if you'd like. Sorry, Annie and I only have one room at our place."

"No problem. I think I'll sleep on the floor in your waiting room in case Lou needs something through the night." Caleb was startled when Lou withdrew her hand from his.

Josh glanced at him and then Lou.

What was his friend thinking?

"Don't need your help," Lou's words were whispered.

"Lou, huh? Why're you calling her that?" Josh's forehead

creased.

"It's a long story." Caleb glanced at her.

Pink tinged her cheeks. It was good to see some color on her face.

Her hoarse voice interrupted. "I'll be fine on my own." She sat up and started to sway.

~*~

Ellie Lou willed the room to stop swirling around her. She couldn't faint when she hoped to convince the men she had no need of their assistance. *Please make my body cooperate, Lord. If they feel they need to watch over me, I won't ever get away so I can start searching for Klaude.*

"Whoa, there." Doc Walker put an arm around her shoulder to steady her. "You need to take it easy, Ellie Lou. And I don't want you going anywhere without using a crutch." He crossed to a corner of the room and brought back an apparatus. "It might take a bit to get the hang of it, but it will help you to keep pressure off the ankle."

"I really should get back to my ranch." She shifted to the edge of examining table, gripping the wood as the room tilted.

"No reason to be ornery. There's plenty of room here, and I can see you're all done in. Let's get you settled in the room." Doc steadied her as she stood.

Caleb positioned himself on her opposite side, hiking his shoulder for her to grab onto.

It took a few stops and starts before she found the rhythm of clasping Caleb's elbow and the crutch and hopping in between.

"It's a miracle you two found somewhere to hole up during those blizzards. Word's been slowly coming in from across the state. Thousands of head of cattle died in the storm. And a lot of wildlife froze to death." Josh stepped around them and pulled the covers down on a small bed on one side of the wall. "People are still missing. A number of folks have been found dead, often within a few feet of their doors. Heard tell they're still working at digging out the trains in portions of the state. Drifts have been as high as ten feet in areas."

A sheen of sweat soaked Ellie Lou's brow by the time she settled on the side of the bed. Her head hurt with each throbbing of her foot, in cadence with her heart.

"How did you two meet up?" Josh pulled a couple pillows from a cabinet and set them on the end of the bed. "You'll want to use those to elevate your foot as much as possible. It will help to get the swelling down. I'll also mix up some laudanum for the pain to help you sleep."

"That's a story for another day." Caleb glanced at her. "I'll go get your pack and take care of the horses. I'll be back as soon as I can. Do you need anything before I leave?"

She shook her head.

"I'll show you where you can put the horses for the night. My brother's stable has plenty of room." Josh's gaze swung back toward her as the men stopped in the doorway. "Did you want me to get the medicine before I show Caleb where to bed the horses?"

"No," she croaked. "I'll be fine."

Caleb frowned.

As soon as the men had left the room, she removed her other boot and swung her feet onto the bed, pulling the blankets over the length of her body. A cough racked her frame. Slowly the throbbing in her foot eased a fraction. Her eyelids drifted shut.

~*~

Caleb hated leaving Lou to fend for herself, especially with how much her ankle had swelled, but there was no avoiding it. The horses needed cared for after hours of travel.

Josh tromped through the snow beside him. "What brings you to Burrton Springs?"

"Wanted to get Lou home." He stumbled over a branch half hidden by a snowdrift but caught himself before falling.

His friend smiled. "I think there's a story behind that."

He shrugged. "Don't suppose you've heard anything about Klaude Kidman's whereabouts?"

"He the one who held up the stagecoach and shot three people? Is he who you've been tracking?" Josh flipped the collar of his coat up as the wind swirled harder. "Guess you're still the U.S. Marshal in Topeka?"

Caleb shook his head. "Yes, Klaude's the one I'm looking for, but not as a marshal anymore. Gave my job up a few weeks ago, but I promised the new marshal I'd see what I could do about rounding up Klaude before I hang up from chasing criminals for a living."

Josh's gaze pierced him. "Never thought I'd see the day you retired."

He chuckled. "You're one to talk. Didn't think you would either, let alone end up as a doctor. How did that happen? Last time I saw you, you were gun shy about entering a town let alone living in one and being a doctor."

Josh adjusted his Stetson, bending his head as the wind shifted. "It was the Lord's doing." He laughed. "His and my Annie."

"Lou mentioned you're married now." Caleb patted each of the horses before he untied the reins from the hitching post.

"Here, let me help you." Josh reached for one of the reins. "Not just married, but I have a daughter too."

"Looks as if you've had a lot of good things come into your life since you left the law profession." Weariness tugged at Caleb's shoulders. He couldn't wait to rest his exhausted body.

"That's for sure." Josh opened a barn door. Inside he clanked against something before a match was lit followed by a lantern. "You can bring the horses in here. I'd help you take care of them, but I should probably get back so I can get the pain medicine for Ellie Lou. As much as her foot is swelled, she must be in a great deal of pain."

The dog drew close to Caleb's side, wagging his tail.

Caleb bent down and petted him. "Don't worry about me. I can take care of them. I'd rather you make sure Lou has what she needs."

Josh chuckled. "You definitely have changed. Never dreamt I'd see the day you were wanting to take care of a woman."

11

Dim light woke Caleb. It took him a few seconds to remember where he was. On the floor in the infirmary. Well, more so the waiting room. His left shoulder and hip ached from sleeping on the hard floor even with his bedroll beneath him. It had been late by the time he'd finished with the horses. Lou had been fast asleep when he'd poked his head in the doorway to check on her. Josh had said she'd been sleeping before he had the chance to give her pain medicine and that rest was what she needed the most.

Caleb groaned as he rolled over and stared at the ceiling. *What should I do next, Lord? I can't find Klaude if I don't know where to start the search. Is it better if I delay a few days to make sure Lou is on the mend before heading out? I feel it's the least I can do since we've been together these past couple weeks. Seems as though she doesn't have anyone to take care of her. Not that I'm applying for the job, Lord. Just hate to see a widow struggling to survive.*

A series of coughs came from a room down the hall.

Lou.

Was it too early to check on her?

Another round of coughing sounded.

Best to take a peek. Maybe she needed him.

Needed. That was something he hadn't felt since before his parents died. He shoved the thought aside and pushed back the blanket.

He groaned as he stood, stretching his arms above his head to try and ease the crick in his neck. His stocking feet didn't make a sound as he walked down the hallway. He hesitated a moment outside of the opened door. Poking his head around the corner, he glanced into the room.

Lou was partially propped up on a pillow, a hand over her

mouth as she coughed into it.

"You don't sound so good."

She jumped at the sound of his voice. "Caleb."

He could barely hear her. Poor thing. "What do you need? How can I help?"

"A glass of water." Her words were a croak.

"Sure thing." He crossed to the cabinet on the opposite wall from her bed where a small pitcher and glass sat. Caleb poured some water into it and handed it to her. "Drink up. Maybe it will help your throat."

She drained the glass and gave it back to him. "Thank you." Her words were a little clearer, but not much.

"Can I get you anything else?" He rested his shoulder against the doorframe.

Color tinged her cheeks.

"What is it? What do you need?"

"Th…the necessary."

Heat soared into his neck. "It's, uh, under the bed. Let me get it for you." His fingers grazed hers as he handed her the pot. An odd jolt shot up his arm. "I'll just, uh, close the door behind me. Knock on the wall when you're, uh, finished, and I'll take care of it for you." He scurried from the room before she had time to answer him.

Best take care of his own needs so he wouldn't be thinking about Lou. He hurried down the hall and tugged the front door open. The night before he'd seen an outhouse behind the building.

The sun hadn't crested the horizon yet, so it had to be early. Caleb heard a dog bark as he took care of business. When he strolled back to the doctor's office, not a soul could be seen. He needed to find something for them to eat this morning. Guess he should've made it clearer last night to Josh that they were out of food. His stomach growled. Lou would be hungry too. Maybe he should search for something for them and allow her a little more time alone. He didn't want to walk in on her and…

He shoved the thought aside.

Caleb strolled down the street. A light shone in the general store. Maybe he could get the owner to open early. He knocked on the door.

A balding man strolled to the window and stared at him. He pointed at the shop hours listed on a piece of paper propped in the store window.

He knocked again.

The man shuffled over and unlocked the door. "Sorry, mister, I won't be open for another hour or so."

"Could you please make an exception?" Caleb pressed closer. "My companion and I haven't had food the past couple days. She's injured and staying at doc's office. I've got money and can pay you."

The man opened the door and motioned him inside. "Name's Hiram Martin. Wouldn't want to turn you away when you're hungry." He indicated to the left side of the store. "Canned goods are over there. Also have some muffins one of the local ladies made yesterday. They didn't all sell. Folks haven't ventured out as much with this weather. I can knock the price down for you since they're a day old. Did you two get caught in those blizzards?" The man shivered. "Lived in this area for a long time and have never seen weather as bad as that."

"Me, either." Caleb studied a stack of cans, selecting a few of them. "I'll just get what I need for breakfast and will be back later."

The man waved. "No need to hurry on my account. I was just getting the fire going so the store would be warm by the time folks hopefully venture outside. The store's been slower than normal. Think most are still shoveling their way from their homes."

Caleb juggled the cans as he studied the rest of the store.

"Where did you say you came from?" The store owner shuffled closer, tying an apron across his expanding belly.

"Didn't say." He glanced at the man. Most times Caleb didn't like to share too much information about himself with strangers.

"Hmm." The man grabbed a broom and started sweeping. "Just trying to make conversation."

Caleb nodded but didn't respond. He started toward the counter when he saw a display of boots. They were sized for children, women, and men. A dark brown leather pair snagged his attention. Fancy stitches and swirls decorated the soft leather. They looked to be about the right size. Before he could talk himself from the purchase, Caleb snagged the boots from the shelf and carried them to the long counter.

"Looks like your companion's a woman." The shopkeeper smiled. "Any gal will love these."

Lou wasn't just any gal.

~*~

Ellie Lou managed to set the chamber pot back under the bed. She'd heard the outside door a few minutes earlier but not again. Caleb must've gone somewhere. She hated him being the one to take care of the pot but didn't figure she had enough energy to deal with it herself. She felt weaker than a newborn kitten. How had the trip taken so much of her energy?

Ellie Lou groaned as she stared at a calendar pinned to the wall. December 20th. Less than two weeks to pay off the bank. Her hands were clammy as she adjusted the covers.

I keep waiting for You to make Yourself known in my situation, Lord. Lately it feels as though I'm talking to the ceiling and my prayers aren't going anywhere. I know Your Word says You are trustworthy, but I haven't been personally experiencing it, God. I need You to write a big sign to tell me what I'm supposed to do next. I don't want to fail Charles's memory. His dream. But I can't do this on my own. Can You send someone to help or at least help me to find the funds to pay off my debts? And give me the words when I tell Betty what happened.

A door creaked open. Footsteps sounded in the hallway.

Someone knocked on the door and opened it. Caleb poked his head at the edge of the doorway. "You decent?"

She chuckled. "Have been for a while."

He bent and picked up the chamber pot.

Heat flamed up her neck and into her cheeks. She couldn't glance his way.

"I'll just take care of this and then I have our breakfast." He disappeared before she could question him.

A minute later he returned. He placed the pot back under the bed. Next, he poured water from a pitcher into the basin and washed his hands. "You hungry?"

Her stomach growled.

He chuckled, his laughter filling the room.

It was the nicest sound Ellie Lou had heard in a long while.

Caleb strolled to the doorway, stooped, and picked up something on the floor from the hallway. "Managed to get some food at the general store. It's an odd collection but should be enough to tide us over until we can get some more substantial supplies." He carted the items to the bed and set them beside her. "Be right back." A few seconds later he reappeared with both of their plates and utensils.

"Is there anything you can't do?" She smiled as he shifted his white Stetson.

His blue-eyed gaze pierced her, making her heart falter for a second.

"Believe me, there's plenty I can't." He placed two muffins on each of their plates followed by some meat he spooned from a can along with carrots. "I know it's an odd assortment of food for breakfast, but I didn't figure you'd be too particular." A grin spread across his chiseled chin. When had he found the time to shave?

She'd never seen a man so fastidious when it came to having a clean face. Even in the soddy, he'd made a point of shaving each morning and evening. It was almost an obsession.

He gripped her hand. "Dear God, thank You for the food You provided. Thank You for getting us to Burrton Springs safely. Help Lou to heal. Give her what she needs. In Jesus's Name, amen." He released her palm and gave her the filled plate. "Dig in."

She took a bite of the muffin.

So, he still called her Lou even though he'd surely heard Josh call her by her full name. Should she ask Caleb about it? Holding her hand while he prayed was new. He hadn't attempted hand holding at the soddy. Well, this wasn't exactly hand holding either. Why did she sense a tiny shift in their relationship? What did it mean? More importantly, was it something she wanted changed?

"You all right?" He rested his palm against her forehead. "You don't feel warm."

Ellie Lou cleared her throat. "I'm fine. Thank you for the food. Did you happen to check on our dog?"

"My pleasure. No, I haven't yet, but I will after we eat."

Silence stretched between them as they filled their bellies. While it'd been an unusual assembly of foods, it was the best meal they'd had in a few days. She set the plate aside and rubbed her full stomach.

He took the dish from her. "I can take care of these in a few minutes. Perhaps we'd better decide our plan for the day first."

"Still working on deciding that. What about you? What will you do?" She shifted the pillows under her ankle.

"Here, let me." He gently lifted her calf and adjusted the pillows before setting her leg on top.

The scent of whatever he used to shave his face wafted her way. She swallowed. Her breathing hitched.

"I need to talk to the sheriff to see if he's heard anything new about Klaude's whereabouts. We also need to get you situated somewhere too." He leaned against the doorframe. "Didn't suppose you'd want to stay here. How far away is your ranch? Do you have anybody there who can help you?"

She shook her head. "Just me, and I live halfway between here and Hutchinson. There's not a lot to do at the ranch right now since both of my horses are here in town. With being winter, there's nothing to do in the fields." How much should she share with him? She hesitated. "Need to talk to Betty too." She didn't look forward to that conversation.

His brows rose.

Was he wondering why a horse rancher only had two horses?

"Is there somewhere you can stay in town here? Do they have a hotel or someone who rents out rooms?"

Her chin came up.

"Lou?"

"Can't afford it."

He nodded and rubbed the back of his neck. "There's, uh, something else I have for you." He fingered the black neckerchief tied loosely around his neck.

Was he nervous about something?

"Close your eyes."

"What?" She studied his face.

"Please."

She obeyed.

The only sound in the room was his boots as he clomped to the doorway and then back to beside her bed.

She heard him set something down beside her.

"You can open your eyes now." His words were soft.

Ellie Lou opened her eyes to find the prettiest set of ladies boots she'd ever seen.

12

Caleb swallowed.

Lou just sat, not saying a word. Didn't she like the boots? Were they the wrong size? Had he overstepped? Should he take them back to the store? No. He couldn't ungive a gift.

He darted a glance her way.

Was that a tear she swiped from her cheek?

This definitely didn't go the way I intended.

"I, uh. I don't know what to say." Lou ran a finger along the fancy stitches. "I can't afford to pay you for them." She sniffed. "I never had a pair of boots like this."

"Well, I figured with being a ranch owner, you needed a pair. Especially after the doc had to cut off your husband's." He touched her hand for a second. "I'm sorry about that. I know they meant a lot to you."

Tears streaked down her cheeks, chasing one right after the other.

He fished a clean handkerchief from his pocket and handed it to her. "I know you can't wear them both for a while yet, but hopefully they'll fit. Do you want to try the one on?"

She swiped her cheeks with his hanky. "I shouldn't but…"

He didn't wait for her to change her mind. Caleb carefully worked the boot on over her stocking foot. "What do you think?"

Her face broke into a smile.

His chest expanded with pleasure to have brought her even a small measure of happiness. From what he'd witnessed in the past few weeks, the widow had had very little positive things in her life since she'd lost her husband.

"They fit perfectly." She tipped her foot from side to side admiring the boot. "And it's so comfortable too."

A grin pulled at his cheeks. "Glad you like them."

She slipped the boot off and hugged it to her chest for a few seconds. "Still, it isn't appropriate for me to accept a gift from you. You aren't a relative or friend, even." Her cheeks flamed with color. "And definitely not my intended."

"After all we've been through together, I think we can at least say we're friends, don't you agree?"

Her brown eyes widened.

Heat rushed to his face. Had he gone too far again? He rubbed a hand along the taut muscles in his neck. Since when had he started getting soft? Next thing he knew, he'd be knitting something in front of a roaring fireplace. Caleb shook his head. The faster he got back on the trail of Klaude, the better. Hopefully Josh could connect him with the sheriff today. Maybe the fella would've heard something new, despite the bad weather the past few weeks.

"I suppose you could say we are sort of friends."

Before he could respond, the sound of a door being thrust open carried to them. "Be right back." Caleb hurried from the room. A woman bustled towards him.

She halted for a minute. "Hello. Where's Ellie Lou?"

He motioned toward the room he'd just exited. "Right there, ma'am."

"Oh, Ellie Lou, I ran into Josh, and he said you'd been injured. You poor thing. What can I do to help you?"

Caleb hesitated, unsure whether to follow the woman into the room or just stay nearby in case Lou needed him. Best to stay within hearing distance, just in case. He edged a few steps away to give the ladies some measure of privacy.

"Gertrude. It's so good to see you."

"What happened? Betty said you've been gone for almost three weeks."

Lou chuckled. "Well, not quite."

"Why would you leave so sudden-like? Surely someone else could have gone searching for Betty's fiancé."

Silence stretched for a few seconds before Lou responded. "You know why. When Betty offered to pay me to find her fiancé, I knew I had to go."

"Oh, Ellie Lou, are you still trying to get the money to pay off the note on your ranch?"

So that was why she'd been insistent on tracking down the fella. Caleb should stop listening to their conversation, but he couldn't help himself. He crept a step closer. Lou hadn't ever mentioned her true reason. It made a lot of sense now.

"Didn't you tell me a while ago you needed to pay the loan back by the end of the year?"

He heard Lou sigh as if she had the weight of the world on her shoulders. "Yes, I don't know what I'll do, Gertrude, if I can't find the money to pay the bank by the end of the year. I don't have anywhere to go." She sniffed. "I'm sure I'd be a disappointment to Charles if he were still alive. But then, if Charles was still alive, I wouldn't be in this mess in the first place."

"I could say something to Enoch if it comes to that. We do have an extra room although we may be needing it before long."

"Are you having a baby?" Lou's tone changed. She sounded happy but there was something else in her voice too. "Oh, Gertrude, that's wonderful. You'll make an incredible mother."

Caleb shifted a step away. He didn't want to hear woman talk about husbands and babies.

The outside door swung open.

Heat flared in Caleb's cheeks as Josh entered the office and saw him standing in the middle of the hallway. He felt guilty like when his ma had caught him snitching cookies from the jar before supper.

Josh's brow rose. "Something wrong?"

He strolled towards his friend. "No."

His friend studied him for a few seconds but didn't ask him anything else.

"If you point me in the direction of the sheriff's office, I think I'll mosey over there and see if he has any more information on Klaude."

"I imagine he's there by now since Gertrude, his wife, was asking about Ellie Lou. I suppose she found her way here already."

"I'm here." The woman poked her head around the corner. "Did you need something from me?"

Josh glanced at the woman, and then back at Caleb. The doc's eyes twinkled.

He could just imagine what his friend was thinking to have found him eavesdropping on the ladies. Caleb grabbed his Stetson and shoved it on his head, buttoning his coat as he headed toward the door. "Where was that sheriff's office?"

Josh chuckled but didn't press him on the matter. "Turn right when you leave the building. It's a few blocks away. You can't miss it."

Caleb nodded but didn't respond.

Cold air greeted him as he meandered through town. Folks greeted him as he made his way down the street. The pastor waved but Caleb didn't stop to chat with the man.

Burrton Springs was a small town, but folks seemed friendly enough.

What would it be like to settle in a place like this, Lord? Away from all the memories of war. Of death. Away from the constant reminders of my failings?

~*~

Ellie Lou listened as Gertrude rambled on, but she also couldn't help hearing Caleb leave the doctor's office. After being together so much the past weeks, she had a moment of loss. Would he return? Would Caleb tell her what he might learn about the outlaw?

She chafed to leave the bed and follow after him, in hopes of discovering whatever information he obtained.

"Ellie Lou, are you listening to me?" Gertrude touched her shoulder. "Was there something I missed?" She glanced at the doorway.

Doc Walker poked his head in. "Sorry to interrupt, ladies, but I wanted to check on Ellie Lou to see how she's faring."

"Of course. I can come back later." Gertrude headed toward the door.

"No need to leave. This will only take a few minutes." Doc motioned toward the hallway. "If you don't mind waiting there until I'm finished."

Gertrude exited the room without another word.

Ellie Lou worked to conceal her cough.

"Still coughing, eh?" He glanced at her before withdrawing a stethoscope from a drawer.

Silence filled the room as he listened to her heart.

"Hmm. That's good. Doesn't sound like pneumonia has settled in your lungs." He draped the instrument around his neck. "I still want you to take it easy and definitely rest your ankle as much as possible."

She cleared her throat. "I can't keep staying here, though." At least her voice was stronger this morning.

"Nonsense. Right now, I don't have need for this room."

Ellie Lou winced as he turned her leg from side to side, gently touching the swollen ankle.

"Still doesn't look great."

She couldn't just lie around all day doing nothing. She'd already done a fair amount of that the past few weeks. Besides, how would she get her meals? If she could somehow get back to the ranch, she'd have plenty of food. Except she didn't think she could saddle Storm by herself. *What're You doing to me, Lord?*

"I'm recommending bed rest until I tell you otherwise. If for some reason we need to move you, we'll deal with that then. For now, I want you staying put here." Doc Walker gripped her wrist, feeling her pulse. "Good. Nice and steady."

"Are you sure you don't want me to leave?" There had to be somewhere she could go.

"I know it's not ideal staying in town when we're so close to celebrating our Savior's birth. I imagine you'd rather be with family." Doc released her wrist. "Is there someone you want me to contact for you? Sorry. Should've asked you last night."

Ellie Lou shook her head. "I don't have anyone."

Doc patted her shoulder. "I'm sorry, Ellie Lou. If there's anything I can do for you, please let me know. Have you had something to eat yet? If not, I can stop by my place. Annie always makes plenty."

Ellie Lou shifted a little higher on the bed. "No need. Caleb made sure we had something."

"Caleb, huh?" The doctor grinned. "Never did hear how you two ended up together."

Heat rushed to her cheeks. "We're not together. That is. We just happened to stumble upon each other before the first blizzard hit. Fortunately, Caleb was able to get us to an abandoned soddy. Don't think we would've made it if he hadn't."

"I'd say it was the Lord guiding you two. Heard tell folks died just steps away from the door to their homes." Doc Walker sighed. "It's a good thing the Lord brought you two together."

She shot a glance his way.

A smile spread across the doctor's face. "Who knows, maybe God had more reason than keeping you safe through the storm. Might have something else in store for you two."

Why did the idea bring comfort?

Ellie Lou shoved the thought aside. She didn't have time for any romantic thinking. The paying off of her debts still needed to be taken care of. Doctor's orders or not, she had to find a way to make money over the next week.

Are You listening, Lord? I don't understand why You'd have me laid up with no way to pay off what I owe the bank. What're You trying to teach me, Lord? I've always tried to follow You and do what I thought You were saying. Why aren't You answering me? Are You there? Doesn't Your Word say You won't abandon me? I know that in my head because of reading it in the Bible, but I sure don't feel it in my heart.

"Ellie Lou? Is something else bothering you?" Doc stooped and stared into her eyes.

Tightness clogged her throat making it difficult to respond to his kindness. Tears pricked her eyes. How could she tell this kind man she felt as though the Lord had abandoned her? Forgotten about her needs. That in a matter of ten days she'd be homeless. But she couldn't expect mere strangers to come to her aid and solve her problems for her. No. She'd have to find some way to manage things on her own. If God didn't show up, she'd somehow find a way to keep the ranch. Maybe the banker would be willing to extend her another month or so.

"Ellie Lou?" His brow furrowed.

She realized she hadn't answered him. "There's uh, a few things I need to take care of in town."

"Is there something I can do?"

She shook her head. "No, I'm sure you're busy with your doctoring."

He rubbed his jaw. "Maybe Caleb can be of assistance whenever he returns."

If he returns.

"Don't worry, Ellie Lou. Whatever your needs are, we'll make sure they're taken care of." He glanced heavenwards. "And I know God can provide for you as well. My brother-in-law would tell you that you can trust God, no matter what you're going through. Sometimes we think God is late in responding, but He's always on time."

Right.

"His time, that is." He smiled. "Believe me, He knows what is best, even when He delays in responding."

13

Caleb knocked before opening the door to the sheriff's office. A tall, dark-haired man sat at the wooden desk.

"Howdy. What can I help you with?" The man stood, the tin star shining on his vest. "I'm Sheriff Enoch Valentine." He reached a hand towards Caleb.

Caleb shook it. The man had a firm grasp. Said a lot about the man.

"I'm Caleb Dawson. Friend of Joshua Walker. He was one of my deputies while I was a U.S. Marshal in the Topeka area."

The man nodded and motioned to a chair. "Have a seat. So, you're no longer a U.S. Marshal?"

He shook his head. "No, just stepped down from the position, although I promised my replacement I'd see if I could round up Klaude Kidman before I officially hang up my gun belt. Was wondering if you'd heard anything about his recent whereabouts. I stumbled across the stagecoach he attacked shortly before the blizzards. I was on his trail until the snow got too bad." No way would he mention how Lou lassoed him.

"Heard tell it was a pretty grisly scene." The sheriff shifted in his seat.

The sight flashed across Caleb's memory. He closed his eyes for a few seconds against all the other recollections it stirred.

"Did they ever determine the names of the passengers?"

"Not the young couple, but I think with the information I recently learned, the one fella was Jeffrey Murphy." He'd best not mention the man had been a fiancé of one of the women in town until Lou had a chance to talk to her. "Have you heard any more recent news on Klaude?"

The sheriff shook his head. "No. Wish I had. But with those two storms, most of the state is still trying to dig out, I think. I'd go looking for Klaude too if I knew which way he headed. Don't want to start on a wild chase when I hear tell the drifts are still pretty bad in places and the trains are struggling to get through."

"I wouldn't doubt it. I know on our way in, there still are drifts above my head in places."

"We?" The man's dark brow hitched.

"Lou Williams." Caleb shifted on his chair. "I mean, Ellie Lou Williams." He willed the heat not to spread to his neck and face.

"Ellie Lou?" The sheriff's forehead wrinkled. "Why would she have been heading to Topeka?"

It wasn't Caleb's place to share things about the woman who'd been his companion the past few weeks.

The sheriff ran his hand along his jaw. "I should've checked on her sooner."

Caleb was thankful the man hadn't pressed to discover why they'd been together. "How do you know her?" Best to get the lawman distracted, even if Caleb already knew some of the history that intertwined Lou and the sheriff.

"I worked at her ranch while her husband was living and for a while afterwards. Before I got this job. Say, if you've been a U.S. Marshal, don't suppose you'd be interested in being a deputy, would you?"

"No." Caleb shook his head. If he hadn't promised to look for Klaude, he wouldn't even have been doing that, but he'd given his word. Besides, if he did catch the outlaw, the reward money could go toward the nest egg Caleb had been saving for a place of his own. "Well, I won't keep you, Sheriff."

"Call me Enoch."

Caleb stood and shook the man's hand again. "Will you let me know if you hear something?"

"Sure thing. Would be nice to have a hand in rounding up the outlaw, especially since my wife's expecting now." Enoch chuckled. "She isn't too excited about me being away from her, let alone tracking down violent criminals, even though she knows from first-hand experience it can be part of the job. But that's a story for a different time if you happen to stay around."

"I'm staying for a few days at least. Hope to hear word so I can get on the man's trail again." Caleb strolled to the door. "Thanks for the information."

"Sorry I didn't know more." Enoch lifted a hand in farewell.

Back on the street, Caleb glanced around the town. Children were making their way to a schoolhouse on the edge of town. A fella stepped on the porch of the building and rang a bell. Caleb imagined they'd soon be taking a short break for Christmas. Hard to believe it was only five days away.

A gaggle of women lingered around what looked to be a lady's dress shop.

Caleb racked his brain, trying to remember what Lou had told him about Jeffrey Murphy's fiancée. Should he ask around town to find who she was? Would Lou be upset if he broke the news to... Betty something or other. He couldn't recall if Lou had ever shared the woman's last name or not. Apparently, Lou was good at not sharing last names.

He flipped up the collar of his coat as a brisk wind stirred up snow from the drifts near him. His breath hovered in the air. Caleb shivered. Maybe he should check on Lou first to make sure she was obeying Josh's orders. He had a feeling she'd be chomping to let Betty know what happened. If he could help it, he'd do whatever it took to keep her off that ankle, so it healed without permanent damage. He'd seen enough injuries during the war to know things didn't often heal well when the body was taxed beyond its limits. Knowing Lou, she'd be hard to tie down to the bed. At the soddy she hadn't had a choice with the weather. Otherwise, she'd been up trying to take care of the horses or whatever else needed taken care of.

She likely wouldn't stay put at Josh's office, especially if other patients needed it. The question was, where could he find a place for her? He didn't want to take her to her ranch to fend for herself. What if she needed help? After all they'd been through, he felt partially responsible for her. And there was no way he planned to let her follow him when he went searching for Klaude. He'd do whatever it took to prevent that.

~*~

Ellie Lou chafed to be free of the bed. How long had it been since Caleb left and why did her thoughts keep traveling to him?

"I'd like to stay longer, Ellie Lou, but I need to go open Ruffles and Stitches. I'll try and stop by again before Enoch and I head home later today. If there weren't steps leading up to my room above the shop, I'd offer for you to stay there." Gertrude buttoned her coat. "Maybe Mrs. Walsh has some room openings. Would you like me to check with her?"

She glanced at the clock on the mantel above the fireplace in the room. "No, looks as if you're late opening your shop. Thank you for stopping by to see me."

"If you're sure." Gertrude hesitated a moment before she wrapped her arms around Ellie Lou's shoulders. "Hang in there. You'll see. God will provide for you somehow. I don't have any doubt you can trust Him to take care of all your needs. I'll see you later."

Her friend left the room.

Ellie Lou's throat tightened. She used to know it too. When had doubts started to creep in, making her wonder if God truly did concern Himself with her problems? She knew she'd told Gertrude in the past about relying on God, so why did she feel so bereft now? Maybe because it was the first time God hadn't shown up in her time of yearning for Him to step in and make Himself known in her situation. She didn't understand why He was refusing to answer. Silent. Almost as if He didn't care. Her head and her heart battled to make sense of her circumstance. She sighed, her shoulders slumping.

A knock on the doorframe pulled her from her thoughts.

She glanced at the open doorway hoping to see Caleb.

Instead, Pastor Montgomery smiled at her. "I hope I'm not interrupting. Wanted to check in and see how you're doing. Also, to see if you need anything. I hope you had a good night and weren't in too much pain." He shifted a wooden chair closer to where she sat propped up on the bed.

She could use a change of clothes and a healed ankle. Ellie Lou glanced around the small room. Where had Caleb put her saddlebags? She shifted her train of thought back to the pastor who'd performed Charles's funeral. "Nothing worth mentioning." The pastor didn't likely have time to hear about all her problems. Best to paste on a smile instead. She hoped what she attempted would come across as that.

Pastor Drew didn't say anything but sat there watching her.

She shifted her foot on the pillow, adjusting the light blanket covering her legs.

The preacher opened his Bible. "Hope you don't mind. Thought maybe you'd enjoy hearing God's Word."

She nodded.

"I read this in Isaiah 43 this morning and thought about you." He shifted the Bible towards the light shining through the window. "'Fear not: for I have redeemed thee, I have called thee by thy name; thou art mine. When thou passest through the waters, I will be with thee; and through the rivers, they shall not overflow thee: when thou walkest through the fire, thou shalt not be burned; neither shall the flame kindle upon thee. I am the Lord thy God, the Holy One of Israel, thy Savior.'" Pastor Drew ran his hand across the page.

Ellie Lou swallowed. "Why did reading that passage of Scripture bring me to mind?"

"I've been thinking about all you've been through the past year or so with Charles getting sick and dying. All you and Gertrude experienced with his cousins trying to take over the ranch." He glanced at her. "Now with this ankle. I'm guessing there could be more you're going through I'm not aware of, too."

Tears sprang to her eyes, and she knuckled them away.

"Do you know what I like about these verses?"

She shook her head, not trusting her voice to talk when it was clogged with emotion.

"God didn't say if you pass through the waters, or if you pass through the rivers or if you go through fire. He knew we'd experience difficult things in our lives. Which I believe is why it says when in this passage. When we go through waters, rivers, fires, He promises we won't be consumed by them." He smiled. "I like how God starts the passage. For us not to be afraid. He has redeemed us. He's called us by name. He's a personal God who cares about every single aspect of our lives."

Her lower lip trembled. "B-but what about those times when it doesn't feel as if He's with us? When we aren't getting any answers? When we feel as though we're pouring our hearts out to Him and He's distant?"

"That's where faith kicks in. He promises in His Word He will never leave us or forsake us. He always answers us when we call to Him." He flipped the pages of his Bible. "Here in Psalm 116:1 it says, 'I love the LORD, because he hath heard my voice and my supplications.'" Pastor Drew flipped a few more pages. "Also in Psalm 145:18 it says, 'The LORD is nigh unto all them that call upon him, to all that call upon him in truth.' God promises to be near to us."

"I think sometimes my head and heart don't always agree on the topic. I know it says in God's Word He'll always be with me. That He's trustworthy…" She bit her lip. "But sometimes it's as though

He's ignoring me. Not answering. Not providing an answer when I'm earnestly seeking Him. When I'm desperate. When I need Him to rescue me."

Pastor Drew chuckled. "And most times that's when we mess up. We think we'll help God along since He's not responding on our timetable. Or we give Him an ultimatum. Expecting Him to perform like a trained animal showing off a trick it's learned. But we must remember, we aren't God. He can do as He chooses. If He's choosing to delay in answering, it's always for a reason. We don't see the big picture. We see only a small part of the tapestry. One day we'll see everything and understand what lesson He was trying to teach us. But it all boils down to trust. Trusting Him even when we can't see evidence He's working in our lives."

Trust. It seemed so easy when the preacher talked about it. So why did Ellie Lou find it so hard?

14

Caleb hadn't intended to eavesdrop twice in one day. He was only a few steps behind the pastor when he'd entered the doctor's office. At first, he thought the man wanted to see Josh, but when he started talking to Lou, Caleb had hesitated. Hadn't she mentioned he was a brother-in-law to Josh?

The man's words about trust washed over Caleb like a gentle rain on a blistering hot summer day. He didn't doubt God cared about him. God had protected him more than one time on the battlefield, but the thing he struggled with was why the Lord had preserved Caleb while letting others suffer and die. He knew evil entered the world when Adam and Eve chose to do their own thing instead of seeking a relationship with God, but it didn't make it easier seeing the ugly results of sin on the battlefield.

A few years back, a preacher had talked about evil. How God allowed folks to make a personal decision to follow Him. He didn't force people to serve Him. God longs for everyone to come to Him, but He is a gentleman. Always loving. Always desiring to fellowship with all of humanity. How evil in the world made those who choose to follow Him long for our Heavenly home.

Caleb's thoughts were interrupted as Josh's brother-in-law continued his conversation with Lou. "In Psalm twenty-two, David asks God why He's forsaken him. He petitions God day and night, and He doesn't respond. Despite feeling as if his strength was dried up like baked clay. David was in utter despair." The man paused. "But still, he remembered his forefathers trusted in God and how the Lord rescued them. He makes an active choice to praise the Lord. To proclaim Him to others. Even when he didn't understand why God wasn't answering, wasn't solving his problems at the moment, he made a decision to praise the Lord. To trust Him with his unknown.

He remembered how God had worked in the past with his ancestors."

Caleb leaned against the wall as he listened.

"I'm sure you've had many answers to prayers through the years, haven't you?"

"Yes." Lou's voice was stronger.

"In those times when we aren't hearing God's voice, ask Him if there's something between you. Perhaps some unconfessed sin you haven't dealt with. Ask Him to remind you of how He's answered prayer in the past. Praise Him even when your answer hasn't come yet. Trust that even if you don't see it for a while, He will come through. Don't allow Satan to throw doubts in there. Keep reading His Word. Know He promises to always be with you, and He never goes against His Word." The preacher chuckled. "You're letting me use you to practice my sermon on. If Josh permits you to get off this bed, I hope you can attend church. Even though it will only be a couple days before Christmas, I feel the Lord prompting me to talk about the faith of Noah."

Maybe Caleb could delay going after Klaude a few more days. That is, unless he got word of a recent sighting of the outlaw. The preacher's words made him curious to stay and find out what the man had to say in his Sunday sermon.

Lou's response must've been too quiet to reach Caleb's ears.

The sound of a throat being cleared interrupted his listening in on the preacher's conversation with Lou.

Josh smiled. "Never figured you'd be one to stand around checking out someone else's communication."

Caleb's ears burned as he took the Stetson from his head. A muscle twitched in his jaw.

"I know Drew has a way of drawing a body into whatever he's saying. I think it's why folks enjoy his sermons so much. Speaking of, do you plan on staying for Sunday? Or did you find some new information from Enoch?"

He took a couple steps away so hopefully Lou wouldn't hear him. He swallowed. Hard. What a hypocrite he was. Wanting to make sure she didn't hear him when he'd deliberately listened to two of her conversations today.

"You feeling off?" Josh's brow twitched.

"No. Just fine." Caleb cleared his throat. "Enoch didn't have any new information. Thinking I might stay around for a few days and hopefully I'll hear something in the meantime. Wanted to get Lou situated somewhere too. I know she won't want to impose on you here. Although I don't believe she's ready to be alone on her ranch either."

Josh didn't answer right away. Just stared at him.

It made Caleb downright uncomfortable. But there was no way he would let his friend know that. "Any thoughts on where she can hole up for a few weeks until she recovers?"

"I can ask around. There's also an older lady in town who has a few rooms she rents out. Although I thought she mentioned she might be busy with folks coming to see family for the holidays. But she said that before the snowstorms hit. It's possible folks weren't able to travel because of the weather. What about you? Will you need a room too?"

He twirled his Stetson. "You know me, I can bed down almost anywhere. Is your barn still an option?"

"It is, but maybe we can come up with something better than my barn." Josh studied him. "Have you thought much about what you'll do after you capture Klaude?"

He liked how his friend didn't say if the outlaw was captured, but when. Kind of reminded Caleb of what the preacher had said about the Bible verse from Isaiah about when folks went through things. "Been thinking about finding a ranch for sale somewhere. I decided it's about time to settle down."

"Do you have anywhere in particular you plan to live?"

Caleb shook his head. "Don't have anywhere specific. I guess one place is as good as any."

"It would be great to have you move into this area."

He warmed to the idea. What would it be like to be in a place where he had a friend and didn't have to be concerned about trouble following him?

~*~

Ellie Lou's throat constricted. Was Caleb trying to get rid of all responsibility for her so he could get on Klaude's trail?

"Well, you must be tired." Pastor Drew smiled. "I'll let you get some rest. Please send word through Josh if you need anything."

"I will. Thank you for stopping by." She returned his smile.

The man gave a small wave as he left the room.

She tried to hear more of Caleb's conversation with the doctor but only a smattering of words traveled to her ears. Nothing she could make heads or tails with.

I know Pastor Drew would likely say there's a reason for this delay, Lord, but I sure can't see what the purpose of it is. I know I shouldn't struggle to follow You when it feels as though You aren't speaking to me. As Pastor said, I know I need to trust You are there working even when it isn't evident for me to see. She shifted on the bed. I am curious to hear his sermon on Sunday about Noah.

Time dragged by as Caleb finished his discussion with the doctor and left. Would he say goodbye whenever he chose to get on the trail again?

A few patients came to visit the doctor's office. They streamed past the doorway to the room where she was staying. While she'd seen some at a distance before, she didn't know any of them by name. The doctor was too busy to stop by her room again.

By lunchtime, her stomach rumbled. She yawned, debating between taking a nap or using her crutch to see if she could hobble somewhere and find some food. Had Caleb used up all the food he'd purchased this morning? Someone stopped in front of her door.

"I hope you're hungry." Caleb stood in the doorway with two plates of steaming food. "Came across the doctor's wife. She insisted I bring some food here for the two of us."

"Mmm. Smells delicious." She winced as she shifted her ankle. "Are you sure it wasn't for her and the doctor?"

Caleb chuckled.

The sound filled the room like a warm hug.

Ellie Lou realized how little either of them had laughed throughout their ordeal.

"No. She said he usually goes home for the noon meal unless he's swamped with patients. She didn't think there'd be many because of the weather." He handed her a plate and utensils and said a quick prayer.

She took a bite of roast beef and mashed potatoes smothered in gravy. Her stomach filled in appreciation after quite a few days of scant food.

A comfortable silence settled over the room while they consumed their meals.

"Any word on Klaude?" She studied him closely to see if he'd be honest with her.

He shook his head. "Sheriff didn't have any new information."

"Are you planning to leave soon to find his trail?"

"Figured I'd wait a few days to see if any news comes in." He scraped the last of his plate.

She smiled. He looked as though he was tempted to lick it. She'd considered it too, not wanting to miss a single morsel.

At least he didn't plan to leave yet. Maybe her ankle would improve quicker than the doctor anticipated, and she could trail after him.

"I found you a place to stay, unless you want to continue here."

She frowned. "I don't need your help and besides, I told you, I can't afford it right now."

His face softened. "I know. And Josh said, if you want to stay, you can. But there's a lady in town who rents rooms. She said it would assist her with having boarders since all the folks who planned to be in town aren't able to with the storm. Said we'd be helping her out since she purchased extra food in anticipation of having a full house for the holiday season and doesn't want the food to go to waste since she's had a lot of cancellations."

"I don't know." Ellie Lou shook her head.

"Her name's Mrs. Walsh. The only folks she has there right now are a young woman and her elderly aunt."

She sucked in a breath. "Betty Hadler and Mary Scott. Betty's the one I told you about, Jeffrey's fiancée. I was hoping you could help me get word to Betty that I need to talk to her. Maybe this will work out after all. I just need to find a way to pay for the room."

"No need to worry about that right now." Caleb took the plate and utensils from her. "I can carry our saddle bags over there and then come back and fetch you. Mrs. Walsh said the rooms aren't big, but she provides all three meals. Thought it might set your mind at ease not having to worry about trying to cook when you're hobbling."

"That will be a relief, although I hate to be in someone's debt." She nibbled on her bottom lip. "I uh, will need to go to the bank today too. Do you think you could help me get there before we go to Mrs. Walsh? I probably should stop in and see Betty too, but I think it might be better for me to tell her about Jeffrey when she's not in the middle of her workday." She glanced at Caleb. "Or would it be better to tell her right away? I imagine she's been anxious to hear how he's doing. She may have heard I'm back in town already."

"By the time you stop by the bank, and we get you settled at Mrs. Walsh's boarding house, you might need a nap before talking to this Betty." He set the plates on the small table. "I'll fetch those in a bit. I need to check on the dog too. I already took care of the horses earlier. But I think the first thing we should do is run your errand. I can always come back and take care of the rest once you're situated."

"You're probably right." Ellie Lou scooted to the edge of the bed and slipped on her new boot.

Caleb handed her coat to her.

She no sooner had it fastened when he swung her up into his arms.

"Oh!" She gasped as she wrapped her arms around his strong chest to steady herself. Her heart pounded in her ears. Could he hear it?

15

Caleb's chest tightened, and he swallowed. Hard. He'd never had a woman in his arms other than the short time he'd carried her the night before. He couldn't deny it was a nice feeling having Lou's arm wrapped around his chest. As though she depended on him to protect her. To care for her. He glanced down at her dirt-smudged face and bit back a smile.

Even when he'd discovered she was a woman, she had kept the dirt on her face, almost as if she still thought it disguised her true identity. He couldn't help wondering what she'd look like with it clean.

Her dark brown eyes sparkled. She dipped her chin, and he got a closer look at her lips.

Caleb dragged his attention away from them. He had no business pursuing a woman until he was free to settle down. Not until the job of rounding up Klaude was completed. "Which way to the bank?" His voice came out gruffer than he'd intended.

She pointed to a building just ahead of them. "We should've brought my crutch. I maybe could have made it without you having to carry me."

"I don't mind." He cringed. The words were out of his mouth before he could grab them back. He shifted her in his arms and opened the door to the bank.

Lou motioned to a desk on the side of the room. "The bank president is there. If you could just take me over to him."

"Mrs. Williams. What happened?" The man behind the desk stood. "I was thinking I'd be seeing you soon, but not injured."

Caleb sat her down in the chair in front of the man's desk, shifting his weight as he debated what to do.

"Mr. Browning, I'm fine. Just stepped in a prairie dog hole and sprained my ankle." Lou smoothed her coat, her fingers trembling.

Caleb took a step backward but decided to stay close in case she needed him. Something definitely had her ill at ease. Was it the man or someone else? Hadn't Lou mentioned something about a bank loan? He racked his brain trying to recall what he'd heard earlier this morning when she was talking to a woman named Gertrude. The sheriff's wife?

Lou glanced over her shoulder and bit her lip. Did she want him to leave? She turned back around.

"Are you here to pay off the note on your ranch? You realize the due date is only eleven days away." The banker shifted some papers on his desk.

She cleared her throat, poking her finger into the small hole in the knee of her britches. Well, probably not hers. Likely they'd been her husband's. As big as they were on her. "I uh, was hoping I could get an extension."

The banker frowned and shook his head. "I'm sorry, Mrs. Williams. Really, I am. I know you've been through a lot with the loss of your husband and being in that shoot-out a few months back, but I'm afraid I've made as many extensions for you as I possibly can." He glanced at a paper on his desk. "In fact, there's someone interested in purchasing the ranch if you aren't able to make the payment by the end of the year."

"But I have nowhere else to go." A tear streamed down her pale cheek. "Charles was given the land by his grandparents. I can't lose it. Please. Surely there's something you can do."

"As I said, I'm sorry. I had tried to get word to you a few weeks ago to tell you someone else is interested in the property, but when I sent someone to your home, they couldn't find you." The man's brow furrowed. "I would've thought you'd be home, trying to gather extra money somehow so you wouldn't lose your spread."

"I was trying to do something to get the money." Lou sniffed. "Unfortunately, it didn't work the way I'd planned."

Bands around Caleb's chest constricted. Surely the banker wouldn't toss her from her home when she had nowhere to go. How could the man be so heartless? He started to step forward to give the man a piece of his mind.

Lou turned toward him and shook her head, tears filling her eyes.

He curled his fingers into a fist.

How could the man throw a widow on the street? It made no sense. Just how much did she owe on the note for her property? He may not find the answer with her here, but he'd stop back later to make inquiries.

"You're sure there's nothing I can do?" Lou's voice was barely above a whisper.

"Other than bringing me the thirty dollars you owe me by end of December? No, I'm afraid not." The banker stood. "You understood the conditions of the loan when you sought funds to cover you. Now, if you'll excuse me, I have other business to attend to." He nodded at Caleb.

He stepped forward and gently swung Lou into his arms.

Her body stiffened but she didn't say anything.

They made it outside before her shoulders started shaking. Tears streamed continuously down her cheeks. Soft sobs shook her frame.

Caleb tightened his arms around her. *Dear God, what can I possibly say to her that will take her pain away? What would You have me do in this situation? Show me how to be a friend to her.*

Lou continued to cry, the sound ripping a hole in Caleb's heart.

He carried her to a side street, away from prying eyes. She didn't need folks talking about her crying while he carried her. He'd do whatever he could to prevent her from experiencing more pain.

Her shoulders shook as she turned her face into his chest, tears dropping on his coat.

He shifted her closer, stroking her hair. "Shh, Lou. It'll be all right."

But was it?

She cried even harder.

He felt moisture on his own cheeks. He couldn't remember the last time he'd cried.

~*~

Ellie Lou's world was shattering. If she lost her home, how could she ever pick up all the broken pieces of her life? *Lord, I want You to fix it all. For my story to have a different ending than losing the ranch. I feel as if everything is falling apart. I want to trust You beyond what my eyes see, but I don't know how. I don't see how this shattering can bring about any good. Oh, God, what are You trying to do here?*

Uncontrollable sobs shook her frame. Losing the ranch was like losing Charles all over again.

I don't see a path forward, Lord. Please help me.

Caleb's arms tightened around her.

What must he think?

She snuggled closer, accepting his comfort. In a few minutes, she'd pull back, but for now she rested in his strength.

"I know you can't see it now, but God will get you through this, and you'll be stronger because of it."

Ellie Lou shook her head. "I." She sniffed. "I used to think that way too…but I'm not so sure anymore." Her lower lip trembled.

He didn't answer right away. Just sat on a tree stump, holding her.

Several minutes passed as she tried to control her weeping.

Caleb's jaw tightened. He stared off at something. What, she couldn't tell. "I saw many horrific things in the war. Things that still haunt me. And my dreams. The killing. Brother fighting against brother. All of them in the battle because they strongly believed in their cause." He grew quiet.

She touched his sleeve, hoping to convey her support for him.

"I couldn't make sense of it for a long time. All I could see was the hurt. The devastation. I cried and asked the Lord about it. For many months, I heard no response. Nothing. I thought maybe God had abandoned me. If He really cared about me, He'd answer me."

"What happened? Did He ever respond to you?" Ellie Lou studied his face.

"Not in a verbal way. But He kept bringing scriptures to my mind."

"What kind of verses?"

He glanced at her. "Jeremiah 33:3, 'Call unto me, and I will answer thee, and show thee great and mighty things, which thou knowest not.' In Isaiah 49 it talks about how He'll never forget us. That He's engraved us on the palm of His hands. In Psalm nine it says the Lord doesn't forsake those who seek Him. Various people throughout scripture have questioned God's abandonment–David, John the Baptist. But in each and every case, God has been there, making Himself known, even when we can't first see it."

Ellie Lou sniffed. "Why do you think He's so slow in letting us know sometimes?"

Caleb glanced at her. "That might be a question better asked of the preacher. But I wonder if sometimes we don't hear a response so He can use the in between time to draw us to Him in a way we never have experienced before. Maybe circumstances that cause us to fall apart are all part of His plan to make something new of our lives. Something better. Deeper. I'm learning to ask Him to hold me together when I feel as if my world is smashed to a million pieces. Only He can take a shattered pot and put it back together and make it something beautiful."

Could God be somehow using this for something good in her life? It seemed an impossibility. But Ellie Lou did know God could take broken things and make them whole again. Jesus had done it many times in the New Testament by touching and healing people. She released a shuttering sigh. "I don't know how God can use this kind of situation for His good."

Caleb chuckled. "I don't either. But I know God can see the big picture. Things we can't envision. A preacher told me one time that what we see is only a small speck compared to the vast scale God can see. We think we know what's best for us in a situation when we don't have any idea what's coming afterwards. He's able to weave an elaborate tapestry and all we witness are snarled threads."

"Are you sure you didn't want to be a preacher?" Ellie Lou smiled. "Sounds as though you would be a good one."

He grinned at her, a dimple flashing in his left cheek.

Her breath hitched in her chest.

"No. Never felt led to preach. God just has shown me a lot through the years. Through difficult times. Losing my folks. Going through the war. Being a lawman. Despite all my pain and sorrow, I asked God to somehow use it for good. To help me make sense of all the pain and loss."

"And He's done this for you?" Ellie Lou shifted in his arms to get a better look at Caleb's face.

A muscle in his jaw flickered. "I'd say I'm still in the process of trying to figure it all out. To learn to trust Him even when I don't understand all I'm going through. Times when I doubt if He's there. If He cares. If He's listening. But I think that's part of what faith is. Remembering the times He has answered our prayers, and trusting He will continue to do so. That when He delays in responding to my prayers, He has a reason for it. I just can't observe it yet. I may never learn the cause. I just have to trust He's working no matter what, because He said He is."

Ellie Lou was tempted to snuggle against him and somehow rest in Caleb's strength and support. Something she hadn't felt since Charles died. She missed having someone to talk things through. Someone who also had a love for the Lord. And could handle her doubts and questions. And didn't judge her when her faith was lagging. Would she ever have it again? And did she ever want to get married a second time?

16

Caleb didn't know what came over him to talk so much. It wasn't like him. There was something about Lou that drew words from him. But then, maybe it was because of all she was going through. He'd do anything to take away her pain if he could.

"I appreciate you sharing with me." She shifted in his arms. Color filled her cheeks. "I'm sorry to cry all over your coat." She glanced down. "I, uh, don't usually break down like that."

He tapped under her chin, so she'd look him in the eyes. Moisture still filled her dark brown eyes. "I think the news you had at the bank warranted a good cry."

A giggle spurted out. "Not very often you hear a fella talking about a woman having a good cry."

Heat sprang to his neck and cheeks. "Well…"

"I guess we'd better get to Mrs. Walsh."

He stood, gathering her closer in his arms, telling himself he only did it so he wouldn't lose his grip on her.

Silence settled between them as he strolled to the outskirts of town where the boarding house was. He pushed through the front door. The scent of baked chicken tickled his nostrils. "Mrs. Walsh? Are you here?"

The gray-haired woman stepped from the kitchen, wiping her hands on an apron tied at her plump waist. "There you are. I was hoping you hadn't changed your mind." She smiled and stepped forward extending her hand to Lou. "Mrs. Williams, I'm so sorry to hear about your injury. I put you in a room on the main level." She motioned. "Hopefully you'll find it to your liking. Please let me know if you need anything."

Caleb entered the room. A blue quilt had been folded back, as if to welcome its new occupant. He set Lou on the bed.

Mrs. Walsh followed him. "Here, let me take your coat, Mrs. Williams."

"Thank you." Lou eased it from her shoulders and handed it to the woman. "Please call me Ellie Lou."

"Supper will be at five. If you need anything before then, just ring the bell there." She pointed to a small bell she'd placed on the nightstand beside the bed. "I'll let you rest. I've got the remainder of the meal to prepare."

"How thoughtful. Thank you. I'm sure I'll be fine." Lou tried to hide a yawn.

The landlady waved and left the room.

"Why don't you take a nap while I get our things?" Caleb

glanced at her. "Do you need help taking off your boot?"

"No. I can get it. You can leave the door open so you can put my saddle bags in here when you return. I'm sure I'll still be awake." She yawned again.

"Don't stay up waiting on my account." He stepped to the doorway. "It's important you get some rest. It'll help the healing process."

She dropped the boot to the floor. "Definitely don't want to delay it in any way. The quicker I'm on my feet, the better. I've got things I need to do."

"We'll see about that." He lifted his Stetson in farewell. "For now, get some sleep."

As he walked back through town, he decided to make a slight detour to the bank.

"Can I help you?" A woman behind a long counter called to him.

"I was hoping to talk to the bank owner. At least I think that's who he is." He glanced around but didn't see the man. "Is he in?"

"Oh, you mean Mr. Browning. He left early today. Did you want to leave a message for him?"

He shook his head. "No. I'll stop back another time."

The woman smiled. "Just be aware with Christmas soon coming, he'll be in and out the next week and a half. Are you sure you don't want to make an appointment?"

Caleb lifted his Stetson and ran his hand through his hair. "If I can't catch up with him in the next day or so, I'll consider it." He shoved the hat back on his head and left the bank.

The doctor's office was quiet when he stepped into the building. "Josh, you here?"

His friend poked his head from one of the rooms. "So, you decided to take Ellie Lou somewhere else to recover?"

He hefted one of their saddlebags. "Yes. Took your suggestion and went to see Mrs. Walsh. Figured Lou would sleep better where she wouldn't be easily disturbed."

"Sorry about that." Josh crossed his arms. "Never know how busy it will be here."

"I know Lou was concerned about you possibly needing the

room too. Thought she might rest easier if she got out of here." He lifted another bag.

"One of these days I want to hear the story about how you two crossed paths."

Heat flared in Caleb's face.

Josh's eyes twinkled. "I have a feeling there's quite a story behind it. Especially since I've never seen Ellie Lou dressed in a man's clothes before now, not even when she worked on the ranch. Never heard anyone call her Lou either. I know Gertrude calls her Ellie Lou." He leaned against the doorframe. "I think the widow is changing you, Caleb. Making a difference in your life."

He shifted the two bags and picked up the other two, refusing to make eye contact with his friend. He didn't need the doctor to think there was something going on between him and Lou. They were just friends. Two folks caught in a storm together. Two people who had experienced a lot in the past couple weeks. Lou was just someone who'd been dealt a bad hand right now and needed someone to encourage her. Help her along the way. Once she was settled and he didn't need to worry about her anymore, he'd be on the trail to catch Klaude. He had to remind himself catching the outlaw was his final destination before he could settle down and think about something other than outlaws, and trouble. If Lou was around after he brought Klaude to justice, he'd see where things led, but that was a big if.

~*~

Ellie Lou woke to the sound of voices in the hallway. She yawned and stretched. A warm, wet nose poked against her hand.

The dog wagged his shaggy black tail and whimpered.

"Are you supposed to be in here, boy?"

Shuffling noises sounded from the hallway.

"I'm sorry, miss, but I think it's best if you give Lou a little longer to rest. She's been through a lot. What did you say your name is?" Caleb's voice was low, but loud enough for her to hear.

"Miss Hadler. I insist you wake her. I've been waiting for weeks to learn what's happened to my fiancé." Betty's voice rose.

"Betty?" Ellie Lou called.

Fabric rustled as the young woman appeared in the doorway. "I'm sorry, Ellie Lou. I just couldn't wait any longer to hear your news. Did you find Jeffrey? When will he be arriving? What has caused the delay? Was it the blizzards? But then, how did you make it here and he didn't? And why are you here at Mrs. Walsh's?" She glanced at Ellie Lou's foot. "Did you get hurt?"

Ellie Lou pushed herself up on her elbows and patted the bed. No use telling Betty about her ankle. It was the least of her concerns. "Why don't you come sit with me?"

Caleb lingered in the doorway.

Give me the words, Lord. Prepare her heart. Ellie Lou took a deep breath.

Betty's face paled, her lower lip trembling.

Ellie Lou rested her hand on Betty's arm. "I don't know how to tell you this, but there's been an accident." She searched for the words to continue. To somehow prepare the young woman for the upcoming grief.

"Oh, no. Please tell me you didn't leave him alone in Topeka. I thought you would've stayed with him, especially if he was injured."

Caleb took a step into the room. His gaze met Ellie Lou's. He opened his mouth, but she shook her head. This was something she needed to do.

"I'm afraid he was on the stagecoach on his way here when it was held up by an outlaw."

Betty let out a sharp cry, her hand coming to her mouth.

Ellie Lou swallowed and continued. "The uh, criminal shot and killed the people on the stagecoach."

Tears streamed down Betty's face. "Are you sure he was on it? Maybe you missed him?"

Ellie Lou glanced at Caleb.

"I'm sorry, miss, but I came across him right after it happened." Caleb came a few steps closer. "Mrs. Williams showed me the tintype of your fiancé. I hate to tell you this, but he was killed. I'm so sorry."

Sobs shook Betty's frame.

Ellie Lou pulled her close and let the young woman cry.

"Betty? What's going on here?" Mary Scott poked her head into the room. "Why, Ellie Lou. I hadn't heard you were finally back." The elderly aunt glanced at her niece. Her face paled. "Why is Betty crying? What did you learn about Jeffrey?"

"Was his name Jeffrey Murphy?" Caleb shifted closer to Betty's aunt.

"Yes. But how would you know that, young man? And who are you? What're you doing in here?"

Betty continued to weep.

Caleb rested a hand on the older woman's shoulder. "I'm Caleb Dawson. Mrs. Williams and I were on the trail together. I hate to have to tell you, but your niece's fiancé was killed in a stagecoach robbery."

Mary wobbled on her feet.

Caleb gripped the older woman's arm to steady her, guiding her to a chair in the corner of the room. "Here, ma'am."

Ellie Lou's eyes filled. Her heart tightened as she was reminded anew of how she felt the day Charles died. It near tore her chest in two having to put these two women through similar grief. "I wish I had found him before…"

The dog rested his head on her leg as if sensing their grief.

She wanted to bury her head in his thick fur and cry too, but she needed to remain strong for Betty and her aunt.

Mrs. Walsh stood in the doorway, her eyebrows raised. "Is there anything I can do?"

"Could you put on a kettle for tea?" Caleb pulled a handkerchief from his pocket and handed it to Betty's aunt.

"Certainly." The landlady didn't ask for an explanation. Instead, she disappeared.

"I d-don't understand." Betty dabbed her eyes with her handkerchief. "W-why would someone want to kill Jeffrey? He didn't really know anyone here other than me and Aunt Mary. It makes no sense. What would someone have against him?"

Ellie Lou's gaze met Caleb's hoping he somehow had an answer for them.

"I doubt it was anything personal. He just happened to be in the wrong place at the wrong time. Klaude, the uh, outlaw has been doing senseless killings and robbing folks. I'll do whatever I can to bring him to justice, so he can pay for his crimes."

"I appreciate your assistance, Mr. Dawson." Mary twisted the handkerchief. "I'd hate for someone else to have to live through this pain." She glanced at her niece.

"I'll be going after him too." Ellie Lou shifted on the bed.

Caleb frowned at her and shook his head. "Going after dangerous criminals is not something a woman should be doing. I forbid you to go."

"You should listen to him, dear." Mary sniffed. "We wouldn't want something happening to you too."

Betty glanced at Ellie Lou's ankle propped on a pillow. "It looks as if you're in no condition to go anywhere. Let this Mr. Dawson be the one to go. You've done what you could. I appreciate you at least finding the news for me." Sobs again shook the young woman's shoulders.

"I plan to see this through." Ellie Lou whispered.

Caleb's face darkened. "You aren't going anywhere. Even if I have to tie you to the bed, I'll make sure you stay safe."

"That's not your job, Caleb." Ellie Lou met his gaze. "You can't stop me."

17

Caleb wanted to shake Lou, so she'd realize the stupidity of trying to track a dangerous criminal like Klaude. He didn't need her to get in his way and potentially get hurt in the process. Because that's what would happen if Klaude got his hands on her. She'd be hurt or killed. He couldn't bear to see something such as that take place. Caleb had to find a way to convince her to stay put. Surely, she wouldn't risk further damage to her ankle.

But then, he'd seen what people often did when they were in a desperate situation–one where they felt they had no way out. He'd seen Lou's tenacity. While she might go off half-cocked and not think through a situation thoroughly, she was determined to follow through on her word when she gave it. He'd seen it on the trail and saw it in her eyes at the bank. She'd do whatever it took to try and bring comfort to these ladies.

"I'll even pay you the money I promised Ellie Lou if you'll bring Jeffrey's killer in, Mr. Dawson." The young woman blew her nose in her handkerchief.

He groaned. That's all Lou needed to hear. "I'm not about to take your money, miss. Besides, there's already a reward offered for the outlaw. There's no reason for you to concern yourself with money."

"I promised I'll see this through, Betty. I just need a couple days to rest up before I can hit the trail again." Lou patted the young woman's arm. "Hopefully it will bring you some measure of comfort once the man is behind bars."

Caleb smacked his forehead. The widow would be the death of him.

~*~

Sunday, December 23, 1877

Ellie Lou awakened early. She sat up and stretched.

The dog whined and wagged his tail, thumping against the floorboards.

"Good morning, boy. I guess you need a name, don't you?"

He wagged his tail even more.

"Let's see about putting you outside." She reached for her crutch, wobbling as she stood. Her limb shook as she hobbled the few steps to the doorway to her room. She swung the door open.

Caleb stood with his arms folded across his chest. He didn't say anything. Just snapped his fingers, and the dog followed after him.

Ellie Lou sighed as she watched them go. It had been three days since he'd talked to her. Ever since she'd insisted on finding Klaude. Her shoulders drooped. *What choice do I have, Lord? I feel as though I have to do whatever I can to at least try and get the money to pay off my loan. The only way of doing so is by going after Klaude. Why can't Caleb understand? If he'd be open to the idea, we could work together to round up the outlaw and maybe split the reward money. Five hundred dollars is a lot of money. I'd be willing to give most of it to Caleb. If only he'd let me have just enough to pay off the bank and maybe purchase a few more horses.* She wanted to ask him, but he'd been closed ever since their conversation with Betty and her aunt.

A few minutes later, the dog raced toward her, his tail wagging. He yipped in excitement. She bent to pet him. The dog wandered between her and Caleb, accepting pets, belly rubs, and attention from both.

An uncomfortable silence stretched between them. What could she say to break it? "Thank you for taking him out."

Caleb nodded, but he wouldn't meet her gaze.

"Are you, uh, planning on going to church today?"

"Yes."

Ellie Lou bit back a sigh. She missed the easy camaraderie they'd shared. What would it take to get it back again? "I was hoping to go too. Especially after what Pastor Drew was telling me about it. I'm curious how he'll tie in talking about Noah and the birth of our Savior."

Still nothing.

Moisture pricked her eyes. "Well, I'll let you go." She turned back toward her room.

The sound of his voice caused her to pause. "If you're ready after breakfast, I'll make sure you get to the church."

Joy surged through her body. Not only was he talking, but he wanted to join her for the church service. At least it was a start to mending their relationship. She prayed it would be.

~*~

Caleb hefted a sigh. He hadn't slept much the past three nights. Ever since he'd had the disagreement with Lou. He hated being at odds with her, but he also wanted her to know the danger in going off half-cocked. It'd been fine when she'd mistaken him for someone else. But she wouldn't be able to get the drop on Klaude as she had on him. The man was ruthless, and Caleb would do whatever it took to persuade her from hunting the man down.

She stood in front of him with her clothes rumpled, and her hair falling around her shoulders. Odd she didn't have long hair like most women. He should've offered to ride to her ranch and get her some other clothes for her to wear. Like a dress. Maybe if she wore it, she'd want to go back to doing womanly things instead of hunting outlaws.

Couldn't hurt to ask her. "Would you like me to ride to your ranch and fetch you a dress?"

Her cheeks bloomed with color.

It made him smile.

"No. It's too far for you to get there and back in time for breakfast and church." She ran her hand along the side of her britches. "I guess these will have to do." Her head dipped. "Never thought I'd be going to church dressed like this."

"You look beautiful no matter what you wear." Now where had that come from? Since when did he start thinking about how she was dressed? He rubbed the tight muscles in the back of his neck. He needed to get away from her before he said something else stupid. "I'll see you at breakfast."

He didn't wait for her response. Instead, he strolled to the front door and pulled it open. Maybe some time mucking the stalls would help to clear his head. Sure couldn't hurt. Shoving his Stetson on, Caleb turned up the collar of his coat to ward off the cold as he strolled towards the opposite end of town. His breath puffed in wisps.

Pink tinged the horizon as the sun started rising in the winter sky. Wind nipped at his nose and cheeks. The wooden barn door creaked as he pulled it open. It took a moment for his eyes to adjust to the dim lighting in the building. One of the horses whinnied. Another nickered in response. The sweet scent of hay somehow calmed him. There was something about a barn that always set his mind at ease. Maybe it was the mindless cleaning of the stalls.

He picked up a pitchfork and got to work cleaning up after the horses and distributing feed to all three of their mounts as well as the preacher's horse. The task didn't take overly long. Caleb patted each of the horse's necks before securing the barn door behind him. Like it or not, it was time to head back to the boarding house.

By the time he washed up, all the other ladies had gathered at the big dining room table.

Mrs. Walsh peered at him. "Would you mind saying the blessing, Mr. Dawson?"

He nodded and bowed his head. "Father, we thank You for this bountiful meal Mrs. Walsh prepared for us. Use it to provide our bodies with what they need. Bless her hands and her home. Provide comfort for Miss Hadler and Miss Scott. Heal Lou. In Jesus's Name, amen." He didn't glance at any of them as he settled his napkin in his lap.

Mrs. Walsh handed him a platter of eggs and bacon. "Eat up. I made plenty."

"Yes, ma'am." He forked a healthy serving on his plate before passing it to Lou.

Her fingers brushed against his as he transferred the dish.

He nearly dropped the plate.

Lou's brows rose. "Is something wrong?"

Caleb shook his head and wiped his hand on the side of his pants. He was tempted to glance at it, trying to figure out the odd sensation he'd felt when her hand had touched his. It made no sense.

The dog flopped in the doorway and watched him.

He'd been surprised Mrs. Walsh had been open to having the mutt in her orderly house. In fact, Caleb had seen her sneaking the dog scraps at the end of each meal. From the looks of it, Lou had a new companion. Maybe the dog would be a good reason for her to stay behind instead of hitting the trail.

He bit back a snort. Right. As if she'd allow herself to be dissuaded from her quest.

"Did you have something you want to say, Mr. Dawson?" A twinkle sparkled in Mrs. Walsh's blue eyes.

"No, ma'am." He dipped his head and started shoveling the food into his mouth. Best to keep his mind on the meal instead of wandering.

Within fifteen minutes, the dishes were empty, and Mrs. Walsh stood. "I'll just put these in the kitchen and then we can head to church."

Caleb stood and pushed in his chair. "Let me help you, ma'am." He grabbed as many glasses as he could carry. "I'll be ready to assist you in a few minutes, Lou."

"I was thinking about trying to use the crutch this morning." She reached for it.

He set the glasses down and moved the crutch from her reach. "I'll carry you there. Don't you think you should obey your doctor's orders?"

Her shoulders drooped, but she didn't respond.

He picked up the glasses again and followed his landlady.

In the kitchen, Mrs. Walsh motioned to a small table. "Just put them there. I'll wash them once church is over."

He did what she'd instructed.

"Can I talk to you a moment?" She untied her apron.

"Sure. What can I do for you?"

"I don't know what's been going on between you and Mrs. Williams the past few days but let me give you some advice, young man." Her gaze pierced like his mama's used to when a reprimand was coming.

He toed his boot along a mark on the wood floor.

"Don't let things fester between you. I can tell you have feelings for her, and anyone can see she feels the same way about you."

"You're mistaken—"

"You can deny it as much as you like, but I think one day soon you'll realize she has a special place in your heart. I lost my husband a few years ago, and I regret not finding love a second time. I had fellas who came calling, but I was always too busy trying to get this boarding house going to give them the time of day. I regret it now. So, listen to an old woman who has a bit more experience than you. Grab hold of love and hang onto it when God brings it into your life. Don't spend your time trying to change her into what you think is best. Accept her as she is and see how you can work together to accomplish great things for the Lord. Trust Him to work in your lives and in your relationship. If she's set on doing something you don't approve of, don't push her into going off and doing it just to prove to you she can. Find a way to convince her your uppermost thought is to love and protect her. Let her know she can rest in your care and know you'll be there for her."

Love? He hadn't known Lou long enough to consider being in love. He respected her. Enjoyed talking with her. Being in her company. Providing for her. Protecting her. And he'd like to continue getting to know her but that didn't mean he loved her, did it?

18

Ellie Lou glanced at her crutch propped in a corner of the dining room. Caleb had gone into the kitchen at least ten minutes ago with Mrs. Walsh and still hadn't returned. A clock on the mantel ticked. If they didn't hurry, they'd be late for the church service. Should she try and hop to the corner to get her crutch to see what was holding him up?

The door to the kitchen swung open.

Caleb's face was stained with color.

Mrs. Walsh came from the room with a smile on her face.

What exactly had they been talking about?

Holding onto the edge of the table, Ellie Lou stood.

Caleb grabbed her coat from a tree rack and helped her into it.

"Thank you." She buttoned it. "If you hand me my crutch, I can take it along in case I need it."

He shook his head. "I've got you." He swung her up in his arms.

She gasped, keeping her body stiff.

"Relax, Lou. You're safe with me." His words were only for her as Mrs. Walsh held the door open.

Silence settled between them as Caleb took brisk strides toward the church on the other edge of town. A few folks lingered outside the doorway. Several children chased each other in the yard, darting around their parents.

Ellie Lou's chest constricted. If only the Lord had seen fit to gift her and Charles with a baby to love. She sniffed.

Caleb's muscled arms tightened around her, and he glanced down at her.

She averted her eyes so he couldn't see her grief.

"Ellie Lou!" Gertrude stood on the steps and waved at her. "I was hoping you'd be able to attend this morning. I should've had Enoch stop by to pick you up, but it looks as if you're well taken care of." A smile spread across her face. "I'm sorry I haven't had a chance to come see you at Mrs. Walsh's house. Oh, hello, Mrs. Walsh."

"We best get you inside." Caleb started up the steps.

Gertrude followed after them. "You can sit in the pew with me and Enoch. I've been wanting to catch up with you, but the shop has been so busy with being so close to Christmas. So many folks are purchasing last minute gifts."

Caleb settled her on the pew beside him, with Gertrude on Ellie Lou's other side. He reached down and gently placed her ankle on his knee.

Her cheeks flushed. What would people think of her sprawling on him? All right, not sprawling, but still.

Enoch smiled and waved. "Howdy Mrs. Williams." He flushed. "I mean Ellie Lou." The man still hadn't gotten used to calling her by her first name after working for her and her husband for so many years before deciding to become sheriff of Burrton Springs.

"Howdy, folks." Pastor Drew smiled as he stood behind the pulpit. "Thank you for coming on a cold day to worship the Lord." He distributed some papers. "Let's start by singing a new song 'Trusting Jesus'."

Tears choked Ellie Lou's voice when they got to the refrain. "'Trusting as the moments fly, Trusting as the days go by; Trusting Him whate'er befall, Trusting Jesus, that is all'."

Garments rustled as folks settled in their seats after the song concluded.

Pastor Drew studied the room, seeming to take the time to glance at each of them. "You're probably wondering why we're singing about trusting today as we're thinking about the birth of our Savior which we'll celebrate in two days. I'd like you to open your Bibles to Genesis six."

The sound of pages being flipped filled the room.

"We'll start with verse five. 'And God saw that the wickedness of man was great in the earth, and that every imagination of the thoughts of his heart was only evil continually. And it repented the Lord that he had made man on the earth, and it grieved him at his heart. And the Lord said, I will destroy man whom I have created from the face of the earth; both man, and beast, and the creeping thing, and the fowls of the air; for it repenteth me that I have made them. But Noah found grace in the eyes of the Lord.'"

"I like the story of Noah." One of the younger children piped up.

Laughter filled the room.

Pastor Drew chuckled. "I like the story of Noah too. But you may be wondering what the story of Noah has to do with Jesus' birth." He paused and glanced at his notes. "I've been thinking a lot about Noah's story. After God gave Noah the specifics of how to build the ark, God made this promise to Noah in verse eighteen, 'But with thee will I establish my covenant; and thou shalt come into the ark, thou, and thy sons, and thy wife, and thy sons' wives with thee.'"

He leaned closer to his audience. "I want you to picture it. Noah is the only righteous man on the earth. The Bible says Noah walked with God. Can you imagine it? Well, God comes to Noah with an incredible assignment. God wants him to build a big boat in the middle of the desert. Up until this time, it's very likely they'd never experienced much if any rain. Some believe the firmament that covered the earth provided a sort of dew that watered the earth up until Noah's time. We'll not know the specifics until we ask God when we're in heaven." He smiled at the congregation. "All God said was that He'd be bringing a flood of waters upon the earth and Noah believed Him."

The preacher started pacing. "Noah had a huge assignment ahead of him. Something that would take him many, many years to complete. But he was faithful in working on it day after day, year after year. The thing I like about Noah is he took God at His Word. He trusted Him. It took over a century for Noah to see the reality of his faith. But with each nail he hammered in the gopher wood as he built the ark, it was if he was saying, "I believe You, God. I trust You. I trust what You told me. I'm Your willing servant."

Ellie Lou shifted in her seat. When was the last time she believed God and His Word? When was the last time she fully trusted He was working in her life, even when she couldn't see Him moving in it?

~*~

Caleb glanced at Lou, wondering what she was thinking.

The pastor continued. "Noah was asked to believe what he couldn't see. But He didn't question God. He remained faithful year after year after year doing the work God had called him to do. I have to ask you, my friends, how are you doing with being faithful to what God has instructed you to do? Are you getting bogged down by circumstances? Are you filled with doubt? Maybe you've been hurt in a situation, or you can't see God working in your life. You're beginning to doubt He cares about you because He isn't answering your prayers. You think, 'the Bible talks about God's love, but He's being silent.'"

Caleb shifted on his seat, adjusting Lou's ankle on his knee.

"God is always faithful. His Word can always be trusted. Turn in your Bibles to Luke two, verses twenty-five through thirty-five. We read here about a man named Simeon. He was another devout man. It says the Holy Ghost was upon him. God revealed to Simeon he wouldn't die before he saw the Lord's Christ. Can you imagine all the years he waited? Perhaps every day wondering if today would be the day he would see Christ. He never gave up. He kept trusting he would see Christ before he died. He believed God at His Word. He trusted even when he couldn't see an answer coming yet."

The pastor made the act of trusting seem so easy.

"I know trusting is often difficult. We have trouble believing what we can't see. We get impatient when we don't see an answer coming our way in our timing. All we see before us are the problems we're experiencing. We can't see a way out from them. It's during times like this that I have to ask myself, 'Are my eyes on Jesus or on my problem? Are my thoughts centered on the truth of God's Word or on my circumstances? Am I building on the shifting sand or the solid rock?'"

Caleb glanced at Lou. Her gaze was intently on the preacher.

"As we draw close to the time of celebrating the birth of our Lord and Savior, I suggest we each examine our hearts and our lives to see whether we're trusting God wholeheartedly as Noah did as he built the ark. As Simeon did as he waited to see Christ. As the Israelites did as they waited on their promised Messiah. Trust God and His Word, not your circumstances. Let's pray. Dear Father, we thank You for coming to this world as a babe to provide a way for us to be forgiven of our sins. Your death on the cross for our sins allows us access to our Heavenly Father. Just as Jesus had to trust God for His timing in His life, help us to trust You no matter what we face. In Jesus's Name, amen."

The congregation stood and sang a final song. Caleb stayed seated beside Lou, sharing a hymnal. Her sweet voice joined the other parishioners. As the final note finished, Lou turned toward him.

"I've never thought about trust the way Pastor Drew mentioned it. Have you?"

He shook his head. "The man has a way of looking at the topic differently than I've heard before. I never thought much about the faith Noah must've had. That's a long time to be working on a project before seeing fruit from the assignment. Makes you think though, doesn't it?"

A small smile spread across Lou's face. "I'm afraid Noah has way more patience than I do. I've been asking God to work on my situation for the past few months, and I've been frustrated He hasn't seemed to have heard me or answered."

"I know what you mean. There are times when I just assume God isn't answering because He's silent. It's not easy to trust when we aren't hearing a response. I guess that's what faith is all about though."

"I'm sorry to interrupt you two." Gertrude touched Lou's arm. "Are you both able to come to our home for lunch? I'd love to catch up with you, Ellie Lou. And we'd like to learn more about you, Mr. Dawson."

He glanced at Lou.

The door to the church banged open. "Doc. Where's the doc? He's needed right away. Just found a fella bleeding bad just outside of town. Said it was some outlaw."

Folks murmured.

"I'm here," Josh said. "I'll meet you at my office."

"I'm afraid I won't be able to make it to lunch, Mrs. Valentine." Caleb shifted Lou's ankle to the ground. "I'll come back for you. Promise me you won't walk on that ankle. I want to go with Josh too. Maybe it has something to do with Klaude."

"I'll be able to keep that promise if you take me along." Her dark eyes pleaded with him.

"No. Go with your friends, and I'll catch up with you later."

"But…"

He squeezed her hand. "Please."

She stared at their clasped hands before she nodded. "You'll be sure to tell me what happens, won't you? You won't go off without telling me, please?"

"I promise."

Enoch and Gertrude shifted out of his way so he could follow after Josh.

Once outside, he hurried down the street.

Dear Lord, please be with whoever has been hurt. Help Josh to be able to help them. And if this was Klaude's doing, help me to find him, and bring him to justice.

He opened the door to doc's office.

The man who'd come to the church exited the last examining room. His shirt was covered in blood.

"Are you friends with the man you brought in?" Caleb removed his Stetson.

The fella shook his head. "No, sir. Just happened to see him at the side of the road. He was bleeding bad. Gut shot. Don't think he'll make it."

"Did he say much about the outlaw? What the criminal looked like? Which way he went?"

"He wasn't making a lot of sense but maybe you can get some information from him before the doc tries to get the bullet removed."

"Thanks." Caleb hurried back the hallway.

19

Ellie Lou would pace if she were able. Time ticked by slowly and still there'd been no word from Caleb. She'd visited with Gertrude and Enoch over the lunch meal but shortly afterwards had asked them to take her back to Mrs. Walsh's boarding house.

Even though Caleb had promised to let her know what had happened, she hadn't wanted to risk not being at the boarding house when he returned. It had been a couple hours and he still hadn't made an appearance.

Mrs. Walsh smiled at her as they sat in her sitting room. "I can see you're anxious to hear from your young man."

"What?" She shifted her gaze away from the window. "No, you're mistaken. Caleb, I mean, Mr. Dawson isn't my young man. We've only known each other for a short time. He's just a friend."

The older woman nodded as she sewed a seam in a dress she was making. "Friendship is often the beginning of courting."

"Oh, no. We aren't courting." Ellie Lou's cheeks felt as if they were on fire. "It hasn't been that long since I've lost my husband."

"It's been over a year, hasn't it?"

"Well, yes, but..."

"Which means you're well past the year of mourning."

"Yes, but..."

The older woman glanced at her. "I lost my husband too. I realize just because a year has passed doesn't mean you don't still miss him. I think you always will. But I can tell you from experience it gets better as time goes on. I can fondly remember all the good times we had together. The Lord has helped me each step along the way. There's been plenty of times when I didn't know which way to turn or have an answer to what seemed like an unsurmountable problem, but every time the Good Lord has come through. He's always answered."

She chuckled. "Rarely in my timetable. But when I look back at it afterwards, I can see He knew what was best even though at the time I didn't feel that way."

Ellie Lou fidgeted with the crutch. "Did you ever think God wouldn't answer you? That He didn't care?"

Mrs. Walsh set her sewing aside. "Often. But when I felt that way, I would pull out my Bible and read through the psalms King David wrote. There are so many that begin with him asking God where He is. Why isn't He answering? But you know what?"

"What?"

"By the end of every psalm, David realizes God is there beside him." The landlady smiled. "Kind of like Mr. Dawson. Sounds like he's been with you. Keeping an eye on you. Concerned about your welfare. Trying to protect you."

Ellie Lou took a deep breath, unsure how to respond.

"If you ask me, the man has feelings for you. I think he just doesn't want to admit it yet." Her gaze pierced Ellie Lou's. "My guess is you don't want to acknowledge it yet either."

Ellie Lou wished her ankle was healed enough she could stand and walk away from the woman's penetrating gaze. "It's too early to think about someone other than my husband."

"I'll tell you what I told your young man this morning. Don't wait too long. I regret I pushed some fellas away after my husband died. I thought I wasn't ready either. There was this one man who waited for a year, hoping I'd change my mind. But I was too stubborn. I believed it was more important to get this house up and running so I'd have security. I spent too long trying to make my own way instead of trusting God to provide for my needs." She shook her head. "I regret it now."

Ellie Lou glanced at the window. "But what if you ended up losing all you hold dear? What then? How do you go on after something like that?"

"All I know is He promises to always be with us. No matter what we go through. There's a verse in Isaiah which says when you pass through the waters and fire, He promises we won't be consumed."

Why did God keep bringing that particular verse up?

"I guess it goes back to Pastor Drew's sermon on trust. We have to trust He knows what we're going through. I like to think everything I experience has first filtered through His hands. He's well aware of what struggles we face. I think it says in the book of Habakkuk that even if the fig tree doesn't bud and there aren't any grapes on the vine or no sheep and cows in the pen, yet we can rejoice in the Lord and be joyful in God our Savior." Tears glistened on the older woman's cheeks. "I'll be praying for you, my dear. I can tell you've been wrestling with a lot of things in your life right now. I pray the Lord will make Himself evident in your life, even if it's only a soft whisper, and He reminds you of all the times He's answered prayer in the past."

Ellie Lou sniffed, wiping away a tear that sprang to her eye. "Thank you. You don't know how much your words mean to me."

Mrs. Walsh crossed the room and sat down beside her. "I believe I do, dear. Trust God with your future." She squeezed Ellie Lou's hand. "And don't be afraid to open your heart again to love. The Lord still has many good things in store for you. And I believe Mr. Dawson will be a big part of it." She pulled Ellie Lou into a hug.

Tears streamed down Ellie Lou's cheeks. The warmth of the woman's hug was almost like an embrace from her Heavenly Father.

Thank You for Caleb. For bringing him into my life. I don't know if You have a plan for either of us, I mean when it comes to some sort of future. But I want to be walking in the center of Your will. I want to follow after You wholeheartedly. Help me to trust You, even when all is shaking around me.

~*~

"Is there anything I can do to help?" Caleb stepped inside the room where the injured man was sprawled on a table, bleeding profusely.

Josh didn't even glance at him. "Wash your hands in the pitcher there. Be sure to scrub them good."

Caleb made quick work of following his friend's orders, wiping his hands on a clean towel beside the basin.

The man mumbled something and groaned.

Caleb shifted closer to the examining table. "Has he said anything that makes sense?"

Josh shook his head. "Think he's in too much pain. Haven't even gotten his name from him. I've never seen him before."

Caleb leaned close to the man's ear. "Can you tell me who did this to you?"

The man's pain-filled eyes flickered open. "Traitor… Kidman…was to s-share…"

"Hold his shoulders down." Josh's voice was gruff as he cut away the man's shirt.

Caleb put pressure on each of the man's upper arms holding them firmly in place.

The fella let out a yowl that brought back memories of walking beside the surgeon's tents during the war when soldier's limbs were hacked off.

Caleb cringed at the sound.

The man went slack.

"You all right?" Josh glanced at him.

He gave a sharp nod. A few times over the years while Josh was his deputy, Caleb had shared some of his experiences during the war.

"Keep an eye on him to see if he awakens. I'll have to administer chloroform if he comes to again."

Caleb kept a careful watch on the patient in between glancing at Josh cutting away the shirt and cleaning the area around where the bullet had entered the gut.

Josh grunted as he shifted the man and checked his back. "No exit wound."

"Not good." Caleb hefted a sigh.

The man likely had little chance of surviving, let alone becoming conscious again so he could get more information from him. With Josh having to find the bullet and dig it out meant greater risk of infection setting in.

He sent up a quick prayer for the man's health and hoped the fella had made things right with his Maker before he'd gotten to this point. But from Caleb's experience as a U.S. Marshal, most fugitives thought they were invincible, saying they'd make a decision for the

Lord at a later date. Most ended up either in jail or like the fella sprawled on the table.

Caleb studied the man's breathing. It seemed shallower and slower.

Josh had made his incision and was fishing around in the man's middle trying to see the bullet. "I can't find it."

The man groaned.

Josh halted. "Grab the brown bottle there on the counter and the rag beside it."

Caleb jumped to obey but by the time he'd brought them to Josh, the fella on the table had gone completely still. Too still.

Josh blew out a breath, wiping the blood from his hands before placing his fingers against the man's neck, searching for a heartbeat. He shook his head a moment later. "He's gone. Guess you won't be able to discover more about what happened. If you fetch Enoch, he could search the trail with you. Maybe together you'll be able to learn which way Klaude went. At least, that's who I assume this man was referring to."

Caleb glanced at the dead man one more time. "Would you get word to Enoch? I'd rather jump on this before the trail gets cold. Just need to collect my saddle bags and fetch my horse."

"Sure. I understand."

"Besides, I know the sheriff has a family on the way now. I'd hate to see any harm come to him on account of Klaude." Caleb glanced at his friend. "There's nobody to miss me if something happens to me."

"You know that's not true." Josh frowned at him. "You have me. And other friends too."

"It's not the same. This Klaude is unstable. He seems to like killing and hurting folks. I'm sure once you tell the sheriff he'll have to make his own decision, but I don't want to have his safety on my conscience. Tell him I'll do whatever I can to bring Klaude in alive."

Josh plunked his instruments into a metal pan before draping a sheet over the dead man's body. "I saw the wanted poster. Klaude's wanted dead or alive. Don't risk yourself. I know you hate having to take a man's life, especially after what you saw…and did during the war, but if killing is the only way to bring Klaude in, the Good Lord will understand."

Caleb fidgeted with the edge of the sheet.

"Look at me." Josh's tone made Caleb turn toward his friend.

"You're a good man, Caleb. Don't ever forget it. God forgives you for what you had to do in the war. Being a U.S. Marshal has been a noble profession, trying to make a difference, bringing criminals to justice, and taking killers off the street so folks aren't hurt. Don't lose sight of all the good you've done. Even the Israelites were instructed to kill their enemies sometimes. To rid towns of evil and its influence it could have on folks." Josh came to stand beside him, dropping his hand on Caleb's shoulder.

A tightness in his throat prevented Caleb from responding.

"Just thought you should remember that." Josh clapped him on the back. "You're an honorable man, Caleb Dawson. I pray the Lord guides you and protects you as you go. Praying He provides you with a good woman to love you. A place to call home. If anyone deserves it, it's you, my friend."

Moisture pricked the corner of Caleb's eyes. He needed to get out of here before he started blubbering like a baby. He gave a brief nod to his friend knowing he'd understand.

On his way out, he grabbed his coat and Stetson, and pulled them on as he hurried down the street. He didn't look forward to the coming confrontation with Lou.

20

Ellie Lou startled as the front door of the boarding house flung open. Her heart quickened as Caleb stepped into the room, his Stetson in his hands. "What happened? Was it Klaude?"

He crossed the room and sat beside her on the fainting couch, gathering her hands in his. "Klaude's the one who killed the man."

She sucked in a sharp breath. "The man didn't make it?"

"Afraid not."

"You're heading on his trail, aren't you?" She started to stand, but he held her firmly in place.

"The man only said a few words. Near as I can gather, he was calling Klaude a traitor. Said something about sharing. Don't know if he meant this fella had joined up with Klaude and then got shot in the process or what. All I know is Klaude's a dangerous killer. One I don't want anywhere near you, Lou." He squeezed her hand tighter. "Promise me you won't follow after me."

"Take me with you. My ankle's getting stronger. I promise I won't get in the way or hold you back at all. I have to see this through too. I made a commitment to Betty and her aunt." She shifted closer to him. "I'll be careful. But I have to find a way to make some money so I can save my ranch."

A muscle in Caleb's jaw flickered. He looked as if he had something he wanted to say.

She rushed to convince him before he spoke against it again. "I won't do anything you don't feel is safe. I'll follow your orders and allow you to lead. I can be an extra set of eyes to help you with following the trail."

His brows rose.

Her face warmed.

He probably hadn't forgotten about her poor sense of direction.

"I can't allow it, Lou. I won't risk your life just so you can make some reward money."

She shifted to the corner of the couch, making her spine straight. "You know it's about more than that to me." She jerked her hands from his grasp. "I thought you were different. Thought you understood how much I have at stake here too. More than you do. You're just out to make money so you can retire in style. I have everything on the line." She stood and reached for her crutch. Tears sprang to her eyes, and she swiped them away. She hobbled across the room, away from him.

"Lou. Come back." He reached a hand towards her. "I don't want to leave with you angry. But I can't chance taking you along. Can't risk your life. It means too much to me. We'll talk more when I return. Please promise me you'll stay here and be safe. Take time to heal. You know going along would only risk your ankle possibly never healing correctly. I won't be responsible for that."

She leaned against a chair and folded her arms across her chest. "I wouldn't hold you responsible for anything."

His face paled, almost as if she'd struck him. "Rest up, Lou, so you'll be strong enough to return to your ranch." He shoved his Stetson on his head. "I-If I don't make it back…" He hefted a sigh. "If I don't make it back to you, I want you to know you're the most interesting woman I've ever known. Don't be afraid to trust God. He won't disappoint you." Caleb turned and walked out the front door, securing it behind him.

Tears streamed down Ellie Lou's cheeks.

He really was leaving.

Without her.

How had this happened?

A sound in the doorway drew Ellie Lou's attention.

Had he returned?

Mrs. Walsh stood at the edge of the room. "I'm so sorry, dear." She crossed the room and hugged Ellie Lou.

Ellie Lou couldn't hold back her sobs, leaning hard against the older woman's shoulders until her tears were spent.

"There. There. You just cry it all out, dear. You'll feel better."

Mrs. Walsh patted her back. "Caleb's made the right decision though. Don't you see how much he cares about you? He wants you safe. He maybe didn't say the actual words about loving you, but they were implied. Sorry. I didn't mean to eavesdrop."

Ellie Lou sniffed. "You're wrong. He doesn't care about me at all. Just cares about rounding up Klaude on his own. He just wants to keep all the reward money for himself." She flicked the tears away. "Here I thought he'd started to care about me and my predicament. But it's all been a farce."

"No, dear, it's not that at all. You're not thinking straight. You're distraught." She put her arms around Ellie Lou's shoulders. "Let's get you back to your room so you can get some rest. You'll feel better once you take a nap. Things will be clearer after you sleep. Trust me."

Ellie Lou drew back. "No, you're wrong. He doesn't care about me. He doesn't want me along so I can't get the reward money too." She secured her crutch under her armpit. "Well, I'll show him I can do this. As soon as I can get my things gathered, I'll be heading out. But I have two favors to ask of you, Mrs. Walsh."

The older woman shook her head. "I don't know, dear. I really don't approve of you going after a dangerous outlaw who has killed people. It's not safe for you, especially as a woman."

Ellie Lou ignored the woman's caution. "Would you keep an eye on the dog while I'm gone, and would you be willing to pack up some food for me? I promise I'll reimburse you for the room and whatever supplies you send with me as soon as I return with that reward money. But like it or not, I'm going after them."

The older woman's face softened. "I promise to watch the dog, and I'll gladly give you food, but you don't owe me anything, my dear. Consider it a Christmas gift."

Ellie Lou shook her head. "I'll pay you back when I return."

"And what happens if you never return?"

~*~

December 28, 1877

Ellie Lou had been traveling through the countryside for five straight days. She hated to admit it, but she was hopelessly lost. Caleb had gotten a big enough lead on her the first day. She'd only seen him at a distance at the very beginning of her journey. Since then, she'd been following horse tracks. Although whether or not they were Caleb's horse, or some random horse, she had no idea.

She was saddle-sore. Her ankle throbbed. She hunched in her coat, shivering. She'd admit defeat and head back to Burrton Springs, if she knew which direction to find it. Snow drifts still dotted the prairie. She'd come across numerous carcasses of cattle and other wild animals that must've been caught in the storms. At best, she had a couple days of food left. If she didn't catch up with Caleb soon, she'd be hurting to keep herself fed. Charles had never taken her hunting, so she hadn't been able to shoot any fresh meat for her supper.

Other than seeing Caleb one time days ago, she hadn't come across a single soul. So much for thinking she could help round up Klaude. She snorted. "What was I thinking?"

Storm lifted his head and whinnied. Did he think they were on a fool's mission too?

Ellie Lou sighed. *Forgive me, Lord for going off without a plan again. All I could think about was helping You find a way to solve my problem and get my land back."* She glanced at the snowy prairie. *I guess You'll keep me where I am until I finally stop being hard-headed and let You work in my life. You know the way that's best for me. Apparently, I don't know much of anything. I guess I'm no different than a young child demanding their way when they don't know what they need. Forgive me, Lord. It's hard to believe and trust when I can't see an answer coming. Forgive my doubts and fears. Help me with my unbelief. I want to be walking in the center of Your will instead of plodding my own path.*

A peace settled upon her heart.

Thank You, Lord. Help me to continue to keep my eyes on You. And Lord, will You help me to either find Caleb or my way back home?

She pulled back on the reins. "Whoa, boy." She patted Storm's sweaty withers. Ellie Lou studied the field around her. Nothing looked familiar. A small dip in the land was ahead along with a copse of trees. Unusual for the Kansas prairie. "I guess we'll check it out,

Storm, before we turn back."

A shot split the air.

Ellie Lou dropped from the saddle to the ground. She whipped a pistol from her husband's gun belt, aiming it in the direction of the trees and fired. Her heart hammered.

Another shot rang out. She sprawled flat on the snow, moisture soaking her pants.

Guide me, Lord. Show me what to do. Protect Caleb. Wherever he is.

Another shot sounded and a rock near Ellie Lou split from the bullet ricocheting from it. Her head pounded. The only place to hide was ahead in the dip of the land where the trees were, but from what she could tell, that was where the shots were coming from. There was nowhere to hide.

Protect me, Lord. Keep Storm safe.

The words became a steady mantra in her head as she kept watch.

No more shots rang out.

How much time had passed? She couldn't tell. It felt like a lifetime.

Did she dare move?

~*~

Caleb had been playing cat and mouse with Klaude for the past five days although he couldn't tell who was the cat and who was the mouse. He'd pinned the outlaw down. Only problem was, he couldn't get a clear shot at the man because of the trees.

Klaude had been shooting wildly for the past ten minutes.

No bullets had come near Caleb.

So, if the outlaw wasn't shooting at him, who was he shooting at? Or was the criminal just trying to confuse Caleb?

Right after Caleb had left Lou to track Klaude, he thought he'd seen a glimpse of her at a distance. But when he hadn't caught sight of her again, he just figured his eyes and imagination had been playing tricks on him. Wishing she was there, but not wanting her to be, so she'd be out of harm's way.

Should he risk lifting his head from his hiding place behind a large rock to see what or who Klaude shot at? He debated.

The outlaw's gun had been quiet. Probably reloading.

He shifted, searched behind him.

A big black horse stood in the middle of the snow-covered prairie and something large was beside the horse, on the ground.

Caleb lifted his body a little higher for a better look.

That sure looked like Storm.

And Lou.

His heart stalled.

Was she injured?

Killed?

Dear God, no!

A shot fired, followed by a hot coal searing through Caleb's shoulder. Another ripped into his arm. He slumped backward, his rifle dropping from his grasp. Caleb struggled to remain conscious. He blinked. He had to stay awake and not give in to the pain. Had to protect Lou. Had to make sure Klaude didn't get to her. He bit back a groan.

Inch by inch, he forced his body to a position where he could keep an eye on Klaude.

The outlaw had shifted somewhere else.

Caleb's heart thudded in his ears as he whipped his head around trying to catch a glimpse of the criminal. Where had he gotten to?

Got to protect, Lou. Got to protect, Lou. Got to protect, Lou. Please, Lord. Help me.

He forced his brain to concentrate on the prayer.

A movement to his left drew his attention.

Klaude was mounting his horse and heading straight toward Lou.

Caleb had to do something. He forced himself to stand. It took every ounce of determination to lift his weapon, sight his rifle, and shoot.

21

Ellie Lou's throat constricted as she watched Caleb stand and fire his rifle before collapsing on the ground. A man on horseback took off in the opposite direction. Was it Klaude? It sure looked a lot like him.

She swept onto Storm, kicking him into motion. A minute later she sawed on the reins, drawing her mount to a halt. She swung from the saddle, her foot catching in the stirrup. Ellie Lou stumbled, but caught herself, stepping on her sore ankle. Pain coursed through her leg. She ignored it and pressed toward Caleb.

Dear God, let him be alive.

He lay on his back, blood soaking his right arm and shoulder.

"Caleb?"

His eyes didn't even flicker.

"Oh, God, what do I do?"

Her limbs trembled, and she dropped to her knees beside him. She cradled his head in her lap, stroking his smooth face. Tears streamed. "Talk to me, Caleb."

His eyes flickered but didn't open.

"Caleb. Come on. Stay with me." Her throat closed.

It took a minute, but his eyelids flickered again.

There was never a better sight than seeing his blue eyes study her.

He licked his lips, lifted his left hand and stroked her cheek. "You're alive. I was afraid Klaude shot you."

"Shh. I'm fine. Don't worry about me. But look at what he did to you."

His face paled. "Klaude's not still around, is he?"

She shook her head. "No, he took off to the…uh…"

Caleb chuckled. "You don't have any idea which direction he went, do you?"

Ellie Lou shrugged her shoulders and smiled. "I guess not."

"Praise God you weren't hurt. But what're you doing here? You promised you wouldn't follow me." His gaze bored into hers.

Heat surged up her body. "I never made such a promise."

He groaned. "No time to argue about it now."

She glanced at his arm. "We need to stop the bleeding."

"Help me sit up."

Ellie Lou wrapped her arm around his back and used all her might to assist him with the process.

His face paled even more.

"You won't pass out again, will you?"

He shook his head, whether in response to her or to clear his vision, she couldn't tell. Sweat beaded above his lip. "You need to take my coat off so we can check if the bullets passed through or are still inside me."

Ellie Lou unbuttoned his coat and managed to get the sleeve off his left arm. His torso shook as she worked the sleeve off his injured arm. He started to sway but she steadied him.

"Might need to take off my shirt too."

She hated to put him through more agony.

Caleb gave a brief nod. "Gotta be done."

Ellie Lou took a deep breath and unbuttoned his shirt, repeating the process she'd done with his coat. Seeing his bare chest caused her fingers to falter in removing the final sleeve. She forced herself to stop staring.

"Look for an exit wound on both." Caleb shivered.

Blood flowed freely from both wounds.

"We've got to get the bleeding stopped."

He shook his head. "Not yet. Tell me what you see."

She walked around him. "I can see a hole in the back of your shoulder."

"Good." He panted. "And the upper arm?"

Her chest constricted.

"Lou?" He glanced at her over his injured shoulder.

She bit her lower lip and shook her head. "No."

He groaned. "That means you'll have to dig it out."

"I can't. I don't have any doctoring experience. Why don't we go back to Burrton Springs so Josh can take care of you?" She knelt beside him.

"Can't wait." He groaned. "Town too far away. You have to do it, Lou. I trust you."

"But I've never done something like this." Tears pricked her eyes again.

"Can walk you through it."

Dear God, he's barely staying conscious, how will I find the bullet and remove it? Ellie Lou blinked away the tears and took a deep breath. "Tell me what I'll need."

"Start a fire. Get knife blade hot. Small bottle of whiskey in saddle bag. Clean wound. Cauterize shoulder to stop the bleeding. Whiskey on hands to sterilize. Dig out bullet. Clean wound. Cauterize."

"You mentioned that twice. What does that mean?"

"Put…hot knife…against skin…where the bullets…went in and out." He panted and swayed, slumping over on his side.

Ellie Lou shifted him so he wouldn't get dirt in his wounds before she ran for his saddle bag, gathering the items he'd mentioned. She also found a small packet of folded handkerchiefs she could use for dressing the wounds afterward.

Some dead branches dotted the snowy ground. She tugged them, breaking them into smaller pieces. Striking flint, it took a few tries before she got a blaze burning. Ellie Lou shifted a stone closer to the flames, resting the blade of her knife on it.

Caleb hadn't moved since he slumped over.

Please help me remember everything he told me to do, Lord.

She shifted a blanket beneath him, protecting him from the dirt and snow. Ellie Lou uncorked the bottle and rinsed her hands, wondering why he had the bottle in the first place. She'd never seen him drink when they were in the soddy. Was it for medicinal purposes only? She poured a small amount on his shoulder wound but still he didn't move.

Next, she used her glove to protect her hand as she picked up the knife from the rock. Ellie Lou sent up a quick prayer as she hovered an inch above the seeping wound at Caleb's shoulder.

Taking a deep breath, she touched the hot blade against his skin.

Caleb screamed and bolted upward.

Sobs shook her frame. "I'm so sorry."

"Not. Your. Fault." His breathing was choppy.

"I need to do the back wound too."

"Do it." He gritted his teeth.

The smell of scorched skin caused her stomach to churn. She willed her breakfast to stay in place.

"Good. Job." He lay back on the blanket. "Bullet now."

Dear God, how can he go through more of this?

~*~

Sweat soaked Caleb's body despite being shirtless in the middle of winter. It took everything in him to stay still while Lou worked on his wounds. He had trouble remaining conscious after the second cauterizing she'd done.

Lou knelt beside him, her hands shaking and tears soaking her cheeks. "I'm so sorry." Her lower lip quivered.

He shook his head. Caleb needed to get her thoughts elsewhere, or she'd never be able to finish the job. "Like searching for a thimble in a mess of feathers."

Her gaze shot to his.

Well, not exactly like that, but hopefully it gave her a different image to think of.

"I think I'm going to be sick." Her face had a green tinge to it.

"You will do no such thing." His words came out harsh.

She winced as if she'd been slapped before a fire lit behind her eyes.

He hated hurting her, but she needed a shift of focus. "You're a strong woman, Lou. One any man would be proud to marry. Any would be happy to have you by their side."

Her cheeks blossomed.

Good, he'd distracted her.

"Now, wash the wound and your hands and start searching until you find the bullet." He braced himself for the coming onslaught of pain.

She nodded and followed his instructions.

He about jumped from the ground as her fingers started probing the muscle in his upper arm. Black spots danced before his eyes. Caleb gritted his teeth to keep from crying in pain. *Should've asked for a stick to bite.*

Her tongue poked out as her fingers continued to probe. "I think I almost have it."

Dear God, please let this be over soon.

"Got it." She held up the blood-soaked bullet with her blood-soaked fingers.

He tried to respond, but his vision was closing in until everything went black.

~*~

Ellie Lou startled when Caleb's body suddenly went slack. "No, please, God." She dropped the bullet in the dirt and rested her other hand against the side of his neck, searching for a pulse.

It took a few minutes to find it.

Slow but steady. *Was it too slow?*

She rinsed her hands and the wound.

Still Caleb hadn't awakened.

The blood slowly oozed.

Should she cauterize it or not? Ellie Lou worried her lower lip between her upper teeth, debating what to do.

Once her hands were clean and dried, she wrapped a clean handkerchief around Caleb's shoulder wound, securing it. The upper arm injury had stopped seeping. She decided to just wrap it instead of searing his skin again. He'd already have two scars because of her ill-equipped doctoring.

As she wrapped his arm, she couldn't help noticing an old injury on his left shoulder. Ellie Lou ran her fingertip along the line of the white scar and couldn't help wondering how he'd been hurt. Had it been during the war or chasing criminals?

Not wanting to wake him, she covered him with a couple blankets. Using her gloves, she placed a hot stone near his feet to help keep him warm, but not close enough he'd be burned by it.

Ellie Lou studied the horizon. Not a soul was in sight. Wherever Klaude had disappeared, he was long gone. Not a single soddy dotted the horizon. The sky filled with color as it made its final descent. It would be dark soon. Looked as if they'd be staying here until Caleb could point her in the direction of town.

She glanced around, suddenly remembering she hadn't seen Caleb's horse. He had to have him tied up somewhere close, since Klaude had only had the one horse when he'd left. It was odd that Caleb's saddlebags had been beside him instead of on his horse.

She glanced at Caleb. He hadn't moved since he'd passed out.

She'd hopefully only be gone a few minutes until she found his mount. Ellie Lou stood and patted Storm. "You keep watch on him."

The horse snorted and tossed his head.

She patted him again and headed toward the clump of trees on the right. At first, she didn't see Caleb's mare, but she heard the horse nicker. "Hello, Chestnut. I bet you thought your master forgot about you." Ellie Lou untied the reins from a branch. "Come along girl, you can visit with Storm." She clicked and the horse walked beside her.

Back at camp, Caleb still slept.

Ellie Lou touched the back of her hand against his forehead.

Did it feel warmer than normal?

Her heart stalled.

Not again, Lord. You know how hard it was watching Charles die slowly. We didn't know at the time he was being poisoned, but I can't watch another man die, Lord. Please help Caleb not to get an infection because of being shot. I can't bear to lose him, Lord.

She needed to do something to keep her mind off worrying. What had Pastor Drew said about going through fires? "This surely seems to be one of those fires he was talking about, Lord. Help me to trust You, God."

Ellie Lou crossed to her horse, removing the saddle bags. She flipped open her sack and withdrew some jerky and old, stale rolls. Uncorking her canteen, she took a long swig of water. "Thank You for the food, Lord."

It didn't take long to eat her simple supper. Throughout the meal she kept an eye on Caleb. He hadn't shifted a muscle.

Taking a deep breath, she checked his forehead again. This time, it felt as if his body had been lying right beside the fire. The blanket had slipped down exposing his left shoulder and part of his chest. Perspiration soaked his skin.

He mumbled something.

She drew closer. "What did you say, Caleb?"

"Got a dispatch for you, Major General Sheridan."

Sheridan? Hadn't she read something in the newspaper years ago about Sheridan's scouts? Had Caleb been one of them during the war between the States? Was it where he'd received the other shoulder injury? How much pain had the man gone through the past years? Her heart ached for him.

22

Images of the battlefield shifted and blurred through Caleb's dreams. Pain seared his arm and shoulder. The slash of the bayonet held him in place, unable to move as he lay on the ground. He had to get away from the enemy before they found and killed him. Had to get word to his commander.

"Caleb?"

The voice didn't sound like any of the soldiers he knew.

He tried to shake his head, but it took too much effort.

"Stay with me, Caleb. I refuse to lose another man."

Something brushed against his cheek.

"Do you hear me?"

He groaned as whoever it was shook his leg.

"You fight this. It's not your time to die."

Sounded like a woman. Crying. Had someone died? He felt as if he should care. But he was so tired. He couldn't make sense of it. He wanted to sleep. Blessed sleep. Just as his eyes fluttered shut, the persistent shaking interrupted his peace again.

"You stay awake. You hear me?"

Caleb pried open a single eyelid.

Darkness was all around him.

Except for someone kneeling beside him.

His heavy eyelids fluttered shut once more.

Again, the shaking. "Leave me." It took all his energy to say the two words.

"Caleb, please." A soft sob met his ears.

He forced both eyes to open this time.

A face swam into his line of vision.

A woman.

She looked familiar, but it took too much energy to remember.

"That's it." She stroked his cheek.

Felt nice. Didn't recall ever being touched like that before.

"Please fight hard against the infection." Tears soaked her cheeks. "I…" She swiped her face. "I can't lose you. You mean too much to me." She ran her finger along his jaw.

Had he shaved? And why did it matter to him?

"Here. Drink some water." One arm lifted his head while the other brought a tin cup to his lips. Water dribbled on his chin, but some cooled his hot throat.

"Where? Who?" His head lolled back against the ground, and his eyes drifted shut.

"I don't know where we are. Klaude shot you, and we're somewhere in the middle of the prairie. I need to get you back to Josh, but I don't know where to go." She was crying again.

He should do something to stop it, but he couldn't think of what that would be.

"I'm Ellie Lou." Her words were soft. "Although you call me Lou."

Lou. Sounded familiar. He kept his eyes closed, listening to her voice. It soothed him. Comforted.

"Never had Lou for a nickname until I met you." She chuckled. "But at the time I didn't want you to know I was a woman."

Ahh. Lou. His Lou.

~*~

Ellie Lou was babbling. She couldn't seem to stop herself.

At least Caleb was alive and had opened his eyes.

She took his left hand in hers, stroking his long fingers. "You have to keep fighting, Caleb. I need you. Do you hear me?"

His fingers tightened.

In the flicker of the firelight, she glanced at their intertwined hands remembering the last time she'd held a man's hands like this. It was the day Charles was dying. She shook her head, shoving the unwanted memory to the dark recesses of her brain. Ellie Lou had no desire to relive that day.

"Klaude?" The word came out gruff.

She continued stroking his fingers. "Took off after he shot you. Guess we won't see him anytime soon. I'm so sorry, Caleb. I wish I could have found you sooner. Maybe I could've prevented you from getting shot."

This was all her fault. If she'd been better at tracking, she could've found him and distracted Klaude, so Caleb would've been able to round him up. She wouldn't ever forgive herself if Caleb died on account of her.

Dear God, please don't let that happen.

"Thirsty." His voice drew her from her thoughts.

She supported his head and helped him with the tin of water again. He slurped it down. His body emanated heat. She had to find a way to bring down his fever. Crossing to the saddle bag, Ellie Lou withdrew a handkerchief. She scooped up some snow, put it in the cloth, and held it close to the fire to melt. She squeezed out the still cold excess fluid and draped the cloth on Caleb's forehead.

"Nice." He sighed but didn't open his eyes again.

She settled beside him. "Are you hungry?"

He didn't answer. His chest rose and fell. Perhaps sleep would be the best for now. At least she prayed it would be.

The hours blurred as she alternated resoaking the cloth and praying for him.

A coyote called and another answered.

The horses shifted.

Ellie Lou reached for Caleb's rifle and set another bit of wood on the fire. Sparks flew up. Ellie Lou yawned. Maybe it wouldn't hurt to sit beside Caleb for a few minutes and rest her eyes. She shivered and pulled the blanket snug around Caleb's shoulders. His body still was too hot. She leaned close to him, his body heat warming her. Her eyes drifted shut. She snapped them open. She had to keep watch. Had to make sure he survived the night.

A Bible verse she'd memorized from Proverbs as a child popped into her mind. *'Trust in the Lord with all thine heart; and lean not unto thine own understanding. In all thy ways acknowledge Him, and He shall direct thy paths.'*

"Why is everything coming back to trust?" She shook her head. "Never thought I had trouble with trusting until the past few months. But then, I've never had the Lord wait so long to answer a prayer either."

The horses snorted. Probably not happy she was interrupting their sleep. She yawned and stretched.

Help me to trust You'll get us through this night, Lord. Help me to trust You will get Caleb through this. Heal his body, Lord. I need him.

Her thoughts and prayers blurred together.

~*~

Caleb's body was on fire. He felt as if poison was thrumming through his veins. Maybe it was. If he didn't find a way to get to Josh soon, Caleb would soon be meeting his Maker. He didn't have the energy to open his eyelids or move a muscle. How would he ever make it to town?

Are You there, Lord?

Words he'd read from his Bible flooded his mind. '*Be not far from me; for trouble is near; for there is none to help. But be not thou far from me, O Lord: O my strength, haste Thee to help me.*' He struggled to remember where it had been in the Scriptures. Somewhere in Psalms. There was something else too.

Caleb groaned, trying to recall. It came to him. '*Turn Thee unto me, and have mercy upon me; for I am desolate and afflicted. The troubles of my heart are enlarged: O bring thou me out of my distresses. Look upon mine affliction and my pain; and forgive all my sins. Let integrity and uprightness preserve me; for I wait on Thee.*'

Forgive me, Lord, for all the things I had to do in the war. If these are my last moments, I don't want to have anything between You and me that's against You. Forgive my sins. Help me to trust in You. If this is my time, will You send someone to protect Lou and watch over her? She needs someone strong in her life. Needs to remember how much You love her and care about her and what she's going through. Help her to recall Your promises. To realize that just because You haven't answered the way she expected, doesn't mean You haven't been with her every step along the way.

Help her to see even in silence and pain, You are there. In the shambles we often find ourselves in, You are still with us.

Caleb struggled to take a breath. His chest was so tight.

When the bottom falls out of our lives, You remain faithfully by our sides. Help Lou to recognize You won't ever leave her or forsake her. Help her to see how You long to lift her up. To care for her as a mother cares for her little children. It's taken me too long to recognize that, Lord.

He struggled to take his next breath.

If You're taking me home to glory soon, Lord, prepare Lou. She's a good woman. One I would've been proud to have as my own.

His chest made a strange sound as he coughed and tried to breathe. It was so difficult to get a breath of air in his lungs.

Something shifted beside him and suddenly his chest eased some.

"C-Caleb?" Lou's voice was shaky. Had she been lying on him?

"Still kicking." His words were barely a whisper.

Lou's hand came to rest on his forehead.

Blessed cool fingertips.

"You're burning up. We need to get you back to Josh."

Caleb doubted he'd survive the journey to town. Maybe it would be better if he died here. A peace settled over him. If it was his time, he felt ready to meet the Lord.

Lou shook his left arm. "You stay with me. It will soon be light enough to see. As soon as it is, we're getting on our horses, and you'll tell me which way to head back to Burrton Springs. And you will not die on me. Do you hear me?" Her voice deepened with emotion.

A small grin tugged his cheeks. That was the Lou he loved.

His heart stalled.

Loved?

When had he started thinking about love?

"Caleb?" She shook his arm again.

"Still alive." His words came out as a slur. He struggled to stay conscious.

She shuffled around as she saddled the horses and strapped saddle bags in place. Each sound of leather scraping and cinches jingling brought comfort. Her tasks would keep her mind off his dying. He'd rather have it that way. *Help it not to be painful, Lord. Take me into Your arms and bear me to Your throne.*

Lou shook him again.

How long had it been?

He struggled to open an eyelid. The darkness had faded away and a splash of color dotted the horizon. *Didn't the Bible say somewhere about joy coming in the morning? Funny the things you think of when you're close to death.*

"You need to wake up, Caleb." Lou's finger ran along his jaw.

She'd done that before, hadn't she?

His memories blurred and fuzzed.

"One way or another, we'll get you on your horse, Caleb." Lou tossed water on the low burning fire before kicking a bunch of snow on the embers. "Before we do that, you need to wake up enough and look around. Which way is it to Burrton Springs? Caleb Dawson, are you listening to me?" She stood with hands thrust on her slim hips and fire in her eyes.

He couldn't help but chuckle. His Lou. What a warrior she was. "I hear you."

She lifted his head, tilted the canteen, and gave him some water. She then fed a bite of bread to him. "You've got to keep up your strength."

It took every ounce of energy to chew the piece of food and swallow. His eyes drifted shut.

"No, sir. Not happening. You stay with me. Now point me in the right direction."

His head lolled as he studied the landscape. Caleb didn't have the strength to lift his hand and point in the right direction. Instead, he motioned with his head. "That way. Head east towards the rising sun and you can't miss it. Best to leave me here."

She shook her head and tears streamed down her pale cheeks. "I won't ever leave you, Caleb Dawson. You're stuck with me to see this through."

He didn't have the heart to tell her he'd likely die on the trip to town. Caleb just prayed she wouldn't blame herself.

23

Ellie Lou's heart constricted. She couldn't bear this. *Lord, I feel as if my heart is shattering into a million pieces. Take this pain. Save him. Help me find the way to Josh. You know how terrible I am with directions. I can't do this on my own strength.*

Never had she felt so alone. Abandoned. Needing the Lord to answer and scared He wouldn't. At least not the way she wanted Him to or when. What if God said no? Then where would she be? She hefted a sigh. Do I trust You only when I see an answer? Or do I trust You in the fires and floods? But when I'm feeling overwhelmed, how do I trust then, Lord?

Ellie Lou squared her shoulders. *Give me strength, Lord.* "All right. Time to get you on Chestnut." She shifted the horse beside Caleb's sprawled body. "I need you to help, Caleb."

He grunted. His blue-eyed gaze sought hers.

She stooped and shifted an arm under his good shoulder. "On three. One. Two. Three." With all her might she helped him get to a seated position. Sweat poured down her back. With as much care as possible, she pulled on his shirt and coat, buttoning it. Her gaze drifted to his bare chest. Heat blazed its way up her body.

He lifted a brow and a small smile tugged at his cheeks.

"I'll give you a second to get your bearings." She sucked in a sharp breath. "Here we go again." She shifted his good arm around her shoulders. "We'll stand, and you'll put a boot in the stirrup."

His body trembled beneath her. Heat emanated from him.

"Are you ready?" With all her strength, she shoved to her feet with her arms wrapped around his waist, pulling him upward. Her limbs quaked as they stood. She panted. "Raise your left foot into the stirrup."

His body started to pitch forward.

She planted her feet in the snowy ground and gritted her teeth. *Please, Lord.*

He steadied and inch by inch lifted his foot until his boot was in the stirrup.

"Grab a hold of the reins."

His fingers reached for them and missed. He tried again. This time he grasped them, wrapping his gloved fingers around the strips of leather.

"Whoa, girl." She murmured to the horse. "Here we go. You pull, and I'll push."

Somehow, she didn't know how, but they managed to get him in the saddle. "Thank You, Lord."

Perspiration soaked her body. She reached for a rope from his saddlebag, looping it around his waist and the horse's torso. "You will not fall out of the saddle, you hear?"

He didn't respond, just slumped over Chestnut's neck, his fingers wrapped in his horse's mane.

Ellie Lou swung onto Storm, gathering Chestnut's reins. "You hang on now, you hear? Giddy'up." She kicked her heels into Storm's side.

Cool wind whipped against her cheeks. She shoved her Stetson tight on her head with her free hand. With a quick glance back at Caleb, she pushed the horses to a trot, praying Caleb would stay in the saddle.

Her heart pounded with each stride. She prayed they were closer to Burrton Springs than she thought. Hopefully, they'd been wandering the countryside just outside of town and she just hadn't recognized it. *Please, Lord.*

She kept the pace as long as the horses could handle before slowing them to a walk. Bringing Chestnut alongside Storm, she studied Caleb. At least he was still breathing. Hopefully his wounds hadn't opened with the jarring.

She urged the horses forward again. If she didn't get Caleb to Burrton Springs soon, he might…

She refused to finish the thought.

"Hyah." She pushed Storm to a faster pace. Tears streamed down her face. Her heart felt as though it had been beaten to a pulp.

As the sun started its slow descent, she caught sight of Burrton Springs. *Thank You, Father. Help it not to be too late. Help Josh to still be at his office.*

The countryside whipped past as she pushed the horses to their limits. Weariness tugged at her limbs.

The town lay just ahead.

They thundered down the main street. Ellie Lou didn't stop until they pulled up to Josh's office. "Whoa, boy." She patted Storm's sweaty withers and swung down from the saddle. Whipping the door open, she yelled as she went. "Josh, you here? Come quick!"

A couple folks were gathered in the waiting room. Hopefully it was a good sign the doctor was in.

"Ellie Lou?" Josh came from one of his examining rooms. "What's going on?"

"It's Caleb. He's been shot." She didn't wait for the doctor to follow, instead heading back outside where Caleb was slumped over Chestnut, sliding from the saddle. She ran over to him.

Josh was on her heels. "Dear God."

Ellie Lou's fingers fumbled as she struggled to untie the knotted rope.

Josh pushed her hands away, making quick work of releasing the cord. He somehow managed to lift Caleb from the saddle and carried him to the office.

She ran ahead and thrust the door open.

Josh headed down the hallway, and she was right behind him.

"He's hurt bad. I'm afraid his wounds are getting infected. I tried my hardest…" Her voice choked with emotion.

"Maybe it's best if you give me space to work and you wait in the other room." Josh placed Caleb on the table.

Caleb was so still. Too still.

"I'm staying."

Josh didn't answer, just started yanking instruments from drawers and removing Caleb's coat and shirt. He shook his head. "Doesn't look good. Only the Good Lord can pull him through this, but I'll do whatever I can. Pray hard, Mrs. Williams."

"I have been." She didn't have any more words. Ellie Lou wrapped her arms around her waist, watching Josh work on Caleb. She kept watching his chest. Was it still rising and falling?

~*~

Caleb thought there'd be softer beds in heaven. But the one he was lying on was harder than sleeping on the ground. He dragged in a ragged breath. The scent of a wound going bad filled his nostrils. His gut churned. The smell had been familiar in the war, one he'd hoped to never experience again. Why would heaven smell like this? And why did he still hurt? Hadn't he read in Scripture about there being no more pain or sorrow once he reached the pearly gates?

"About time you woke up." Josh's voice pulled him from his semi-consciousness.

Definitely not in heaven yet.

He opened his eyelids, and a bright light pierced his vision. Caleb pinched his eyes shut.

"Hang in there and keep fighting." Josh prodded his upper arm.

Caleb about jumped off the table. "What're you doing to me?" Sweat soaked his face.

"Applying a potato poultice." His friend adjusted cloths wrapped around Caleb's arm.

"I'll lose my arm, won't I?"

Josh's lips pierced together, and he shook his head. "Not if I can help it."

Caleb knew better. Might as well admit it to himself even if his friend couldn't. It had been rare for any of his fellow soldiers to come back from an infection inflicted by a bullet or saber wound without losing a limb. He knew it firsthand. He'd be no good to Lou with only one arm, and his predominant one at that. Might as well die. He turned his head away, not wanting to see his putrid flesh.

His friend tightened the bandage.

Caleb gasped at the throbbing coursing through his limb. He glanced around the room, trying to get his mind off the pain pulsating through his entire body.

His chest rose and fell with a heavy sigh. He thought for sure Lou would've been here, concerned about him. Maybe she didn't feel the same way about him as he did about her.

"If you're looking for that gal of yours, I made her go to Mrs. Walsh to get some sleep. She's been here for the past seven days straight." Josh grasped Caleb's wrist. "Good. You're heart's nice and steady now."

"Wait. Did you say a week? What day is it?" His gaze met his friend's.

"January fifth." Josh studied Caleb's eyes. He nodded his head. "Much better." He made a notation on a piece of paper before he put the stethoscope in his ears and rested it on Caleb's chest.

Josh finished and removed the earpieces.

"What do you mean, it's been a week?" He shifted his head to stare at his friend.

"You've been unconscious for seven days, ever since you were brought in." Josh rubbed his chin. "For a while there, I didn't think you would pull through. But Mrs. Williams kept praying. She stayed by your side, refusing to leave. Not for meals. Nothing." He motioned to a wooden chair beside the hard table Caleb was lying on. "Sat there and slept there the entire time. Although she's done very little sleeping. That's why I made her go to Mrs. Walsh's for the night." He chuckled. "Took some doing. She's one determined woman when she gets her mind set on something."

Caleb knew all about Lou's stubbornness. He swallowed. "She'll think twice once my arm is gone." He'd seen it many times in the war when sweethearts or wives came to visit in the military hospital. After seeing their loved one with a missing arm or leg, or sometimes both, they left saying they'd never return. His jaw tightened. He couldn't bear to have Lou do the same to him. "Best if you tell her not to come back again. Don't want her to have to make a difficult choice. I'll make it for her." He turned his head away.

Josh shook his good shoulder. "Now, you listen here. You aren't dying. And you aren't losing your arm. The poultice is making a difference."

Caleb shook his head. "It's not. The smell…" He couldn't finish.

A frown flashed across his friend's face. "The wound was putrid, and I really thought I'd lose you, but things are turning around. I'd like to say my doctoring made the difference, but I think it was the prayers your woman has been praying for you. She's been pleading with the Lord to save you. To save your arm. Never saw a woman pray as much as she's been doing. I haven't meant to listen in on her prayers, but it's hard not to when she's been bold in praying. You should count yourself blessed to have such a dear woman in your life. I won't stand here and watch you throw that away. If you don't want her to visit any more then you'll be the one to tell her, because I refuse to do it."

Caleb had never seen his friend so adamant about something.

"But I want to tell you something, if you follow through with this and push her away, you'll be making the biggest mistake in your life. One you'll regret all your days. I'm telling you. I won't be a part of you making a foolish decision." He slammed his fist on the counter and stalked from the room.

Caleb hadn't been reprimanded in such a way since he was a little boy. He'd gotten caught by his mother when he'd been teasing a little girl at school, pulling her braids and dunking them in the ink well. In general, he made the girl's life miserable. He hadn't known why he'd done it. But the teacher had made sure his mother knew what had been going on in the schoolroom. Caleb still remembered the switching he'd gotten from his pa, and how Ma had cried. She'd told him she knew he was better than his actions. How he needed to change his behavior. It was her prayers and reprimanding that had led him to decide to follow Christ. To ask Jesus to forgive his sins. Since then, he'd worked to help others and not hurt them. So how could he hurt Lou now, even if it was best for her?

24

January 5, 1878

Ellie Lou sighed as she packed the last crate, carefully wrapping Charles's family Bible so the pages wouldn't be torn. She glanced around the room. A tear trickled down her cheek. She sniffed and whispered, "I'm sorry, Charles. I tried my best to hold onto the place, but I guess it isn't to be."

A sigh escaped. The furniture would have to remain for the new owner since she had no place to take it to. She glanced at her few crates containing her clothes, a tintype of her and Charles on their wedding day, both of their Bibles, and a few odds and ends. Keepsakes from their ten years together.

Oh, Lord. I thought You'd show up and somehow save the ranch for me. For Charles. But I guess it isn't to be. Guess this is one of those times when the answer is 'no.' Help me to accept it and not grow bitter in the process. She bit her lip. Sure is hard though, Lord.

She carried the crates to the wagon. Storm snorted and tossed his head. "I know, fella. We're about ready to head to town. Good thing Enoch let us borrow his wagon." She winced as she climbed onto the high seat. While her ankle was improving, it still pained her. But she couldn't keep babying it. She had to find a way to support herself. Couldn't keep living off the generosity of Mrs. Walsh no matter how much the woman insisted Ellie Lou didn't owe her anything.

She yawned. Josh had commanded she go back to the boarding house to sleep, but she'd laid awake for an hour, her mind whirling. She'd gotten up and asked to borrow Enoch's wagon instead of tossing and turning on the bed. She didn't tell Enoch why she needed it. Just said she had to get some things from the ranch. Fortunately, he'd brought it into town for the day.

Mr. Browning, the banker, hadn't told her who'd bought her

property, and she really didn't want to know. She hadn't been able to face him. What more could she say other than she didn't have the money to pay her debt? She couldn't imagine anyone else owning the property than herself, which was why it was better not knowing who'd purchased it. She took one glance at the corrals and fields as she headed back to Burrton Springs.

Ellie Lou squared her shoulders and sat straighter in the seat. "G'yup, Storm." She snapped the reins, urging the horse forward. Away from her hopes and dreams. Onto an unknown horizon.

She'd been away long enough. Best to get back to the doctor's office so she could keep a watch over Caleb. When she'd left him earlier in the afternoon, there hadn't been any change. Ellie Lou was beginning to wonder if he'd ever wake up or would he just stay asleep and one day be gone. She shivered. Seeing Caleb lying on the examination table brought back too many memories of Charles' last days before he died from poisoning. His death had been the result of his cousins and one of their ranch hands trying to get the property away from her.

But Caleb's poisoning from his wound and likely death all fell at her feet. Her responsibility. He was in this position because of her poor doctoring skills. She had nobody to blame but herself. If he died, she'd never forgive herself.

She couldn't seem to get away from the crushing weight of guilt. She questioned what she'd done wrong or what she should've done differently. One thing she had determined though, was she would do whatever it took to see Klaude brought to justice. One way or another. Maybe Enoch could give her a couple lessons on tracking, following a trail, shooting, hunting, and not getting hopelessly lost. Ellie Lou snorted. Who was she kidding? It would take her a lifetime to learn all those skills.

"Yoo hoo."

Ellie Lou jumped. She hadn't paid attention to where she was traveling.

"Ellie Lou, is that you?" Gertrude waved. The wind whipped her skirt, revealing the slight bulge below her waistline.

Ellie Lou waved and pulled back on the reins. "I thought you'd still be in town with Enoch."

Gertrude's brow furrowed. "Did you forget the shop closes at four on Saturdays?"

She hadn't noticed the time when she'd left for the ranch. In fact, Ellie Lou had no idea what time it was now either.

Her friend frowned. "Ellie Lou, are you feeling all right? Is there anything I can do for you? Were you at the ranch? I hope Mr. Browning was willing to give you an extension." Gertrude drew closer to the wagon. "Please come in and visit with me. Enoch said he had to patrol tonight. He's been more on edge with Mr. Dawson getting shot. I know he won't have his mind at ease until Klaude is rounded up and behind bars."

"I don't know. I should get back and check on Caleb."

Gertrude rested her hand on Ellie Lou's knee. "How is he doing? Enoch told me Caleb was shot pretty bad. That you hadn't left his side."

She blinked the ever-present tears away. "Not good. I'm afraid he's not…" Her voice broke, and she couldn't continue.

"Aww, come inside, Ellie Lou. Sounds as though you need a friend and maybe a good cry too." Gertrude grabbed hold of Storm's bridle and led him to the front of her small house.

Ellie Lou sniffed as she climbed from the wagon seat. "I can't stay long. Just tie the reins to the hitching post there, and I'll soon be on my way."

Storm tossed his head as he stamped his hairy white hooves. She patted his mane. "You behave. I promise I won't be long, boy."

Warmth from the cookstove greeted her as they entered the small kitchen. Ellie Lou hadn't realized how cold it had gotten. She shivered as she unbuttoned her coat and pulled off her gloves. She crossed to the stove and held her fingers near the warmth.

"Can I get you a cup of tea? If you can stay a while, supper will soon be ready." Gertrude bustled about the small room. "Once you warm up, have a seat." She motioned to a chair. "I want to hear all about Mr. Dawson and whether you think he'll pull through. We'll pray about it and hopefully the Good Lord will spare him."

~*~

Caleb's sleep had been fitful ever since Josh had last checked on him. Without a clock in the room, he had no way of knowing how much time had passed. Where was Lou? Was she still sleeping? If she hadn't been sleeping much during the time he'd been unconscious, she likely needed it. But it didn't seem right for her not to be with him. He shook his head. If it really was the fifth of January, he'd known her for a month now. With all they'd been through, it seemed as though it had been longer.

Rustling came from the doorway. Turning his head, he smiled in anticipation of seeing Lou. Even though he needed to convince her to stay away he couldn't help being excited to see her.

"Howdy." Pastor Drew walked into the room. "Josh said you might be awake. Thought you could use a little company."

"Of course."

The preacher settled on the wooden chair. "I bet you're getting tired of sleeping on the examining table now that you finally woke up. I know Josh said it was touch and go for so much of the time, he was afraid to move you to the bed in the other room. Josh had offered Mrs. Williams the chance to sleep there each night, but she refused. Didn't want to leave your side."

So that's why he was still on the hard table.

The preacher chuckled. "You can always tell when a woman is in love. She sticks to her man like butter on a corncob. Especially if her man is hurting in any way."

Heat flared in Caleb's neck. Whether from embarrassment or a sudden return of his fever, he couldn't tell for sure. Somehow it didn't seem right talking about this with a preacher.

"Heard it's been a rough week for you." Pastor Drew motioned to Caleb's right side. "How's the shoulder and arm doing?"

Did he really want to talk about the potential of losing an arm? He stayed quiet hoping the preacher would take the hint and drop the topic.

Silence stretched, but it didn't seem to bother the man.

"Josh mentioned you've been through a lot in the war."

That was not something Caleb wanted to discuss at all. It was bad enough his injuries brought up memories of it.

Pastor Drew took off his coat and Stetson, placing the hat over his knee. "I'm guessing you are kind of like King David."

Caleb's gaze snapped to the preacher's. "What makes you think that?" Apparently, the man knew very little about him.

"I imagine David was grieved by all the killing God had him do as well. But despite all that, he's known as a man after God's own heart. David had plenty of difficulties, but he still strove to be the man God called him to be. Even when a jealous king was chasing him. When he had to flee for his life. When he sinned with Bathsheba. When the child from their union died. Each time, David continued to turn to the Lord, to trust Him with his life." The preacher shifted the chair closer.

"If you read many of his psalms you can see his openness and honesty. He wasn't afraid to tell God his laments. Wasn't afraid to ask God to take care of his enemy." The preacher smiled. "But at the end of all those psalms when he lists what he's upset about, each time he comes back to God. Recognizes God is worthy of praise. Even in the midst of battles and difficult times. He knows God has his best at heart when he's going through things."

"Guess I never thought of it that way." Caleb shifted, wincing as pain shot through his arm. "But what if I end up losing my arm? What good will I be to anybody then?" He pinched his lips shut. He'd actually voiced his concern. His struggles. His doubts. His fears. "Who would love a one-armed man?"

The preacher didn't say anything but studied Caleb for a few minutes.

It made Caleb nervous. If he felt better, he'd fiddle with something. Anything to get the man's penetrating gaze off him.

"Is your mother still living, Caleb?"

He shook his head. "No. Both of my parents died before I left to fight in the war." One they would have been opposed to his participating in. Not because of his desire to help people, but over concern for his safety.

Pastor Drew nodded. "If your ma was still living, would she love you any less if you came home from the war without an arm or a leg?"

"No. Ma loved me no matter what. She always made it clear her love had no conditions on it. Pa, too."

The preacher smiled. "Figured as much. I think most parents are that way."

"But I saw many times during the war, sweethearts and wives who didn't want to be with their man when they saw the extent of his injuries."

The preacher twirled his hat. "I suppose that's true for some. But I would wager it was only a few who responded that way. I'd guess their love wasn't founded in the love God calls us to in His Word. We don't love with restraints attached. We're able to love wholeheartedly because of the unconditional love Jesus had for us when He took on our sins and died on the cross for us. He was the ultimate example of sacrificial love."

"But I couldn't ask Lo… I mean a wife to have to deal with a gimp husband her whole life. To need help with the menial tasks. It's supposed to be the man taking care of his wife. Even scripture talks about it."

Pastor Drew grinned, almost as if he'd heard Caleb's slip of tongue when he'd nearly mentioned Lou by name. "You're right there, the Bible does say the husband is to love and care for his wife, but also it says we're to be a servant to each other too."

"How can I serve if I only have one arm?" Embers flared in his chest. Why would God bring Lou into his life, only to have him lose an arm and a chance at love? Marriage. Happiness. Having someone to walk through life with.

"I think it's a good possibility that won't happen. But tell me, Caleb. Can God still use you if you only have one arm?"

Caleb shifted to his side so he could see the preacher better. "I don't know what job I'd be able to do with only one arm, and my good one at that. It'd been better if I'd died along the trail." Shame washed through him. His mother would've washed his mouth out with soap for talking like that.

"But you're here and breathing. Can you still talk? Were your legs injured?"

"No." He glared at the preacher.

"Seems to me there's still a lot good with you. Your mind is still working." The preacher stopped twirling his hat and stared at Caleb. "I'm guessing you have a lot of knowledge and experience you could share. Perhaps train other lawman to know what kinds of things to look for. Show them the best way to trail an outlaw."

Caleb wanted to linger in his anger, not to be told ways he could still make a life without a limb. Besides, he couldn't ask Lou to marry him if he only had one arm. He refused to put her in that kind of situation. She might say yes initially, but one day she'd grow to regret her decision. Grow to despise him. He couldn't bear that to happen. It might be like a knife in the gut to cut her loose now, but one day she would understand. One day she'd forgive him and be glad he'd done it. She'd learn to move on without him.

"I know you probably can't see it now. But do you trust God brings things into your life for a reason?"

"What do you mean?"

The preacher rubbed his hand along his jaw.

Caleb brought his hand to his own jaw. Stubble scraped against his fingertips. He couldn't remember the last time he'd been clean shaven. Ever since the war, it was the one thing in his life he could control. He snorted. So much for that. He barely had the energy to lift his arm, let alone shave himself. And he'd have a difficult time doing everything one-handed.

"When Shadrach, Meshach, and Abednego got thrown in the fiery furnace, was it part of God's plan for their life?" Pastor Drew stood and came closer to the table where Caleb lay sprawled. "I'm sure you heard the story from the Bible when you were a boy. Daniel's friends who refused to bow down and worship the image Nebuchadnezzar had made. They knew there would likely be harsh punishment for refusing to worship the image but still they didn't do it because they only worshiped God."

"I remember the story." Caleb shifted again. "But what does it have to do with me?"

"Do you admit they had strife into their lives?"

He nodded.

"That they had to make a decision whether to follow God or obey an earthly king?"

"Yes. But what's your point, Pastor?"

"They had a situation in their lives that could make or break them. They had a choice to make. Follow God or bow down like everybody else. God used that event to save their lives, and change the heart of a king. So, my question for you is, can you see that God brought you to where you are now even if you end up losing an arm? Are you willing to let Him work in you? Or will you be bitter like Jonah?"

25

Caleb couldn't get away from thinking about the discussion with the pastor. The man had left some time ago, but his words still lingered. Josh had been back to check on his poultice and change it. Said something about potatoes being good at drawing out infection. Caleb had told his friend that while Josh was cooking potatoes, he should fix Caleb a big old steak to go along with it. Instead, all he'd gotten was a cup of broth. His stomach still rumbled, wanting something more substantial.

He yawned and stared at the window, trying to get comfortable on the hard table. It was still dark outside and no Lou. Josh had said if Caleb was doing well in the morning, he'd see about getting him moved to the bed in the next room.

Caleb glanced at the window again. He'd encouraged Josh to go home for some shut eye. From the looks of his friend, he'd been losing sleep this past week too. He yawned although he shouldn't be tired considering he'd been sleeping the days away.

A door creaked.

Had Josh decided to come back and check him again?

Caleb shifted. His eyes were adjusted to the darkness. Only a slim light from the moon filtered through the window.

Steps sounded in the hallway.

He shifted.

Had Klaude tracked him down? Had he come to kill him? As far as Caleb knew, Klaude hadn't let anyone live since his run in with the stagecoach. Even the fella who'd been gut shot hadn't lasted more than an hour if that.

The footsteps halted just outside the doorway to the examining room.

Caleb's pulse spiked as he searched for something within reach he could use as a weapon. He didn't find anything. Should he lay here as if he was sleeping or try to sit? Just the thought made his heart speed up. *God, keep Lou from coming in. I don't want to see her get hurt, if Klaude's here.*

Sniffling sounded outside the door. It made no sense. Had the dog he and Lou rescued found his way to the doctor's office? Caleb shook his head. No. He'd heard boots, not the soft padding of an animal's feet. He may have been out of commission for a week now, but he hadn't completely lost his edge. More sniffing and something else. He cocked his head, trying to discern what or who was making the noise. He closed his eyes, straining to hear.

Crying. Someone was crying.

"Lou?" His voice came as a gruff whisper.

The noise halted.

He tilted his head closer toward the direction of the door. "Lou, you there?" He raised his voice.

"C-Caleb?" She hesitated in the doorway.

"It's me." He lifted his head higher.

She rushed in and came straight to the table, hugging his good arm.

It felt right. Good. He had to put a halt to it.

"The light was off. I was so afraid s-something happened to you. Josh left a lamp burning low each night in case I needed to do something for you." She sniffed and pulled back a little, staring into his eyes.

His heart hammered. Could she hear it?

"But you're awake. How're you feeling?" She touched his arm again. Almost as if she wasn't sure if he was really there or something.

He cleared his throat. The quicker he discouraged her and made her leave, the easier it would be on both of them. Although he doubted he'd ever get over caring about her. "I'm fine. Doc hopes to move me to the bed in the morning."

Her face softened, and she smiled. "That is good news. I knew you'd pull through. I kept pleading with the Lord to answer my prayers for you. He hasn't answered when it came to things for me, but I hoped He'd have you get better. Didn't think I could stand it if something happened to… I mean… I know I did a lousy job of taking care of your wounds. It's my fault." Tears welled in her eyes.

He covered her hand with his left. "Look at me, Lou."

She sniffed and shook her head.

It took every ounce of energy he had to lift his hand and run it along the side of her face, tapping on her chin until she met his gaze. "I'm only still here because of you, Lou. I would've bled out and died if you hadn't been there."

Tears continued to soak her cheeks.

"I don't want you blaming yourself, you hear me?" His arm trembled as he touched her face one more time, trying to memorize each feature. "For whatever reason, God left me here." At least for the time being. But there was no use bringing up he could have a setback. He'd seen it many times in the war. A soldier was on the mend and improving only to die in the middle of the night. If the Good Lord came to take him home, he'd be ready. But he didn't want Lou here to witness it. Best to get her to forget all about him. She'd be better off not tying herself to a one-armed man. Even if he kept the arm and didn't die, he had a long recovery ahead. He might never get full strength back.

"But it's my fault you're lying here." She sniffled.

His arm dropped to his side. Too weak to lift it any longer, he sought the fingers of her hand, intertwining his with hers. "I said no thinking like that. I will always have you to thank for saving me." *Saving me from Klaude, but also pointing me back to the importance of keeping short accounts with the Lord. Not allowing things to get in the way of my relationship with God.*

She rubbed his fingers. "You've come to mean a lot to me."

He needed to stop this before she said more about how she felt about him. Before she started thinking about hitching her caboose onto his train car. *Help me do this, Lord.* He took a deep breath and withdrew his finger from hers. "I don't want you worrying about me anymore, Lou. In fact, I want you to leave and never come back. You have your own life to live, and I have mine. There's no future for the two of us to be together. Best we admit it now. Thanks for all you did for me, but it's time for you to stop coming around."

She looked as if he'd slapped her.

His gut churned. "Don't come back."

~*~

Caleb might as well have thrust a knife in Ellie Lou's heart. Her throat closed. Surely, he wasn't serious. Not after all they'd been through. Maybe Josh had given him some strong medication to make Caleb not feel any pain, and talking nonsense was the result.

"You heard me. I want you to leave and never come back." He shifted on the table and no longer met her gaze, his body stiff.

"But..."

"Leave Mrs. Williams."

His calling her by her proper name, pricked like an open sore that refused to heal. "Caleb, please..."

He turned his head away. Dismissing her.

She couldn't hold back the sobs. Ellie Lou flew from the room, banging her hip against the doorframe as she ran down the hallway and threw the door to the doctor's office open.

Cold air fought with the heat of her tears. She leaned against the hitching post, giving in to the tears. The heartbreak.

I should've never allowed myself to get close to a man again, Lord. Should've never gone on a fool's errand to find Jeffrey. Should have never taken out a lien on the ranch. Should've found a job to pay my debt instead of thinking I could make fast money. She sank to the ground and buried her head in her folded arms. *I should have trusted You, God. I've made a mess of things, and I don't think I can ever change it now.* Her body shook as she cried about missing Charles. About losing the ranch. About losing Caleb. About being a complete and utter failure. *The fires and floods are overwhelming me, Lord. Are You there?*

"Ma'am? Can I help you?"

She sucked in a breath. "E-noch? Is that you?" She lifted her head and squinted at the dark shape standing a few feet away. The moon had gone behind the clouds, making it difficult to tell who it was, but it sure sounded like her former ranch hand.

"Mrs. Williams." He hurried over and reached for her arm. "Here, let me help you, ma'am."

"Ellie Lou, remember?" A shuddering breath escaped. She grunted as she pushed to her feet, keeping a tight hold on the sheriff's hand for a few seconds.

"What happened? Are you hurt?" Enoch took her arm in his. "We'll head to Josh so he can look you over."

She dug in her heels. "No. I'm fine."

The dark-haired sheriff shook his head. "You're far from fine, Ellie Lou. Can I take you back to the ranch?"

She couldn't stop the tears that started again. Ellie Lou was surprised there were still more tears in the well. "No. Can't go there."

Enoch shifted his Stetson and studied her. "I'm sure Gertrude wouldn't mind talking to you." He started walking, urging her along.

She shook her head. "No. She needs her rest now that she's with child."

He ran a hand along the brim of his hat. "Then where can I take you? Did you want to come back to my office and tell me what's going on? Did something happen to Caleb? Are you sure I don't need to get Doc?"

Ellie Lou wiped her tears with her fingers. "I-I'll be fine, Enoch. I'll just make my way to Mrs. Walsh's. Don't you worry about me." She started to shift away from him, but he held fast to her.

"No, ma'am. I can't let you go on your own when it's the middle of the night." Enoch glanced at the abandoned street. "It's not safe."

"Have you heard anything more about Klaude?" Ellie Lou started in the direction of her landlady's home.

"Promise me you won't take off and try to catch him, Mrs. Williams." Enoch drew them to a halt and stared at her. "He's a dangerous man."

Ellie Lou couldn't stop a shiver from running down the length of her spine. "Believe me, I'm well aware of his cruelty. I promise I won't go after him."

Enoch's brow lifted before he finally nodded. "Good. I don't want to be worrying about you going off and getting yourself hurt or killed. Besides, Caleb would have a piece of my hide if I let something happen to you while he's laid up."

He won't care. She wanted to say the words, but Ellie Lou didn't want to talk about it tonight. Probably not ever. "So have you heard some news about Klaude's whereabouts?"

The sheriff nodded. "He shot another man. Killed him." He shook his head. "I can't figure why he didn't kill Caleb. He's the only one who's survived. I'm afraid if Klaude hears he's still alive, he'll come after Caleb."

Dear God, not that.

"You need to be careful too, Ellie Lou. Do you think Klaude got a glimpse of you when he was shooting?"

She swallowed. Her legs trembled. "I-It's possible. I could tell it was him when he took off after shooting Caleb. I recognized him because of seeing the wanted poster." She pulled back and studied the sheriff. "But he wouldn't have any idea who I am, would he?"

He patted her hand. "I wouldn't think so. And most outlaws tend to have a code about not hurting women, so I don't think you have anything to worry about, Ellie Lou. We'd best get you to Mrs. Walsh though."

Except Caleb had told her one of the folks Klaude had killed on the stagecoach was a woman. She'd been shot in the back of the head.

Her mouth went dry. She glanced over her shoulder.

Was that a man standing in the shadows a couple doors down from the doctor's office?

She gripped Enoch's arm tighter and stopped, looking for a flicker of movement.

26

February 16, 1878

Six long weeks and Caleb was chomping at the bit to hit the trail again. "Come on, Josh, it's been long enough."

"You haven't gotten back full strength yet. I don't want you overworking it." Josh placed his stethoscope back in its case. "You and I both know once you hit the trail, you won't let up until you capture Klaude."

He paced the tiny office. "And you know why I have to go after him." He waved his good arm. "While I've been laid up here, Klaude's killed three more folks. Folks are mourning their loved ones, and I want to give them a measure of comfort by knowing the outlaw is behind bars."

"I still say you should wait until the end of the month before you take off after him." Josh crossed his arms and leaned against the examining table. "Or let Enoch go after him. It's his job. Not yours."

Caleb sighed. "You know he has a wife, and a child on the way. He's got too much to lose."

"And you don't?" Josh's brow rose. "All you have to do is say the word and Ellie Lou will come running back to you."

"Will you leave it be?" He ran a hand along the tight muscles in his neck, trying to ease them. "Why do you have to keep bringing her into every conversation we have? I told you many times, it's over. There's nothing between us."

"Never thought you'd be foolish enough to not see when something or someone good is in front of you. It's obvious you care about her, and she cares the same. She's been watching you at every church service you've attended since you've been strong enough to be on your feet. Your reason for pushing her away was because you thought you were losing your arm." He motioned. "But the wound has completely healed. There's no sign of infection. You just need to gain strength in the arm muscle. There's no reason to keep pushing her away."

Caleb paced the small enclosure. "I can't bear for anything to happen to her." There. He'd said it.

"What makes you think something will?" Josh's gaze seared.

He refused to glance away, meeting his friend's stare. "Because you've heard about all the people Klaude has killed. If I manage to capture him, then maybe I'll consider speaking to Lou, but I refuse to do so before."

"And what if you never come back?" Josh's tone softened. "Doesn't she deserve to know you have feelings for her?"

He shook his head. "Of course, I want her to know how I feel, but I won't do it until Klaude is behind bars. Where he won't be able to get to Lou. Only when I know she's safe and I've fulfilled my duty will I say something to her. I won't have her hurt by telling her I care about her only to not make it back."

"I still say you're a fool to wait. The woman has been through a lot the past couple years. She needs the hope she'll feel if you tell her you have feelings for her. Especially since she isn't living at her ranch anymore. She's lost too much."

Caleb came to a halt. "Wait. What? Why isn't she living at the ranch?"

Josh shrugged. "I haven't heard the specifics."

It made no sense.

A door in the main room slammed. "Caleb? You in here?" Footsteps thudded down the hallway. Enoch came to a halt. "There's word Klaude is in the Hutchinson area. Are you willing to ride out with me?" He glanced at Josh. "Providing Doc says you're cleared to go."

Caleb slapped his Stetson on his head. "Don't need his clearance. I'm good to go. I won't hold you back. My horse is out front. See you, Josh." He didn't wait for his friend to respond, hurrying down the hallway and outside.

Enoch quickly untied his horse. He mounted, waiting. "You sure you're up to the trip?"

Caleb held back a wince as he pulled up and onto his mare's back. "I'm just fine. No need to worry on my account." He turned Chestnut around and kicked her into motion.

A gaggle of women stood at the edge of the street, Lou among them. Her face was drawn.

He longed to go over and say goodbye. To tell her not to worry. That he'd be back. How he desired to take her in his arms and kiss her.

His thoughts halted.

Just when had he started thinking about kissing Lou?

~*~

Enoch and Caleb thundered to the edge of town, made a turn, and soon were out of sight.

Ellie Lou had no words to speak what she was feeling, but the other ladies had plenty to say.

"Where do you think the sheriff and Mr. Dawson are heading?" Mrs. Walsh brushed the dust from her skirt.

"I hope they have a lead on the outlaw who..." Betty Hadler dabbed her eyes.

"It's about time someone catches that criminal." Mary Scott patted her niece's arm. "Let's just pray the Lord keeps them safe, and they can finally round up that scoundrel."

Ellie Lou's chest ached from the pain of Caleb's rejection, and with concern about him confronting Klaude. What if Caleb wasn't strong enough if he got into a shoot-out or fighting match? Had he been practicing shooting his gun since his arm had healed? She hadn't heard much about his progress, especially since she'd forbidden Gertrude or the ladies at the boarding house to give her any information about Caleb. She'd thought it would help her to forget him. Instead, it was a constant reminder of what she'd lost. A great friend who had cared about her. At least, at one time she'd thought he had some sort of feelings for her. Clearly, she'd been exposed to the cold and elements too long. Or something. Ellie Lou didn't know what to blame it on.

She shoved the thoughts aside.

"Well, we'd better get to the shop." Mary tugged on Betty's arm. "Come along, dear. I'm sure if the sheriff and Mr. Dawson capture the scoundrel, we'll hear all about it. For now, we should keep them both in our prayers." She waved. "We'll see you two later this afternoon."

Mrs. Walsh returned their wave and then glanced at Ellie Lou. "You ready to go to the general store with me?"

Ellie Lou stared where the men had disappeared. "Um. Yes. I just think I'll make a quick stop first. Can I catch up with you in a few minutes?"

Mrs. Walsh patted Ellie Lou's face. "Go ask the doc what the news is. I'm sure you won't rest until you know what's going on."

Her cheeks flamed. Was she that obvious?

The older woman chuckled. "Come when you're ready." She strolled in the direction of the general store, not glancing back.

Ellie Lou sucked in a deep breath, squared her shoulders, and went to the doctor's office.

She opened the door and breathed a sigh of relief to find the waiting room empty. "Josh? You here?"

"Ellie Lou?" He came from the examining room. "Are you feeling poorly?"

Heat flamed her cheeks making her wish she had the excuse she was coming down with something. She shook her head. "I just wanted to know…" She dropped her gaze.

"Yes?"

"That is. I was wondering…" She sighed. "Oh, never mind." She turned back toward the door, her hand on the latch.

"You wanted to know how Caleb is." He came closer to her and smiled. "And perhaps wanted to know where he went just now?"

She caught the inside of her cheek between her teeth and gave a small nod.

"Sheriff heard Klaude's in the Hutchinson area. They took off to track him."

A silence settled.

"Thank you. I should probably go."

"I know he's been pushing you away the past several weeks, but you have to know he cares about you."

Her gaze darted to his. Could it be true?

"He was afraid he would lose his arm." The doctor leaned against the doorframe. "Probably not my place to say but since he's being so bullheaded..."

"What? What do you mean?" Her pulse quickened.

"Caleb saw many a man lose a limb in the war. I think it's been one of his greatest fears. He was convinced when his wound went bad, he would die. Or in his eyes, worse would be going through life without an arm. He didn't want…" Josh didn't continue.

Caleb had been afraid she wouldn't want him if he only had one arm? When had she ever given him such an impression? Tears pricked Ellie Lou's eyes.

"Don't think it had anything to do with you. More so his own fears because of what he went through in the war." Josh smiled. "I had my own things I ran from because I was scared. Not something most men want to admit."

"Charles always tried to be strong." She swallowed. "Even on the day he was dying."

"Guess that's partly how God made us." Josh chuckled. "Although sometimes I think it's part of our hard-headedness too. We think we know better than God. Or we don't want to do what He's called us to do. We think we can figure out things on our own. He doesn't answer the way we expect, so we throw a tantrum like a young'un. I guess it's what Paul said in Scripture—I think that's who it was. He ended up doing the things he didn't want to do. And what he wanted to do, he didn't do. I think we're often no different. We get caught up in protecting people and end up not being honest with them or ourselves. Or we decide to rebel and turn against God. It's what I did for a while."

"What do you mean?"

"I was angry God took my parents and my little sister. I wanted to be a doctor until He snatched away most of my family except for Jules. I ran for years, thinking I could run from God and what He wanted me to do. But you know what?" A smile flashed across his face.

"What's that?" Ellie Lou leaned closer, eager to learn what he had to share. She'd never heard the story of why he'd changed from being a lawman to becoming the town doctor.

"I couldn't ever distance myself from God. No matter where I went, or what I tried. Couldn't get away from my fears, for that matter either. I ended up having to face them when Annie took sick with the rest of the children she was teaching at the time. Don't know if you remember the quarantine the town had a while back?" He motioned to one of the chairs. "Why don't we sit down for a few minutes?"

She settled into one. "We didn't come to Burrton Springs often back then, so I never heard about it. Maybe Charles had, but I haven't."

"Well, when Annie got sick, I was afraid I would lose her. Sickness is what kept me from going to towns. Thought if I avoided them, I wouldn't get sick, or wouldn't be able to take anything to Jules when we were living along the trail." He glanced at the window. "But God knew all about my fears. My doubts. My choosing to disobey Him and not follow His direction to be a doctor. He ended up thrusting me into a situation where I had to choose whether I would trust Him or not. Where I had to decide if I would keep sinning and ignore the call He put on my life or I would start trusting and following Him again."

Ellie Lou wiped away a tear. "I had no idea."

Josh nodded. "Most people don't. And I rarely go around spouting my story. But for some reason I think God wanted me to share it with you. Hope it helps."

"You've given me a lot to think about."

He stood. "While you're thinking, also be praying for that numbskull. Pray the Good Lord keeps Caleb safe, and he wakes up to see what's been in front of him ever since you were trapped in the blizzard together."

27

March 1, 1878

Another dead end. Caleb shoved his hands through his hair in frustration before slapping his Stetson in place. Two weeks wasted trailing after Klaude around the countryside, and always one or two steps behind.

Time to check in with Enoch to see if he'd heard anything new since they'd parted ways a couple days ago. They'd been on the trail together for the better part of a week before it was clear they weren't making any headway. Enoch opted to head back to town to see if any more information came in as well as providing an opportunity to check on his wife, Gertrude.

Caleb couldn't blame the man for wanting to stay close to his wife. He'd felt a tug numerous times over the past two weeks to check on Lou and make sure she was unharmed. He couldn't stop thinking about Klaude not letting people live. Once the outlaw got wind of Caleb pulling through, the man would likely be on his tail. Caleb prayed the man wouldn't ever find out about Lou. He smashed the door shut on that train of thought.

Glancing at the moon, he kneed Chestnut to the small ranch ahead. A light still shone in the window. Hopefully he'd caught them before they turned in for the night.

Chestnut knickered. Another horse at the hitching post responded in turn.

The horse was dark as the night with snowy white hooves.

Caleb only knew one horse with hooves like that. He held back a sigh. *Keep it together, man.* He tugged Chestnut to a halt and swung down from the saddle. Looping the reins over the hitching post, he patted his mare.

He gave two short raps on the door.

A few seconds later, it swept open. Enoch shifted aside. "Come in."

Caleb stepped inside, sweeping off his Stetson.

The sheriff's wife and Lou sat at a table, with mugs in front of them.

Lou stood when she saw him and her hands fluttered at her side. "I should probably be getting home."

"Don't leave on my account." When had it become so uncomfortable to be in the same room together? And when did he start thinking more like a woman? He must be overtired from all the days along the trail with no tangible results.

"Any progress with finding Klaude?" Enoch motioned toward the table. "Have a seat, and I'll get you a cup of coffee. You must be beat."

"A cup of coffee would be welcome, but I won't stay long since it's getting late." He tugged out a chair and sat.

Lou glanced at him as if unsure what to do next.

Enoch handed Caleb a steaming cup of coffee.

"Thank you." Caleb blew across the top of the mug and took a swallow. The hot liquid warmed him down to his toes. Just what he needed.

"So, what's new?" Enoch sat beside him.

He hefted a sigh. "Nothing. Every time I think I have Klaude, he's already left." He studied the women. The sheriff's wife hadn't said anything since he'd arrived.

"Any more folks die because of him?" The sheriff's face hardened. "I haven't heard any additional word on his shenanigans."

Caleb nodded. No use telling the grisly details while the women were present. Best to protect them. He didn't want Lou hurt. And the sheriff wouldn't take too kindly to his woman being involved either.

Wait. His woman? Did that mean Caleb thought of Lou as his? He shoved the idea aside. He must be way overtired to keep going off on coyote trails like that.

"I best head back to town." Lou glanced at the window. "It's much later than I realized."

"Town?" Why would she be heading to town instead of her

ranch?

She shoved in her chair. "I just want to check on Honey before I leave, especially since Enoch said she might be foaling any time now." She reached for her coat.

Why did she have both of her horses here? Didn't she have the expertise to assist with the foaling if need be? Although most times a mare had no trouble bringing a foal into the world without any help. Something God built into them.

He gulped down his coffee and stood, pushing in his chair. "I'll go along to check on her with you before I hit the road again."

Lou frowned at him. "That won't be necessary. I'm sure Enoch will help if needed."

The sheriff's gaze bounced between the two of them. A twinkle shone in his dark eyes. "Why don't you two go and check on Honey? I'll help Gertrude with the few dishes and get her to bed. Maybe Caleb can see you home, Ellie Lou. If not, let me know and I'll ride along with you." He handed a lantern to Caleb.

She thrust the door open and stomped to the barn.

He trailed behind her, swinging the lantern to help direct their steps.

The barn door creaked as Lou swung it wide. She hesitated in the doorway, probably trying to have her eyes adjust to the darkness.

He passed her and trailed down the small path between the stalls until he came to the last one. Caleb hung the lantern on a hook.

Honey paced the small enclosure. One second, she was standing and the next, she laid down. A minute later she was on her feet again, only to repeat the process.

Lou's hand grasped the wooden door enclosure for the stall. "What's wrong with her? Has something happened to the baby?" She glanced at him and blinked back tears. "You don't think she'll lose it, do you?"

He patted her hand. "Don't worry. She's just in labor. By my guess, she'll have a new foal within a few hours."

"Really?" Lou's gaze bounced between him and the mare. "I've never seen a foal being born before."

How could that be? She and her husband owned a horse ranch. It was why she'd been pushing to get money to save it after Charles died. How had she never witnessed the beauty of a new life coming into the world? Had her husband shielded her from it? Should he do the same?

~*~

Ellie Lou gripped the door to the wooden stall tighter, as Honey alternated between standing and laying down. At times the mare reached back to bite or kick at her belly. "She's hurting." Ellie Lou reached for the latch.

Caleb's hand halted her. "Let's leave her be for now. Most times a mare doesn't need our help. We just need to be patient and keep an eye on things."

"But..." Her heart went out to the mare that was clearly experiencing pain. Why else would she be writhing so much?

"I know it looks as though she's suffering, but it's all part of the process of positioning the foal for the birthing. God instilled in her to know what to do." Caleb shifted closer.

Ellie Lou had no idea how much time passed as they observed the travailing mare. "What's that?" Her words came out in a whisper as she pointed to a yellowish sack at the horse's hind end with two of something visible.

Caleb chuckled. "It's the foal getting ready to be birthed."

She watched in wonder as Honey lay back down, the sack visible. A few moments later Ellie Lou could clearly see hooves through the membrane. Next came the foal's nose followed by its head and neck. Ellie Lou squeezed Caleb's arm. "It's coming."

He grinned.

A short bit later, the shoulders appeared and then the hindquarters. The foal was still encased in the yellowish sac.

"Do we need to help get it out of there?" She whispered.

"No." Caleb's tone was low. "Just watch."

Another contraction had the foal completely delivered and lying on the straw in the stall. The foal thrashed, breaking through the sack.

The mare shifted and sniffed the newborn, nuzzling the foal's side and ears.

"It's beautiful." Tears pricked Ellie Lou's eyes as she stared at the chocolate brown foal with a white blaze running from its forehead down to its muzzle. "Aww, he's struggling. What's happening?" Her fingers gripped the tight muscles of Caleb's arm.

He placed his palm over top of her hand. "The critter's just fine. Just learning to get up and get his legs under him so he can stand."

Her gaze collided with his. "Already? I know Charles mentioned one time that foals stand early but this soon?"

He chuckled again. "I can't believe you live on a horse ranch and have never seen a foal being born."

She bristled. Obviously, he'd forgotten she lost the ranch at the end of the year. No use bringing it up now. Best to focus on something happier, like the little foal. "Oh, look, he's almost got it."

The foal shoved with his back legs but only raised a few inches from the straw floor. He tried again but didn't move any more than he had before.

"He still has some of the sac around his middle." She pointed.

"Keep observing." Caleb's gaze was on the mare and the foal.

The mare shifted and gently pulled the sac off the foal.

The foal moved his front forearms under him, kneeling on his knees. With a sudden burst of energy, his back legs shoved him forward, and sprawling.

"Oh, no. He's not getting it." She sniffed.

The foal tried again, this time managing his back legs under him before collapsing back on the floor again.

Honey stood and sniffed the foal, nuzzling against its side and head as if encouraging the foal to get up.

With another bit of strength, the baby pushed to all four hooves, wobbling and trembling, its short tail wavering.

"You have yourself another colt, Lou." Caleb turned to her. "That should help to develop your line of horses."

If only she could still live out Charles' dream. Tears pricked her eyes.

Honey licked the foal's head and ears as the pair bonded.

What would it be like to have a child?

The colt wobbled a few steps closer to its mother.

"She's getting to know his scent." Caleb pointed.

"Why hasn't he nursed yet? You'd think he'd be hungry after all he's been through the past few hours."

"Give it time."

The colt nudged closer to his mother, sniffing her back leg.

She laughed. "He seems a little bit mixed up."

Honey laid back down on the straw floor.

"She's worn out. Poor mama." Ellie Lou edged closer to the stall.

"She'll rest for a little while." Caleb turned toward her. "Did you want me to take you home?"

She shook her head. "No, I don't want to leave yet. I don't want to miss anything."

Honey rested and the foal wobbled on his legs, trembling one moment and the next hopping little steps around the stall, never wandering far from his mother.

Ellie Lou didn't know how much time had passed. She yawned and stretched her spine.

Caleb smiled at her. "I don't know why, but most times a mare gives birth overnight. There's many a time when you don't see any sign of active labor at their nighttime feeding only to find a foal in the morning."

"I guess they prefer the quiet to give birth." Ellie Lou leaned against the side of the stall. Weariness tugged at her frame. She couldn't imagine how tired Honey must be feeling. She wrapped her arms around her middle. What would it have been like to give birth to a child of her own? She sniffed. She'd never experience that joy. Tears trickled down her cheeks. Ellie Lou flicked them away hoping Caleb hadn't seen them.

The mare stood on her feet and the foal wandered close, nudging his mother's side before finally finding nourishment.

"Aww. So sweet," Ellie Lou whispered. Her heart filled to bursting watching the mare and foal interact. If only she'd been able to fulfill Charles' desire for a thriving horse ranch. Moisture pricked her eyes again. She blinked several times, willing the tears not to fall. Now was not the time to give in to her emotions.

"The beauty of new life never gets old." Caleb's voice grew deeper.

Was he affected by what they'd just witnessed too? Even after he'd likely seen it numerous times through the years?

He cleared his throat. "What will you call the little fella?"

28

Caleb waited for Lou's response. Silence stretched between them.

"Blaze." A mixture of joy and sadness filled her eyes when she turned to meet his gaze. "Somehow, I think he'll be blazing his own trail." She shifted her attention. "Something I need to do too." Her words were so quiet, he barely caught them.

What did she mean? He wasn't sure he wanted to know.

The barn door creaked open.

Caleb rested his hand on his pistol. He relaxed when Enoch appeared from the shadows.

"I see you two are still here. Saw your horses yet. Did the mare foal?" He continued down the aisle and joined them beside the stall. He smiled when he saw the mother and colt. "Ahh. I see why you both stayed. Always loved watching a mare give birth when I worked on your ranch, Ellie Lou."

"It was my first time to witness a birth." She smiled. "I'm so glad I could see it since I won't likely see it again."

All right. What was going on here? Why was she talking so cryptically? Caleb aimed to find out.

"Gertrude told me to ask you both to stay for breakfast. She saw your horses and thought maybe the mare had gone into labor overnight. We'd love to have you." Enoch curled his fingers around his suspenders.

"I probably should get on Klaude's trail again."

"Nonsense. You won't do any good if you don't have a full belly first." Enoch raised an eyebrow.

"I should get back to town. I'm sure Mrs. Walsh is worrying over what happened to me." Ellie Lou glanced at her mare and foal before studying Enoch. "Besides, I don't want to be gone too long from Blizz."

"Blizz?" Caleb stepped closer to her.

A small smile flashed across her face before it was gone. "Figured the dog needed a name since nobody has claimed him. Although I think Mrs. Walsh would take him in if she had a choice."

"Why Blizz?"

She glanced at him. "I thought it was appropriate since he showed up in the middle of a blizzard. That's what Blizz is short for."

He chuckled. "Glad he finally has a name and an owner." Caleb lifted the lantern off the hook as they walked down the aisle towards the barn door.

When they stepped outside, the gray light of predawn lit the horizon. Wouldn't be long before the sun made its appearance. His stomach rumbled.

"There you all are." Gertrude stood in the doorway. "Everything's about ready. Why don't you wash up and we can eat?"

They trooped inside. Caleb and Enoch waited as Lou washed her hands, drying them on a towel beside the basin. He made quick work of cleaning up wishing he had time to shave the whiskers from his chin. It would have to wait.

After they sat at the table, Enoch bent his head. "Father, we thank You for the gift of new life. Thank You for the mare delivering safely. Thank You for friends and family. Bless the woman who prepared the meal. Guide us to capture Klaude, so he can't hurt any other folks. Help us to follow and serve You in all we do. Amen."

The rest of them murmured amen in response to Enoch's prayer.

Gertrude passed a platter of eggs, bacon, and fried potatoes to Caleb. He scooped a healthy portion onto his plate before handing it to Lou. Their fingers touched and that same lightning zinged through his hand and up his arm. He shook his hand.

"Are you hurting?" Lou's words drew his gaze to tangle with hers.

Lord, help me to resist her. I can't commit anything to her until Klaude is rounded up. It isn't fair to her. I don't think I'll lose my arm, and I'm grateful for that, but I can't ask her to consider me until I know she'll be safe. And the only way to be sure of that is when

I get the scoundrel behind bars.

"Caleb?" She rested her fingers on his injured arm.

His throat tightened. "I'm fine."

"I hear you made a miraculous recovery, Mr. Dawson." The sheriff's wife smiled at him.

"Please call me Caleb. If it weren't for the Good Lord and Lou, I wouldn't be here." He dropped his gaze to his plate of food and started shoveling it in, hoping it would detract from someone else asking him a question.

The sheriff's wife laughed. "I've never been able to get from Ellie Lou how you came up with that nickname for her."

There was no way he would tell the story. He peeked at Lou.

Her lips were tight.

Didn't appear she wanted to share their tale either.

"Any thoughts on where Klaude would go next?"

Caleb breathed a sigh of relief at the sheriff's change of subject. He'd rather focus on the criminal than his feelings for Lou. "Spoke to the sheriff in Hutchinson. He said he'd get word to you if he hears anything new. I guess there's talk of a payroll coming through the area soon. They're trying to keep the details hushed so Klaude doesn't get wind of it."

"That's wise." Enoch forked some eggs into his mouth.

"Didn't you and Charles used to do most of your shopping in Hutchinson?" Gertrude's gaze sought Lou's.

She nodded. "He was partial to going there since he tried to avoid run-ins with his cousins by coming to Burrton Springs very often even though he was raised around here."

"I think I've only been to Hutchinson one time." Gertrude picked up a piece of bacon. "It's a bit bigger than our town, isn't it?"

Lou nodded. "More opportunities there too."

What did that mean?

"I suppose." Gertrude nibbled on her piece of bacon and swallowed. "But you have friends here who care about you."

Lou shifted the food on her plate.

Had she even taken a bite?

"I, uh, have been thinking about making a fresh start there." Lou kept her gaze on her food.

Wait. She what?

~*~

There. Ellie Lou had finally said it.

Caleb's mouth gaped open for a few seconds before he snapped it shut.

"But why? What about your ranch?" Gertrude reached for Ellie Lou's hand. "What would I do without you?"

"Now may not be the best time to consider a move, Ellie Lou." Enoch's voice interrupted his wife's. "I realize you've had a hard time lately, but I think it'd be better if you stayed here a while longer where we can protect you. Especially with Klaude on the loose. I don't like that he saw you when he shot Caleb. However, I think it's only a matter of time before the scoundrel learns you both are alive, and you're targeted."

Gertrude sucked in a sharp breath. "Surely he wouldn't hurt a woman."

The men exchanged a look.

Clearly Enoch hadn't told Gertrude how cruel Klaude had been. Best her friend didn't know.

"He wouldn't expect to find me in Hutchinson." Ellie Lou pushed the food on her plate with her fork. She couldn't stomach it right now.

"Maybe. Maybe not." Enoch shifted in his chair. "All he has to do is ask around, and I'm sure there's someone in Hutchinson who knows you and where you live."

"Maybe you should stay with Mrs. Walsh until he's rounded up instead of being alone at your ranch." A fierce expression crossed Caleb's face.

That was at least the second time he mentioned the ranch. Didn't he know she'd lost it? But then, she hadn't told anyone else about her predicament. Not even Gertrude. Just had said she needed time away from it and the reminders of Charles. Her friend hadn't pressed her for more information, and Ellie Lou hadn't shared any either. It was too painful to share about her failure. "I wouldn't want to bring trouble to Mrs. Walsh, Betty, or her aunt either, especially when they don't have a man living there to defend them."

Caleb shifted in his seat, clearly irritated.

At her or the situation, she couldn't tell.

"Where do you think he's holing up?" Gertrude shifted closer to her husband. Her hands trembled. "D-do you think he'd come after you?"

Enoch gathered his wife's hands in his. "You have nothing to fear, my dear. I'll protect you and so will the Lord."

"Yes, but we know bad things still happen sometimes." She exchanged a glance with Ellie Lou.

She was sure they were both remembering months prior when they'd been taken captive and tied to a tree. Ellie Lou still had some bad dreams recalling the events from that day. Fortunately, Enoch had come to their rescue, but what would have happened if he hadn't gotten there in time?

Trust in Me.

It was almost as if God Himself had whispered the words in her heart. Why did every situation seem to go back to that topic? She hefted a sigh. She was tired of thinking and struggling over the spiritual truth.

"Where's the payroll originating from and where's it going?" Enoch kept a hold of Gertrude's hands as he sent a look Caleb's way.

"Starting in Topeka. Don't know whether they'll use the Atchison, Topeka, and Santa Fe Railroad line to ship it to Newton or whether they'll use the stagecoach." Caleb finished the last of his food. "I should probably head out soon and get back to Hutchinson. They most likely have more recent information. Just wanted to stop by so I could update you. Too bad Burrton Springs doesn't have a telegraph office like Hutchinson does. Otherwise, it'd be easy to get word to you, Enoch."

"I know. It's something I'll be pushing for, especially after all that's been happening with Klaude. We need to have a faster way of getting information when something like this happens." Enoch patted Gertrude's shoulder. "Now, I don't want you worrying, sweetheart. You must trust God has me in His care."

Ellie Lou studied her friend. She prayed God would protect Gertrude. The last thing her friend needed was to be tangled up with the outlaw. Ellie Lou would rather have a run in with the criminal if it meant protecting Gertrude and her unborn child. She shivered. Not that she wanted to get close to the man either.

"Well, I'll be heading out." Caleb stood. "Thank you for the food, Gertrude. I really appreciate it. Didn't realize how hungry I was." He set the cloth napkin beside the tin plate. "Did you want me to put these somewhere?"

Gertrude waved her hand. "No, just leave it there. I have time to wash dishes before we head to town. Ellie Lou, why don't you ride with us. We can tie Storm to trail the wagon."

She shook her head. "No, I need to get to Mrs. Walsh right away."

Caleb hesitated. "I could see you safely there first."

"Nonsense. It's the opposite direction of where you're going." She stood and pushed in her chair. "Although I can help with the dishes if you'd like, Gertrude."

"No. I know you both want to get on your way. But please, both of you, be careful." Gertrude's gaze rested on Ellie Lou and then Caleb. "I don't want anything to happen to either of you when it's clear the Lord has something special in mind with bringing you together."

Caleb coughed like he'd swallowed a bug or something.

Was he that opposed to being with her?

She turned away before he could see the hurt piercing through every fiber of her being. The sooner she faced the fact she had no future with Caleb Dawson the better off she'd be. Really. So why did her heart keep rebelling and trying to tell her otherwise? She needed to get away from Burton Springs and the memory of Caleb Dawson. That would hopefully ease the pain. Time for a fresh start. No matter how much her heart protested.

29

Caleb rode hard towards Hutchinson. It had been almost three months since he'd started the search for Klaude. Far past time to find the criminal and round him up. *Please, Lord. I don't want him to hurt anyone else.* He rested his hands lightly on the reins.

Help Lou not to leave the area, Lord. I don't know what she was talking about this morning when she mentioned moving to Hutchinson. She has a perfectly good ranch to run. Maybe it was her grief talking. I still have no idea why she's been staying with Mrs. Walsh though. He shook his head. *I must've missed something, Lord.*

Show me where to go in finding Klaude's trail. I want it all to be over with so I can plan a future with Lou. Do You think she'll consider me, Lord? It probably will take some convincing since I've been giving her a lot of mixed signals lately. I guess I haven't been too great at trusting either, Lord. Trusting You have a future for me and that I still would have had one if I'd lost my arm. Why is it so easy to trust when we can see and so difficult when we can't? He puffed out a breath as he studied the prairie around him. Patches of grass poked through the snow. Before long, spring would arrive in full force. A time for fresh starts. If only he could convince Lou to make a fresh start with him.

I might as well admit it, Lord. I love her. Can't imagine my life without her. But I don't know if she's ready to consider a man. The memory of losing her husband is still fresh in her mind. I don't think I could find a woman any finer than Lou. I'm asking You to guide me as I try to find Klaude. I don't want him to constantly be a concern, wondering when he'll crop up in our lives and wreak havoc. I want Lou to feel safe. Help her…and me to learn to trust You fully. Because above all else, Lord. I want to be in the center of Your will for my life…our lives, providing Lou will have me.

His prayer brought peace, something he hadn't felt in quite a while. The few hours it took to reach Hutchinson gave Caleb plenty of time to think and pray. Determination swelled in him as he reached the outskirts of the prairie town. Folks bustled about on the street as he headed to the sheriff's office.

He swung from Chestnut's back and tied her to the hitching post out front. Caleb pushed the door open and stepped inside the small office. "Howdy, Sheriff. Wanted to check in and see if there's any news about Klaude or that shipment coming through."

The man set a stack of paperwork on the side of the desk and stood. "Good to see you again, Dawson." He reached across the desk and shook hands. "Was hoping you'd stop by again. Wanted to get word to you and Sheriff Valentine that news just came in from Topeka. The payroll will be arriving via the stagecoach. Figured it'd be easier to have guards on the stagecoach since we can choose which stops to miss, unlike the train. My men will be riding on the stagecoach. Thought you and Valentine might want to get in on the action too."

"Just say the word and we'll do whatever we can to help." Caleb sat on the chair in front of the desk. "What did you have in mind? Are you planning on laying a trap to capture Klaude?"

"We're getting word out about the payroll going on the train, figuring Klaude will hit it before it gets to Newton. Thought maybe you and Valentine would be willing to ride the train and keep a watch for the outlaw. We've already given instructions to the conductor not to stop for anything other than the normal stops. There will be other men on the train to help you too."

"Are you sure it's a good idea to divide us up like that? Why not delay the shipment and set a trap for Klaude where we all can be available?" Caleb rubbed the back of his neck.

"Oh, the shipment won't be on either the train or stagecoach. The money's already being moved to Newton. Don't you worry about that." The sheriff propped his boots on the edge of his desk.

"What do you mean?" Caleb leaned closer.

The sheriff held up his hand. "I won't tell you the details. Trying to keep it close to the chest if you know what I mean." He scraped some of the mud off one of his boots, letting it plop onto the floor. A small piece dropped onto one of the papers on the man's desk.

"How do you know it got there without Klaude hearing about it?"

The lawman stared at Caleb. "I've checked into you, Dawson, if that's who you really are. I just don't feel real comfortable letting you know the specific details when I don't know what you aim to do with it."

It didn't make any sense. Could the sheriff somehow be a part of Klaude's shenanigans? It wouldn't be the first time a lawman went over to the dark side and joined with criminals. Caleb just had a bad feeling about the whole thing. He couldn't get past the impression something terrible would happen.

He had an itch at the base of his skull. Caleb had it every time something didn't add up. He'd had it occur several times in his years of being a lawman. Caleb had learned to trust it even when it looked as if everything was sewn up tight like a button on a coat.

Help me to get this figured out, Lord before someone gets hurt or killed.

~*~

Ellie Lou held back her tears. Something that was happening way too often lately. After her recent conversation with Caleb, it was clear he didn't care about her. Never would. The quicker she accepted it, the better. It was time to move on with her life. She squared her shoulders. Question was, what should she do since she'd lost the ranch?

"Ellie Lou, are you busy?" Mrs. Walsh interrupted her thoughts. "Oh, there you are." She smiled.

Blizz stood and wagged his tail. He padded over to the older woman and sniffed the pockets of her apron.

Mrs. Walsh bent down and rubbed his fluffy black head. "I don't have any food for you just now. You'll have to wait until later."

The dog sat on his haunches and stared at the older woman.

Ellie Lou laughed. "You have him spoiled. What did you need help with?"

Mrs. Walsh grinned at the big animal. "I've always been partial to dogs. Had one as a little girl and always wanted to have one when I got older. But Mr. Walsh, well, he wasn't partial to them at all. Preferred cats." She wrinkled her nose. "They were never my favorite."

"So, what can I do?" Ellie Lou set aside the pad of paper and pencil.

"I was wondering if you'd run to the general store and pick up a ten-pound sack of sugar and some cinnamon. I thought I had enough to make a batch of cinnamon rolls for after our supper meal, but I'm lower than I thought." Mrs. Walsh petted the dog again. "Blizz can stay with me. He's a dear and won't get into trouble, I'm sure."

Ellie Lou glanced at the dog. While he'd been fairly well behaved over the past few months, she couldn't vouch he'd remain on good behavior. Couldn't hurt to remind him. "You be good, Blizz."

He cocked his head and stared at her.

She smiled, fluffing his ears. "I'll get those items for you right away, Mrs. Walsh."

"Have Hiram put in on my tab, and I'll settle with him at the end of next week." Her landlady turned back to the kitchen. "Come on, boy."

Blizz wagged his tail and followed the older woman.

Ellie Lou grabbed her coat from the hook beside the front door, slipped it on, and buttoned it. While the weather had been warm one day and cold the next, today had been one of the colder ones. She flipped up the collar and reached into her pocket for gloves. The wind whipped her hair. She should've pinned it up before she left. Too late now. Besides there wasn't anyone she was trying to impress.

A bell chimed as she opened the door to the general store. "Hiram, you here?" She hadn't had much need to visit the shop, especially since she didn't have any money to spend. Best to just ask where the items were and get back as soon as possible. The longer she delayed, the more likely she'd long for things she didn't need and couldn't afford.

"I'm here." He poked his head from a back room. Brushing aside a curtain, he walked toward her. "How can I help you today, Mrs. Williams?"

"Mrs. Walsh sent me. She needs a tin of cinnamon and a ten-pound bag of sugar. She asked if you could put it on her tab, and she'll come in next week to settle the difference."

"Why sure. Let me get those things for you." He scurried to a shelf and carted the two items to the front of the store, laying them on a long counter. "Is there anything else you need?"

Ellie Lou glanced around. "I don't suppose you're interested in hiring someone to help you, are you?"

"Do you have experience working in a store?"

She shook her head. "No. But I'm a fast learner." A flush crept up her neck.

"I wish I could help you, Mrs. Williams, really, I do. Truth is, things have been tight lately. Have you tried asking over at the bank or with Mrs. Valentine? Maybe she could use some assistance since she's in the family way." He made a notation in a book and placed the pencil behind his ear.

"Thank you." She couldn't meet his gaze. It was embarrassing enough she'd lost her home, and now to beg for a job. Ellie Lou bit back a sigh. Maybe she should start over in Hutchinson. It was bigger and might have more opportunities for her to work there. Although she'd have to find a job to cover the cost of renting a room too. At least here she didn't have to pay for her place at Mrs. Walsh's boarding house. Except she couldn't keep depending upon the generosity of the older woman. Ellie Lou had to support herself and surely her landlady wasn't making much money with having only two paying boarders.

She tucked the cinnamon can in her pocket and hefted the sugar bag. The bell rang as she exited. It didn't sound as merry as when she'd entered.

Ellie Lou couldn't ask Gertrude to give her a job. Not when her friend was already competing for business with Betty. Besides, Ellie Lou refused to take advantage of her friend. She'd rather move away than do that.

Snow crunched beneath her boots as she walked along the street. She smiled when she looked down at them. Caleb had found a pair that fit perfectly. She'd always be thankful for the time they'd had together.

She studied the bank as she drew closer. Running her teeth along her lower lip, she debated about going inside. What did she possibly know about banking? Although she'd always been good with math. Charles had asked early in their marriage for her to keep track of the accounting books for the ranch. Taking a deep breath, she stood before the ornate door of the bank.

30

Ellie Lou collected her nerve like a mother hen gathering her chicks before a storm. She glanced down at the grocery items. Maybe she should've taken them to the boarding house before asking about a job. Nonsense. Better to know now whether a job was available before making the trip to Mrs. Walsh and then back here again.

"Can I help you?" A woman from the counter called.

She didn't recognize the young girl. Ellie Lou caught her lip between her teeth and glanced around. Mr. Browning was busy at his desk. Should she go over to him or…

"Miss?" The woman's brows rose.

"I'm sorry." Ellie Lou stepped forward. "I was wondering if there's any job openings." She shifted the sack of sugar to her other arm.

The young woman frowned and shot her gaze toward the bank owner. "Today might not be the best day to ask." Her words came out low.

"What's going on here, Miss Cutler?" Mr. Browning stood a few feet away with his nostrils flaring. "Why are you not doing your job? I've already warned you about frivolous chit chat."

"Yes, Mr. Browning." The young girl dipped her head and went back to counting money.

"Ahh, Mrs. Williams. What can I do for you today?" Mr. Browning edged closer.

Ellie Lou's mouth felt as parched as if she'd been wandering in a desert for days. She swallowed to get some moisture into her throat. "I uh… That is, I was wondering if you happen to have any jobs available." She forced herself to throw her shoulders back and look the man square in the eyes.

He studied her.

She refused to fidget under his direct perusing. Instead, she lifted her chin a little higher.

"Why would you need a job?"

Was he serious?

"You should know why."

His brow furrowed. "Thought you'd be married by now."

What was he talking about? What did that have to do with needing a position? She shook her head. The man made no sense. "No, I'm not."

The banker shrugged. "Guess it's a matter of time, then. I supposed you were staying in town until you were married, although I'm surprised you didn't live at the ranch and have your young man stay in town. Of course, from what I've heard, he hasn't been around much."

Had something happened to the banker that he kept talking nonsense? Surely, he remembered she hadn't been able to pay off her debt and had lost the property. She hadn't heard anything about Mr. Browning having memory issues, but from the looks of the young lady cowering behind the counter, maybe Ellie Lou didn't want to work for the banker. She adjusted the sack of sugar again. "I best be on my way and get this to Mrs. Walsh. Good day, Mr. Browning."

He nodded.

She hurried to the door. Just as she opened it, the banker's words reached her.

"I hope you'll invite me to the wedding."

Ellie Lou quickly closed the door behind her, breathing a sigh of relief as she made her way to the boarding house.

It must be a sign, Lord. I can't find a job here. It's time to move on, isn't it? Help me to be strong. Help me to trust You with my future.

She shoved the kitchen door open. "I'm back." Ellie Lou set the grocery items on the long kitchen table. Odd. Mrs. Walsh was usually in the kitchen. Ellie Lou unbuttoned her coat as she strolled through the dining room. "Mrs. Walsh?"

Nothing.

"Blizz?"

The dog whimpered but didn't come.

Ellie Lou's heart accelerated. She should've strapped Charles' gun belt to her waist before she'd left. Glancing around the room for a weapon, all she came up with was a broom propped in the corner. She slipped her fingers around the wooden handle and crept along the hallway leading to the bedrooms.

Blizz whined again.

Her heart thundered so loud it was difficult to hear anything else. Ellie Lou inched along the hall, glancing at each open doorway. Nothing. The only room left was the one she'd been staying in for the past couple of months.

Dear God, help me.

Her prayer halted when Ellie Lou spotted Mrs. Walsh sprawled on the floor beside the bed. Blizz sat up, his tail wagging. Still, he didn't move to greet her.

Ellie Lou took another step closer to the doorway.

Was there an intruder?

Was he still present?

Gripping the broom tighter, Ellie Lou crept forward.

Blizz laid back down, his head resting on the landlady's waist. His tail still wagged.

Surely it meant there wasn't anyone else in the room. The dog would growl or attack if there'd been an intruder, wouldn't he?

Her breathing was choppy as Ellie Lou inched closer to the door. She held her breath as she stuck her head into the room. Just enough to make sure nobody was hiding behind the door.

Air whooshed from her lungs when Ellie Lou saw they were alone. *Thank You, Lord.* She rushed forward and knelt beside the older woman. Her fingers trembled as she fumbled to find the landlady's pulse. At first, she couldn't feel anything beneath her fingertips.

There.

Faint, but clearly the woman's heart was still beating.

"Mrs. Walsh?" Ellie Lou gently shook the landlady's arm.

Blizz edged his body closer as if he was protecting Mrs. Walsh.

Ellie Lou glanced all along the length of the older woman's body. There. Blood oozed from a nasty looking bump on the side of Mrs. Walsh's head.

Her landlady groaned.

"Don't move, Mrs. Walsh, until we can make sure you don't have any other injuries." She laid her hand on the elderly woman's arm. "Can you tell me what happened?"

Mrs. Walsh moaned and shifted. "Head hurts."

"Did you fall?"

Please let it be as simple as that and not the crazy ideas rushing through my mind, Lord.

"Klaude. Was here." Mrs. Walsh's eyes flickered open. "Looking for you."

~*~

Caleb couldn't get past the feeling he was missing something. Something big that might end up getting someone hurt if he didn't solve the puzzle. And soon. He'd never had any dealings with the sheriff in Hutchinson when he was a U.S. Marshal. In fact, the fella was newly elected to the position, so there was no telling for sure if the man was honorable or not.

"Why don't you ride back to Burrton Springs and let Valentine know what's going on. We'll set up the trap on the stagecoach and train midweek. Best get back so you two can get ready and make your plans." The sheriff dropped his feet to the floor and stood. "I'll send a rider to Burrton Springs if something comes up before then. If you don't mind, I've got things to see to."

In other words, the sheriff didn't want Caleb hanging around his office. He'd overstayed his welcome. Caleb shifted his Stetson and gave a brief nod. For now, he'd let the lawman believe he was in control of the situation.

He exited the building and glanced around the town. There was no way Caleb planned to leave until he checked into some things. First stop was the telegraph office. He headed to the small building.

The machine was clacking when he entered. A small fella furiously wrote on a piece of paper. He tucked the message into an envelope and stood. "I'll be with you in a minute, mister." The man stepped onto the porch and whistled.

A young boy came running, his hair sticking up in the back.

It reminded him of the cowlick Caleb had had as a child, and how his ma was forever trying to tame it. The memory made him smile.

"Take this to Dunham over at the general store." The telegraph operator handed the envelope to the boy.

"Yes, sir." The lad grabbed it and clutched it tight to his chest as he tore off in the opposite direction.

Caleb chuckled. "Looks as if you have an eager worker there."

The telegraph man smiled. "Sam has a good heart. Trying to earn money to help his ma ever since his pa got killed."

"How did his pa die?" Caleb swallowed. *Please don't let it have been Klaude who's responsible.*

The man sighed. "Sam's pa had a fondness for drink."

Best to leave it at that. "Was hoping you could send a telegram for me to Topeka."

The fella shifted his visor. "Come in and you can decide what all you want to say."

They stepped into the building. The warmth of the small stove in the corner helped to take the chill off the room. The fella handed Caleb a piece of paper and a pencil. "You can use that to figure out what you want to say and who you want to send it to."

Caleb took the items and sat on a wooden bench. He twisted the pencil for a few minutes.

ANY UPDATES ON OUTLAW? EXPECTATIONS ON PAYROLL? PLEASE ADVISE. WAITING FOR RESPONSE.

He glanced at each word. Hopefully it conveyed all Caleb wanted to ask, but he didn't feel as free mentioning everything with not knowing who all would read the message along the way. He handed it to the clerk. "Can you send it to the U.S. Marshal's office in Topeka?"

The man's head came up.

Was he somehow a part of whatever was going on with the sheriff?

Caleb stared at the man. He didn't appear wealthy or living above his means. But he could be hiding behind wearing simple clothes.

The fella nodded and started typing on his machine.

Or maybe Caleb was thinking everyone was guilty. Maybe he'd been in law enforcement too long and couldn't distinguish between who was innocent and who was an outlaw anymore. He took off his Stetson and thrust his hands through his hair. When was the last time he had a decent night's sleep? Caleb couldn't recall. Would his body know how to relax once he caught Klaude and all the manhunts came to an end?

"Are you staying at the hotel? Where can I find you when a response comes back?" The fella finished typing and straightened some papers on his desk, as though he had no concern about what he'd just sent.

"I'll be waiting here." Caleb sat on the bench, leaning his head against the wall, and shifting his Stetson over his face. "Will get some shuteye in the meantime." He didn't plan to actually sleep, but the clerk didn't need to know it.

"Suit yourself."

Silence settled on the room and Caleb quieted his breathing, as if he was sleeping.

The door flew open and banged against the wall.

"Sorry, Mr. Lewis. I did what you said. Here's the money."

Had to be the kid. Caleb remained still.

"Keep it, Sam."

"Yes, sir." The boy's voice was exuberant. "Thank you, sir." His next words were whispered, almost as though he'd just noticed Caleb. "Is there anything else I can deliver for you, Mr. Lewis?"

"Not right now, son. But stay close, and I'll let you know if something comes up." The clerk spoke in a normal tone.

Did he suspect Caleb was awake?

Caleb must be losing his edge. Definitely time to get out of the law business.

The door opened and closed. More than likely the boy went outside.

Silence settled again. For how long, Caleb wasn't sure. He had a crick in his neck and would soon need to move.

The machine started clacking.

The scratch of stroke marks on a page competed with the sound of the machine.

A few seconds later, the clerk cleared his throat. "You can quit you're faking. Looks as if word came back about your criminal."

Caleb made a point of yawning and stretching, as though he'd just been awakened by a noise.

The clerk's brows hiked on his forehead, as he handed the paper to Caleb.

So much for fooling the man.

31

Ellie Lou felt for Mrs. Walsh's pulse again. Still steady. "You stay here, Blizz and watch over her."

The dog gave a short yip.

She shoved to her feet and took off, sprinting through the house and flinging the back door open. Her legs tangled in her skirt as she ran towards the doctor's office. *Please let him be there, Lord, and not on a call somewhere.* Her heart thundered as she thrust through the door to the office. "Doc? You've got to come quick."

"Mrs. Williams? Are you injured? What's going on?" Josh held a piece of paper as he stood in the waiting room. Several folks looked on.

"It's Mrs. Walsh. Someone hit her on the head. She's knocked out." She panted. "Bleeding."

Josh disappeared down the hallway, and reappeared with his coat and doctor's bag. "Let's go. I'll be back when I can, folks."

They didn't talk as they trotted the short distance to the boarding house. Ellie Lou shoved through the back door first, leading the way. "She's in here." She stepped back to allow the doctor access to the room.

Blizz stood and wagged his tail.

"Come here, boy." She snapped her fingers.

At first the dog didn't budge.

Josh patted the dog. "I'll take good care of her, boy."

His words seemed to reassure the mutt.

Blizz padded over to Ellie Lou. She reached down and petted his fuzzy head, and he leaned his body against her leg.

Silence settled as Josh examined the head wound and made sure the older woman didn't have any broken bones. He opened his bag and withdrew a bottle and a small rag, dabbing it on Mrs. Walsh's forehead. "Has she awakened at all? Said anything about who did this?"

Ellie Lou took a step into the room. "She said it was Klaude."

The doctor's gaze crashed into hers. "That's not good."

Exactly. Which meant Klaude had found where she was staying. None of the women would be safe if Ellie Lou remained at the boarding house. She had to leave if she was to be able to protect them. The sooner she did so, the better it would be for all of them. She swallowed past the lump in her throat. How could she abandon the older woman who'd taken Ellie Lou in as if she was Mrs. Walsh's own daughter?

After Josh listened to the older woman's heart, he pulled the stethoscope from his ears. "Did she say anything else besides who did it?"

She licked her lips, trying to get some moisture in her mouth. "He was, uh, looking for me."

"We'll need to get you somewhere safe." Josh glanced at her before he gently shook the prostrate woman. "Mrs. Walsh. Can you hear me?"

It took a few minutes, but finally the woman's eyes fluttered open. "Josh? What're you doing here?" She struggled to sit up, but the doctor put pressure on her shoulders.

"Just lie there a few minutes until you get your bearings." He reached for a pillow from the bed and propped it under Mrs. Walsh's neck. "I want you to take it easy. You've been hit hard on the head. I'm concerned about a possible brain injury. We'll need to keep an eye on you for a while."

"Nonsense. I'll be fit as a turkey in no time." She smiled and glanced past the doctor. "Ellie Lou, are you all right?"

She stepped closer. "Never mind about me. I'm concerned about you and how you're doing. I'm so sorry I've brought trouble to you and your home." Tears filled Ellie Lou's eyes.

"Don't you dare take the blame for this." Mrs. Walsh's eyes snapped. "This was not your fault. It was that scoundrel. I think the fella's getting desperate. From what all you've told me, he's getting sloppy."

Josh studied both of them. "A desperate outlaw is a dangerous one. One you can't predict what they'll do next, especially if they feel their back is up against a wall. In my experience, it's never a good scenario."

There was no way Ellie Lou would stand by and let her friends be injured on her account. It was bad enough Mrs. Walsh had been hurt. She couldn't bear for anyone else to come in harm's way. Next time it could be Caleb.

Her heartbeat increased, blood throbbing through her veins. She'd do whatever it took to make sure nothing happened to Caleb. He may not be interested in a future with her, but she could get far away from here, so she'd keep him from getting shot or worse.

She had to come up with a plan. And fast. Ellie Lou glanced around the small bedroom. "Is it safe to move her, Josh? She'd be more comfortable in her own bed instead of the floor."

"Good idea. I just wanted to make sure she was stable before we shifted her." He stood. "Do you think you could help me?"

"Of course." She hurried over. "Just tell me what to do."

Mrs. Walsh struggled to sit. "I'll be fine. No need to worry over me. Besides, I need to get a meal prepared."

"No cooking for you today. I want you resting in your bed. I'll stay and keep an eye on you." He stooped to assist the woman in sitting.

"But..."

"No arguing." Josh gave the woman a fierce look. "There's nothing pressing at my office. I'll just send word to the folks there to come back to see me tomorrow. Now, let's get you situated so you can rest."

Ellie Lou came around to Mrs. Walsh's other side. "Here, let me help you."

Together they managed to get the older woman standing. She wobbled for a moment.

Ellie Lou wrapped the landlady's arm around her shoulder. "Lean on me. We've got you."

A few minutes later they managed to situate Mrs. Walsh on her bed. Ellie Lou removed her shoes and covered her with a blanket.

"Rest. And don't worry about me."

Mrs. Walsh's eyes flickered shut and then open. "Promise me you won't take off and try to solve this on your own."

~*~

Caleb shoved the response to his message into his pocket. He'd known Clint Peters, the man who replaced Caleb as the U.S. Marshal in Topeka, for at least ten years. There was no way the man was wrapped up in whatever evil plans Klaude Kidman had. Peters was a stand-up fella always making sure he did things by the rules. The question was, did the sheriff in Hutchinson have a part in whatever Klaude was planning next?

One thing was clear. There was no payroll going from Topeka to Newton, nor had there been one. Clint would've known about any money movement in his area. And he had no reason to lie. Any time a sizable amount of money was being transported across country, it made lawmen nervous. All kinds of things could go wrong along the way. And any sheriff or marshal worth his salt wouldn't divide resources between the stagecoach and the train. The sheriff's plan made no sense. Maybe the man had simply been fed wrong information to get their attention off whatever Klaude planned to do next. Or he was too inexperienced to handle unknown and dangerous situations.

"Do you need me to take care of your horse for you, mister?" A child's voice interrupted his thoughts.

While Caleb had been woolgathering, Sam had sneaked up on him and was petting Chestnut's mane. "You sure have a pretty mare." A twinkle flashed in the boy's eyes. "Always wanted a horse of my own." A range of emotions flitted across the lad's face. "Guess it won't happen now."

Caleb flicked a coin the boy's way. "I'll be heading out of town soon, but I was wondering if you could do me a favor while I'm gone?"

Sam smiled. "Sure, mister. I'll do whatever you want."

He bit back a laugh remembering how eager he'd been to please when he was Sam's age. "It's a big job. Do you think you're up to the task?"

The scrawny boy thrust out his chest. "I can do it. By the way, I'm Sam." He shoved a small hand forward.

Caleb grinned at the lad as they shook hands. "Can you read and write, Sam?"

The boy's cheeks flushed. "Yes, sir."

He nodded. "Good, because I need you to keep an eye on the sheriff for me."

Sam's mouth gaped open before he snapped it shut. "You aren't a criminal, are you?" He edged toward the building.

Caleb placed a hand on the boy's shoulder, halting his movement. "No. I just retired from being a U.S. Marshal, but I still have one more criminal I need to track down before I call it quits."

"Can't the sheriff help you?"

He scrubbed a hand along his stubbled chin. Time to shave again. How could Caleb word things so the boy could be reliable? "The sheriff's new to the job so he may not understand all it entails. I just want you to keep an eye on him and write down where he goes. What he does. Who he talks to. Do you think you could do that for me?"

Sam nodded. "So, I'll be kind of like a deputy U.S. Marshal or a Pinkerton detective?" His eyes gleamed.

Every boy wanted to be a hero.

Caleb held back a smile. "Sort of, although you need to keep your distance, so you aren't spotted." The last thing he needed was for the boy to somehow get caught up into whatever was going on and be injured in the process. "Do you think you can keep track of the sheriff's movements without being caught?"

"Yes sir. You can count on me." He straightened his spine. "What if I see something suspicious?"

"You don't do anything. Do you understand? All I want is for you to write down what's going on here in town. You promise me you won't get caught up in anything."

The boy dug his shoe in the dirt.

"You wouldn't want your ma worrying over you, would you, Sam?"

His chin came up. "No sir. I'd do anything to prevent Ma from being hurt."

"That's a good boy." He clapped his hand on the lad's back. "If you follow my instructions, when I come back to town, I'll make sure you get another coin like that one."

Sam's eyes rounded. "That's a lot of money, mister."

It really wasn't, but Caleb remembered when he'd been given a coin when he was about Sam's age. "I trust you to do the job and stay safe."

"Oh, yes, sir. I won't let you down." He started jogging towards the sheriff's office.

"Sam?"

The boy halted in his tracks and turned back to Caleb.

"You make sure you get your rest and go home for meals, so your ma won't worry. And if the telegraph operator needs you to make a delivery, you do whatever he says. Sometimes you can learn more about what's going on in town by listening to conversations folks are having. If you're always near the sheriff's office, he might get suspicious, so don't be afraid to take breaks away from it too." Caleb prayed he wasn't putting the boy in harm's way. If Caleb had a tin star, he'd pin it to the boy's shirt.

"Yes sir." Sam saluted him.

It brought back memories of the war. Things Caleb wished to forget. He shoved the thoughts aside. "Stay safe, Deputy Sam."

The boy couldn't stop a grin from spreading across his face, bringing out a dimple in his right cheek. "Yes, sir. And what do I call you?"

"Dawson." Best if he didn't give his first name just yet.

"I'll have a full report, Mr. Dawson, whenever you get back to Hutchinson." Sam's face grew serious. "I'm a man of my word." With that, the boy was off like a shot.

Caleb hoped the lad would remember to stop at his house and pick up some paper and a pencil. He chuckled and turned toward Chestnut, swinging onto the saddle. *Keep the boy safe, Lord, and help me to unsnarl this tangle before someone else gets hurt.*

32

"What do you mean she's gone?" Caleb thrust his fingers through his hair. "Where did she go?"

"Now, settle down." Josh glanced down the hallway. "Keep your voice low, or you'll wake Mrs. Walsh. She needs her rest yet after being awake most of the night worrying about Ellie Lou."

"But how could Lou be gone? Why would she leave? What happened while I was in Hutchinson? I haven't been gone more than a day." Caleb paced the small sitting room in Mrs. Walsh's boarding house. He should've never left.

"She slipped away while I was getting Mrs. Walsh settled after Klaude knocked her unconscious."

Caleb stilled.

Klaude had been here?

He knew where Lou lived?

The realization pierced him like an arrow.

Caleb sank into a chair. "You better tell me everything from the beginning."

"There's not much to tell. Ellie Lou went to the store for Mrs. Walsh, came back, and found her on the floor with a gash on her head. Ellie Lou came for me. Mrs. Walsh said Klaude had been here, asking for Mrs. Williams. From my guess, in frustration, Klaude hit Mrs. Walsh and took off. Or maybe the dog startled him before he could do more injury. Good thing too." Josh shook his head. "Hate to think what this outlaw would've done if he'd gotten his hands on your woman."

Caleb frowned at his friend's comment before continuing, "But why would she up and leave when she knew it was dangerous?" It made no sense. Wasn't the woman thinking straight?

"From what I can tell from the note Ellie Lou left, she wanted to protect Mrs. Walsh and the other boarders. Said they'd be safer if she wasn't staying here." Josh glanced at the doorway.

Blizz stood guard.

"She didn't take her dog along?"

Josh scrubbed a hand across his forehead. "No. She should've taken the mutt with her to help keep her safe. That dog hasn't left Mrs. Walsh's side other than to see to his needs." He walked over to the front door, opening it. The dog ran outside. "He'll be back in a minute and go right back to watching over Mrs. Walsh. I've had to take the dog's meal to him back there. He refused to go to the kitchen to eat."

A minute later scratching sounded on the door.

Josh swung it open, and Blizz shot back down the hall, disappearing into a room.

If only Lou had taken the dog along. At least then Caleb would have some measure of comfort in knowing she had some extra protection. He stood and paced the room again. "Did she say where she was going?"

Josh shook his head. "No. Said it was better if she didn't tell us in case Klaude came back again and wanted to know where she went. Ellie Lou thought she could keep the ladies safe if they had no idea where she was heading."

"Will Mrs. Walsh be all right?" His chest pinched. He should've asked about the landlady long before now.

"She's fine. Still has a headache, but it's to be expected. She's chomping at the bit to get out of her bed, but I insisted she rest longer since she didn't get any sleep after I found Ellie Lou's note." Josh sat down and stretched his legs out. It was obvious that weariness tugged his frame. He likely hadn't gotten any sleep overnight either.

"Is she sleeping now?" Caleb glanced at the doorway again.

"Hard to say. You can sneak back and take a peek at her. Just don't wake her if she's sleeping." Josh yawned. "I think I'll rest my eyes for a few minutes."

Caleb left his friend and tiptoed down the hallway as quiet as possible. One door stood open. Caleb hesitated in front of it.

Mrs. Walsh sat propped up on her bed, eyes wide. "Oh, Mr.

Dawson, you finally got here."

Blizz lay beside the bed. The dog lifted his head and wagged his tail.

"Please, come in." The older woman extended her hand toward him.

Caleb took a few steps inside the room, gripping his Stetson. "How're you feeling, ma'am?"

She waved her hand back and forth. "Don't you worry about me, young man. You must go after her. She's not thinking straight. I know she was only trying to protect me and Betty and Mary, but I just have a terrible feeling something bad will happen to her while she's along the trail."

Caleb could attest to the amount of trouble Lou got into when she was on her own, especially with her horrible sense of direction. She'd be easy prey to a violent man like Klaude. Caleb steered his mind away from the thought.

"I'd feel better if she'd taken Blizzard along." Mrs. Walsh rested her hand on the dog's head. The mutt leaned against her. "She knows how I've been partial to the dog, but I never said I wanted Ellie Lou to give him to me. I'd rather know she had Blizz along to keep her safe. There's no telling what kind of trouble that woman might find herself in." She shuddered.

Knowing Lou, she'd intentionally left the mutt to protect the ladies. "Did she give any indication where she'd go? Has she talked about moving?" Caleb scrunched the rim of his hat.

Mrs. Walsh shook her head. "I wished she had. I know she's been lost for the past weeks. Ever since…"

She didn't need to finish her sentence.

This was all his fault. Ever since he'd pushed Lou away when he believed he would lose his arm, she hadn't been the same. He couldn't blame her. Maybe she'd been serious about moving to Hutchinson. It didn't make sense when she had the ranch.

The ranch.

Had anybody checked there?

"Don't you worry, Mrs. Walsh. I'll do whatever I can to bring her home safely." Caleb clapped his Stetson on. "You take care of yourself, Mrs. Walsh." He walked down the hallway, stopping in the sitting room to ask Josh whether anyone had checked her ranch to see if she'd gone there.

Soft snores pierced the silence.

There was no time to lose. Caleb shoved open the door and swung onto Chestnut. "Come on, girl. We've got to find Lou."

~*~

Ellie Lou hadn't been able to resist stopping at the ranch before she left the area. She felt the need to see the place for a final goodbye before she departed the area for good. Also, she'd be able to remember the way to Hutchinson because she and Charles used to always travel from their ranch there. If she'd attempted finding her way from Burrton Springs, she'd end up hopelessly lost.

It was dark by the time she reached her former homestead. She'd knocked on the door, but nobody answered. Ellie Lou had debated for a long time before she turned the doorklatch to her former home. Hopefully whomever had taken up residence wouldn't mind her looking around one last time.

The house smelled musty as if it hadn't had occupants in months. Remembering where she'd left a lantern and matches, she was surprised to find the items exactly where she'd always had them. Ellie Lou struck a match. Light flashed as she ignited the wick to the kerosene lamp. A thick layer of dust coated everything.

Odd.

Why would someone purchase the ranch and not move into it? It didn't make any sense. Maybe the new owner had been delayed moving in because of the snowstorms.

Ellie Lou strolled through the rooms, touching pieces of furniture in each room, memories flooding her mind of all the wonderful years she'd had with Charles.

Tears pricked her eyes and flowed down her cheeks. She let them drip off her chin. "Goodbye, Charles." Her throat tightened. "I still miss you and always will. But it's time to move on. Time to start a new life." The tears came faster, and she blinked rapidly. "I've made a mess of things, Charles. I've lost all you held dear. I'm sorry I couldn't keep your dream of making this one of the most reputable horse ranches in the state. I don't have the experience and without you here…" She sank onto their bed, gathering the pillow where Charles had rested his head each night. Hugging it tight to her chest, she cried until the sobs ceased.

Ellie Lou sniffed and hugged the pillow tight one more time before setting it back at the head of the bed. "I loved you dear one, with every fiber of my being…but now it's time to say goodbye." She kissed her fingertips and then rested them on the pillow.

With a sigh, she stood and reached for the lantern.

She secured the door behind her and stepped outside. The lantern was the only light. The moon could no longer be seen. The wind kicked up. Ellie Lou shivered.

Storm knickered.

A chill filled the air. It felt like a squall was on its way.

She walked toward Storm, untying the reins. "Come on, boy, let's check the barn before we head on our way." Holding the lantern aloft, she tugged him forward.

The stallion tossed his head.

She set the lantern down on the grass to try and maintain control over the horse. Storm had never been partial to bad weather, hence how he'd gotten his name. "Whoa, boy." She placed a hand on his muzzle. "Nobody will hurt you." Ellie Lou kept a tight grip on the reins as she opened the barn door. The wooden door creaked on its hinges.

Storm tugged and broke free from her grip, rushing into the barn.

Ellie Lou stooped and picked up the lantern, holding it high as she entered the barn. Her nose wrinkled at the smell of stale hay. She sneezed.

A rustling noise sounded from the back stall.

Her heart thundered.

Hand shaking as she lifted the lantern higher, angling the light toward the back of the barn. Air whooshed from her lungs at the sight of Storm in the stall. She strolled toward him. "You silly horse. We can't stay here. I only wanted to see it one last time. I know this is where you usually slept in the winter, but we must get going."

Lightning flashed and the building shook with the rumble of thunder.

Storm's eyes widened so much; Ellie Lou could see white rimming the dark. He tossed his head, stamping his feet.

She set the lantern down on a barrel and stepped closer to the stall. "Shh, boy, it's all right. There's nothing to be afraid of."

Storm shifted, kicking against the wood side of the stall.

Ellie Lou sighed. From the looks of it, they weren't going anywhere tonight. She locked the gate in place, securing the skittish stallion.

The likelihood of finding her way to Hutchinson in the dark wasn't great, particularly with no moon to light the way. And being caught in a storm didn't hold any attraction, especially when Ellie Lou knew it would take every ounce of energy to control the fearful stallion. She didn't have the fight in her tonight.

"You've got your way. We'll spend the night, Storm. But just tonight, you hear?" She scrubbed her hand across the horse's forehead.

He calmed a little bit with her touch.

With a sigh, she crossed to the barn door and closed it. Ellie Lou didn't feel comfortable staying in the house even though it looked as if nobody had lived in it since she'd left. No. It would be better to stay in the barn and then leave at first light. Hopefully by then the storm would have passed, and she could make her way to Hutchinson. And a new life. A fresh start.

She went into the stall beside Storm's and bunched hay together. She hoped it would give the stallion comfort knowing she was close by. She sat down on a mound of hay, weary and exhausted to her bones. A yawn escaped. *I'll rest for a minute, and then I'll unsaddle Storm.*

She was awakened sometime later by a creaking sound. She sat up, trying to remember where she was. Darkness filled the barn. Had the lantern burned through all the fuel already?

Shuffling footsteps thumped down the aisle.

Had Storm somehow gotten out of the stall? Should she get up and check? A feed bag was thrust over her head. Ellie Lou screamed.

33

Lightning flashed across the night sky followed by a crash of thunder. The storm was getting too close for comfort. Caleb urged Chestnut through the pouring rain. They were soaked to the skin. He was beginning to question his decision to search for Lou in the middle of the night. And in a storm no less. But he couldn't get past the feeling she was in danger.

Thunder boomed again, and Chestnut skittered sideways. It took a firm hand to keep the mare from rearing and bolting. The mare was rarely high-spirited, but even Caleb was nervous with how quickly the lightning was followed by thunder. With the storm right over top of them, Caleb needed to find cover and soon. With a wide-open prairie, sitting on a horse would be a tall attraction for a lightning bolt.

While Mrs. Walsh had given general directions to where she thought Lou's ranch was, she hadn't been overly sure. Caleb should've awakened Josh to confirm, but he hadn't wanted to disturb the man's sleep. Probably should've let Enoch know where he was going too.

If he didn't find the ranch soon, he'd head back to town, and start again at first light.

The sky lit with a blaze again.

There. Ahead was a set of buildings.

If it wasn't Lou's ranch, at least he should be able to take cover until the storm passed by. Caleb urged Chestnut forward. "Come on, girl." The mare increased her speed. Apparently, she was as eager to get out of the elements as he was.

A few minutes later, Caleb pulled on the reins. He dismounted and kept hold of Chestnut as he pounded on the door to the house. No light came on. Nobody came to the door. He tried once more.

Nothing.

He slogged through the puddles and pouring rain as he hurried to the barn. Caleb yanked the barn door open, tugging Chestnut forward. The horse didn't need any encouragement. The mare shoved her way ahead of him, deeper into the wooden structure.

Water streamed from Caleb's Stetson and slicker and dripped onto the hay-covered floor. He wrinkled his nose at the scent of stale hay. Whomever owned the property wasn't doing a great job of keeping the barn clean.

With a flash of lightning, he saw a kerosene lamp sitting on a wood barrel. He worked his way over to it. With the next flash of light, he searched for matches but didn't find any. As each subsequent gleam of light, he struggled to find where matches might be kept.

Another blaze revealed a tin box hanging by a nail on the side of one of the stalls. Caleb found several matches.

It took a few minutes before he could see to find his way back to the lantern. Lifting the globe, he struck the match. The wick caught and a flame flared to life. He held the light in one hand as he searched the enclosure. Chestnut had found an overturned bin of feed and was eating.

A stomping noise came from the back stall. Caleb crept down the aisle until he got to the last one. When he lifted the lantern, Storm stared back at him.

"Storm? What're you doing here, boy?"

The horse shook his head, and the metal rings on the bridle rattled.

That was strange. Why would Lou keep the tack on the horse?

He shifted the lantern.

Wait.

A saddle still rested on Storm's back.

A chill ran down Caleb's spine.

Something wasn't right.

He searched through each stall but came up with nothing. No signs she'd been there other than her stallion in the stall fully geared up and ready to go.

"Calm down, Dawson. Maybe she forgot something in the house

and went to fetch it. Perhaps this is a friend's ranch and they're all asleep in the house." Caleb took a big breath and blew it out. "Maybe she didn't hear the knock on the door with all the thunder." While he spoke aloud with hopes of calming his nerves, it didn't help. He threw the barn door open and ran through the sheets of rain.

He pounded on the back door and then reached for the doorlatch. It opened easily. Caleb stepped inside. "Lou, you here?"

Rats. He should've brought the lantern with him. His search of the house was delayed, waiting for flashes of lightning to guide him. Every room he came to stood empty and abandoned. Caleb continued to call, but in his heart, he knew he wouldn't find her. Somehow Klaude had gotten to her.

His shoulders sagged as he tramped through the rain again to the barn. The horses knickered as he entered it. He searched the length of the barn one more time, looking in every nook and cranny. In one of the stalls, he found an impression in the hay. Had Lou laid there?

He kicked at the mound with his boot. A small slip of blue shone from beneath the stack. Caleb bent over, and picked it up, shaking hay loose from a slip of fabric.

He brought it closer to the light. It was the handkerchief he'd given her when they were stranded in the blizzard. He recognized the small tear in one of the corners. Caleb had forgotten she had never returned it to him. Did it mean she still cared about him? Had kept the piece of fabric because it reminded her of him?

If he found her, he'd make a point of letting her know how he really felt about her. That he loved her. Wanted to spend the rest of their lives together.

Wait.

When I find her…not if.

Caleb swallowed.

Dear God, help me to find Lou. Don't let her to be lost to me forever. Please give me a second chance with her. Give me the opportunity to let her know how much I love her. That I've been a fool by pushing her away.

A roll of thunder shook the barn as a tear ran down Caleb's cheek. *I know I don't deserve for You to answer my prayers, Lord, but I'm asking anyway. Your Word says to call to You, so that's what I'm doing.*

Guide me. Help me find her. Bring her safely home.

~*~

Ellie Lou struggled against the rope binding her hands to the saddle horn. Her throat was raw from screaming for help, all to no avail. The feed bag covering her head was so rain soaked, she had to angle her head just right, so it didn't cut off her breathing. Her shoulders sagged. She wanted to fall asleep and find this was just a bad nightmare.

Even through the feed sack she saw lightning flash immediately followed by thunder. The storm was right on top of them.

I'm definitely passing through the waters right now, Lord. It feels as though I'm passing through the rivers with all this rain. Are You here, Lord? Your Word says You won't allow either of those to sweep over me. Never have I felt so abandoned. Isn't it enough I lost Charles? That I lost the ranch? Am I to lose my life as well? She shivered at the thought of what else could be lost in the violent hands of the outlaw. *I need a miracle. I need You to break through the darkness surrounding me. Could You send Caleb to find me? Or Enoch? Somebody, Lord?*

The sound of swearing filtered to her ears despite the storm raging around her.

Ellie Lou's heart thudded.

Keep me safe, Lord. Keep me safe, Lord. Keep me safe, Lord.

~*~

Caleb made quick work of saddling Chestnut. The gray light of dawn had yet to dot the horizon, but he couldn't wait any longer. Pouring rain had pelted the barn throughout the night, washing away any hopes of finding tracks to see which direction Klaude had taken Lou.

Slipping the bridle on Storm, he patted the stallion's muzzle. "We'll find your master, but for now we'll take you to Enoch to care for. I guess there's no need for the saddle." He glanced at the dimly lit barn. "Might as well leave it here until later. We don't want anything to slow us down. The quicker I contact Enoch and start searching for

Lou, the better."

The horse snorted.

Caleb threw open the barn door and stepped outside. A light drizzle fell. He tugged the reins of the stallion and mare. They plodded after him. Caleb stooped and studied the mud near the barn.

He released a sigh of frustration. It was as he figured. The rain had erased any kind of tracks–man or horse. He swung onto Chestnut's back, tugging Storm's reins. "G'dyup." He forced himself to keep the pace steady without overtaxing the horses in the soggy terrain. Caleb never saw a more welcome sight than the town laid out ahead of him. He urged the horses forward.

The streets were quiet as he pulled back on the reins, stopping in front of the sheriff's office. He swung down, wrapping both sets of leather around the hitching post. Shoving the door open, he stepped inside. "Enoch, you here?"

"Caleb? What are you doing here?"

His breathing relaxed a little after seeing the sheriff. "Lou's been taken."

"What?" Enoch set down his coffee cup. A bit of liquid sloshed onto the desk. "How do you know about it? When did it happen?"

"I'm guessing sometime yesterday afternoon or evening. I'm not sure." Caleb bowed his head for a second. "Josh said Klaude stopped by the boarding house yesterday. Knocked Mrs. Walsh out cold. He was looking for Lou. I guess she was running an errand at the time."

Enoch frowned as he reached for a rag and sopped up the spilled coffee. "Why am I just learning about all this now?"

Heat flushed Caleb's cheeks. No lawman liked being the last one in the loop. He knew better. "I didn't hear about it until early evening when I got back from Hutchinson. She took off with some fool notion thinking she'd protect everyone if she set out on her own."

A muscle in the sheriff's jaw flickered, but he didn't say anything.

"I hoped maybe she'd just gone to her ranch, so I went to find her last night. I thought for sure she'd be there." He took off his Stetson and curled his fingers around the brim.

"But you didn't find her?"

Caleb shook his head. "No, I didn't, but I found Storm, fully saddled and standing in a stall."

"Was he wet when you found him?"

Caleb scrunched his eyes, trying to remember. He'd touched Storm's head, hadn't he? *Please help me to remember, Lord.* He pinched the bridge of his nose. "Dry. No, he wasn't wet when I took off his saddle and tack. Which means she had to have put him in the barn before the storm hit."

"My guess is she'd tried to leave but that stallion's always been a big baby when it comes to rainstorms. Hates them. He'd have been hard to handle with the gully washer we had last night. She probably decided to hold off until the weather let up." Enoch picked up his mug and took a swallow. "What time do you think you got to the ranch?"

He shrugged. "I don't rightly know. It had been long dark. I was caught in the middle of the storm. Took me longer to get to the ranch than I anticipated, with not being able to see in between the lightning flashes. It was slow going."

Enoch ran his hand along his jaw for a few minutes before he spoke again. "You didn't find any tracks, or anything left behind other than her horse?"

Caleb tugged the handkerchief from his pocket. "Just this. It's mine. I guess she's been hanging onto it for a while now."

The sheriff's brows rose. "It's not much to go on."

He hefted a sigh. "I know."

"You didn't happen to learn anything new in Hutchinson, did you?" Enoch sat down and motioned to the chair. "I know you want to head out and find her, but we really need to come up with a plan first."

Except there was no indication of where Klaude had taken Lou. No clues.

34

Ellie Lou strained against the ropes on her wrist. The skin there was rubbed raw from numerous times of trying to break the bonds holding her. Her back and legs ached from hours in the saddle with very little breaks to water the horses. While she considered herself a good horsewoman, she hadn't been on a horse this long since she'd injured her ankle and had ridden for hours to return to Burrton Springs months ago.

When daylight broke, Klaude had stopped for a few minutes. He'd removed the feed bag and wrapped a filthy handkerchief around her mouth, preventing her from calling for help. Before he'd gagged her, she'd begged him not to put the feed bag back over her head, but he'd ignored her. Hadn't said a word.

Between the bag over her head and the gag in her mouth, Ellie Lou felt like she couldn't get a breath of air. Panic rose. She took a small breath, gasping. *Dear God, help me. I can't do this on my own. Help me to stay calm. To be smart so Caleb can find me. Give him wisdom on knowing where to look. Prevent Klaude from hurting me.* She forced herself to breathe in and out slowly, trying to calm her rapid pulse.

Tears soaked her cheeks, and her nose grew stuffy from her weeping.

"Stop your yammerin', or I'll do it for you."

She swallowed, trying to control her tears.

"Fool woman. Why'd you have to get in the way? Can't believe you shot me."

I shot Klaude? When? It had to be when the outlaw had injured Caleb. She'd gotten off a couple of wild shots, never dreaming she'd actually hit him.

Had Klaude not killed her yet because he wanted her to pay for injuring him?

A chill shimmied up her spine.

Not good.

He'd let her see his face which meant Klaude wouldn't let her live.

~*~

"We can't keep going on like this. Searching with no clues. Klaude could've taken Lou anywhere." Caleb reined Chestnut to a halt in frustration.

Enoch shifted in the saddle. "You're right. So, what do you recommend? You've been doing this longer than I have. Too bad Josh had a broken arm to fix, or he could've ridden with us too."

"Sure would've loved to have his experience helping us." Caleb adjusted his Stetson, starting at the barren prairie.

"Heard tell his sister, Jules, is a great tracker too. Although, her hands are full with the twins and a new baby. Besides, I doubt Pastor Drew would've let her ride with us, although I heard she often has a mind of her own."

Caleb shifted his head from side to side, trying to ease the tight muscles in his neck. "If only we knew where Klaude's been hiding all this time. Surely someone has heard something. If we don't get to her soon…"

"I know."

There was no reason to complete his sentence. They both understood the consequences if they didn't get to Lou.

"Maybe you should head back to Hutchinson. See if the boy learned any more information on the sheriff. Perhaps the young lad has heard whether the sheriff is a player in all Klaude's mischief, or if the lawman just doesn't have enough job experience yet to come up with a decent plan." Enoch glanced back at the way they traveled. "Without having a trail, or something to go on, we can't just wander around the countryside hoping we'll stumble across a clue."

Caleb hefted a sigh. "I know you're right. I just hate feeling as though I'm not doing anything to get her back. Just spinning like a top and going nowhere."

"You've been praying, haven't you?" Enoch's dark gaze met his.

"Of course!"

"That's something then. How about I say a word before I head back to Burrton Springs?"

Tightness settled in Caleb's throat. He bowed his head, not trusting his voice.

"Dear God, we come before You, asking You to keep Ellie Lou safe. You know where she is. Help us to discover some clues to know where to search for her. Protect her, Lord as only You can. Guide us. Give Caleb peace. Help him to be able to turn Ellie Lou over to You, knowing You love her even more than he does. In Jesus's Name. Amen."

Caleb nodded his appreciation, as he adjusted his Stetson in an effort to control his emotions.

"I'll head back to Burrton Springs. If you find something in Hutchinson, send someone with news, and I'll catch up with you." He turned his mount. "And Caleb." Enoch waited until they made eye contact. "Don't go off half-cocked when you find her. Use your head so you'll be able to share your heart with her afterwards."

Did Enoch think Caleb didn't have any experience when it came to situations like this?

The sheriff held up a hand. "Now don't get your feathers ruffled. I'm just giving you advice since I've been in a similar situation. I thought I'd go crazy when Gertrude was taken captive. But the Good Lord helped me to find her. Guided my steps. Kept me calm. I'm praying He does the same for you." He tipped his Stetson and kneed his mount into motion.

Caleb patted Chestnut. "Come on, girl, we've got to find Lou." He kicked his boots against the mare's side. She set off at a gallop.

Lord, I pray Sam has learned something while I've been gone. Keep the lad safe. I need something to go on to know where to search, God. I'm asking You to go before me. Lay out Your plan for Lou. For me. I pray it's a plan that has us coming together in the end. Protect her, God. Prevent Klaude from taking any vengeance on her.

~*~

Ellie Lou was as parched as a prairie flower after weeks of no rain. Having her mouth partially opened because of the gag, made her tongue dry out even more, especially with having to breathe from her mouth. Her nose had been stuffy ever since her tears. How long ago, she couldn't tell.

Light barely shone through the dark feed bag covering her head making it difficult to discern how long they'd been in the saddle. She needed the necessary, and to stretch her legs. Her back screamed at being in one position for so long. If only she had something she could drop along the trail, praying someone would find it and follow them. Except she didn't have anything.

Might as well face it. Nobody was coming.Caleb wasn't coming.

He'd left for Hutchinson and hadn't even said goodbye. And she'd given no indication where she planned to go when she left Mrs. Walsh's boarding house. Other than her comment at breakfast the other day to Enoch, Gertrude, and Caleb about moving to Hutchinson, nobody would be searching for her. And besides, they would search for her in Hutchinson, expecting to find her there. They wouldn't be looking for her now.

Tears pricked again, and she tried to hold them back, to no avail. Things couldn't get any worse.

~*~

Caleb groaned in frustration. Of all the times for Chestnut to throw a shoe. He dropped the horse's hoof and patted her side. Caleb bent and retrieved the errant horseshoe. He should've brought along a second mount. Instead, he'd focused on speed to get to Lou before Klaude did something to her.

From his calculations by studying the terrain around him, he was still at least two miles away from the outskirts of Hutchinson.

Tugging on the reins, he forced himself to walk at a slow pace so Chestnut wouldn't be injured.

I don't understand, Lord. I'm trying to protect Lou. Why do You keep throwing obstacles in my path? It makes no sense at all. I thought Your Word said something about in all things, You work them for our good for those who love You. Well, I love You, God, but I certainly don't see any good in any of this.

Silence was the only answer. If Caleb could call it an answer. He sighed.

What're You trying to teach me, Lord? Help me not to fight against it. I want to learn and grow. I want to be in the center of Your will.

He ran his hand along his clean-shaven jaw.

His gut clenched.

After all he'd been through in the war, he'd felt the struggle to control something in his life. Throughout the years and battles, he'd had no command over much of his life. Caleb had been told where to go, what to do, what to eat, when to sleep. Since then, he had taken to shaving twice a day. In the morning and early evening. It wasn't much, but it was something he could dictate in his life. Except for when he was recovering from the saber wound during the war and when he'd been shot by Klaude.

It had taken weeks to be strong enough to hold the straight edge, let alone wield it without cutting himself in the process. Since he'd regained his strength, Caleb had gone back to shaving twice a day. Controlling the situation.

He swallowed. Hard.

Are You trying to tell me I need to let go of striving to be the one to be in charge of my life, Lord? I should know it by now, shouldn't I? He bit back a sigh.

Chestnut knickered and butted her head into his arm.

He scratched her mane. "You trying to tell me something too, girl?"

She bobbed her head up and down.

He laughed, and his heart eased up a bit.

Pastor Drew's sermon about Noah filtered back through Caleb's memory. *What would it take to have faith like Noah?* To trust and obey God without seeking to control the circumstances, and believing God had a plan for his life? Letting go of his worries and placing them in his Heavenly Father's hands. Leaving them there instead of snatching them back again. Trusting and obeying.

He glanced at the sky. Rain had moved off and white puffy

clouds scurried across the blue sky. The ground squished with each step. The only sound that could be heard was the steady steps of Chestnut and Caleb's. He checked behind them, seeing the impression of their footprints in the prairie grass.

Help me to walk in Your steps, Lord. I want to walk by faith as Noah did. He rubbed his chin again. *I want to be fully trusting and obeying You instead of relying on my own strength and direction. I know I won't even find Lou without You intervening. I give my life to You, Lord, to do with as You see fit. I pray You bring Lou and me together. But if for some reason it's not in Your plan for us, close the door just as You shut the door to the ark.*

From this day on, I'm giving up control to You. I trust You, Lord. And as an act of my obedience, I won't shave again until You give me a sign of some sort. Probably sounds silly, but it's my way of sacrificing my desire to control things. Forgive me for taking so long to recognize my faulty desire to be the one in charge. Silly, when I know You're the only One who knows what's best for my life. He held his hands open and lifted them to the sky. *I'm Yours, Lord. Use me how You best see fit.*

Caleb felt as if a weight had been lifted from his shoulders. His chest eased. One way or another, God would work on Lou's situation. He just knew it beyond a shadow of a doubt.

35

Ellie Lou moaned as Klaude dragged her from the horse. He threw her body to the ground, kicking her in the side. Pain seared through her chest.

"You no-good Jezebel. I should shoot you now."

Her heart stilled with the sound of a pistol being cocked.

Dear, God, no.

"Take care of your business and don't try anything funny. All it takes is one shot to the head, and you'll no longer be my problem."

She fingered the sack wrapped around her neck.

He ripped the bag off.

Light exploded. Ellie Lou squinted, trying to adjust her eyes to the sudden change. Tall prairie grass brushed against her skirt.

Klaude stood a foot away. "I'm not leaving, so you better take care of your needs quick-like."

She mumbled against the gag and lifted her tied hands.

He shook his head. "I'm not stupid. Get on with your business." He shifted another foot away from her.

Surely, he'd at least turn away instead of watching her.

She swallowed.

He stood with his pistol trained on her chest.

All right, then. She took a few steps into the taller prairie grass, stooping down low. Ellie Lou glanced over her shoulder unable to see through the tangle of weeds and grass. Since she couldn't see the outlaw, she assumed he couldn't see her either. She made quick work of taking care of her needs, being careful to be sure she was modestly covered throughout.

When she stood, she studied the terrain around her. Unfortunately, she didn't recognize anything. If only she'd been better versed in following a trail, and knowing what was around her.

"Stop your stalling." Klaude stomped over to her, grabbing her by the arm. He thrust the sack back on her head again. "Fool woman. Can't wait until I can shoot you and that man of yours. Neither of you will ever get the drop on me again."

Her pulse stuttered.

Klaude knew about Caleb? How could Klaude have learned Caleb was still alive? Or was the outlaw mixed up?

"Thought for sure shooting him in the shoulder and arm would've killed him with the infection. Too bad he was hunkered behind those rocks, or I would've been able to shoot him straight through the heart or head." His cackle set Ellie Lou's nerves on edge. It gave her the impression of someone not in control of his sanity any longer. But then, shooting people with no regard to their lives had to take a toll on a person's mind and body.

God, please don't let Caleb come anywhere near Klaude. I couldn't bear for him to be injured or killed. I love him. Keep him far away.

She stilled. When had she started loving Caleb, especially when he hadn't wanted anything more to do with her? Nothing like setting herself up for failure and heartbreak, if either of them survived this.

Klaude tugged her forward.

She stumbled and fell.

His boot connected with her side again in the same place he'd kicked her before. Spots danced before her limited sight as pain seared through her chest and lungs.

Klaude yanked her to her feet, shaking her body hard.

Ellie Lou felt like marbles were rolling around in her brain as she tried to halt the throbs coursing through every muscle in her body.

"You useless piece of manure." His fingers curled around her arms, digging in.

She winced, afraid to make a sound. Fearful to even breathe. His fingers would leave bruises.

He loosened his grip, and she fell to the ground again.

"You're as worthless as any other woman. Only good enough to wipe the dirt from my boots." He slammed his boot into her side again.

Air whooshed from her lungs. Her vision blurred.

Help me, Lord.

The sound of his boots stomping across the prairie grass brought some measure of peace. At least he wasn't right beside her anymore.

If only she could get away from him.

Next thing she knew, he was shaking her violently again.

Her head buzzed.

A relentless sound.

Not letting up.

If only relief would come.

Help me to hold on, Lord. I don't think I can last much longer.

"Why don't you scream?" Klaude gave her another shake. "Are you still alive?" He ripped the feed sack from her head again.

She blinked at the light.

"Ahh. Still kicking." His face flushed and an evil grin tugged at the corners of his mouth. "Maybe we can have some more sport with you."

Dear God, not that. Protect me, Jesus. Come against the evil one who only has desires to steal, kill, and destroy.

He started to loosen his pants with one hand while keeping hold of her with the other.

She swayed on her feet. *God, I'll gladly take another beating, but please don't let him do this to me.* Her heart hammered so loudly she could barely think.

A shuffling noise sounded in the grass behind them.

Klaude turned and stared where the sound had come from.

The scraping came again.

He tugged her along with him as he pulled her through the thick prairie grass.

She stumbled, falling to her knees.

He grabbed her hair, yanking her to her feet.

Ellie Lou moaned. She wobbled.

Please let it be help, Lord. I don't think I can hold on much longer.

Scripture she'd read before flooded her mind. *'When thou walkest through the fire, thou shalt not be burned; neither shall the flame kindle upon thee. Behold, I will do a new thing; now it shall spring forth; shall ye not know it? I will even make a way in the wilderness, and rivers in the desert.'*

Thank You, Lord. I trust You to make a way in the wilderness, or in my case, the prairie. I can't see a way out, but I know You're beside me and haven't left me.

Klaude grunted.

Ellie Lou stumbled and fell to the ground.

His fist connected with her head.

Blessed darkness swept across her vision.

~*~

Caleb's feet complained with each step through the soggy prairie grass. His boots were soaked. At least the town of Hutchinson lay just ahead. He tugged Chestnut's reins. "Come on, girl. We're almost there."

She nickered in response.

A few minutes later, he reached the blacksmith's shop. Heat smacked him as he opened the door. "Howdy."

A burly man with a leather apron plunged a horseshoe into a bucket of water. Sizzling sounded as the metal cooled. "What can I do for you?"

"My horse threw a shoe on the way to town. I was hoping you'd have time to shoe her. I'm kind of in a hurry."

The man scrubbed a hand across his cheek, leaving a black streak. "Everybody's always in a hurry." He grinned. "Guess it's the nature of my business."

"A young woman's life is in danger." Caleb hadn't meant to share that part.

The blacksmith's brows shot higher on his forehead. "Give me an hour."

Caleb tipped his Stetson. "Thank you. I appreciate it."

The man reached for Chestnut's reins.

Caleb left the shop, securing the door behind him. Wind cooled the beads of sweat on his face that had pooled with the heat from the forge. Caleb lifted his Stetson and swiped the moisture away.

An hour gave him time to find young Sam to see if he'd learned anything, although Caleb doubted the lad would have discovered much in the short time since they last spoke.

Caleb glanced at the street. Should he try and talk to the sheriff again or stop by the telegraph office first? He decided on the latter and turned toward that side of town. Couldn't hurt to see if any messages had come in for him, and it was the best way to track down Sam.

A gaggle of women giggled as they studied him. One waved.

He turned away from them, hoping to discourage conversation, not wanting to waste any time. A minute later, he turned the doorlatch to the telegraph building.

Clicking filled the room as the clerk bent over a piece of paper, hurriedly recording the message. The man was wearing the same visor he'd worn the last time Caleb saw him.

He waited, not wanting to distract the man.

After the clicking stopped and the fella wrote the last word, Caleb stepped forward. "Howdy. Not sure if you remember me."

The clerk glanced up and nodded. "I remember. In fact, I got a message here for you. Didn't know how to get hold of you, but Sam mentioned you'd be back although he wasn't sure when." The man shuffled through a small stack of papers. "Now where did I put it?"

Caleb shifted from foot to foot while the man continued to sift through paperwork.

"Ahh. Here it is." He scooted a small slip of paper across the desk.

Caleb reached for it and tucked it in his pocket not wanting to read it in front of the man. "Thank you." He handed him a coin. "Don't suppose Sam's around, is he?"

The operator glanced at the doorway. "Should be back any minute. He's delivering a message for me."

"Thank you. Think I'll wait for him outside." He turned toward the door.

"Let me know if you have a response to send," the fella called.

"Will do." Caleb closed the door behind him, slipping the note from his pocket. He studied the street, making sure nobody was watching him. Once he was satisfied the townspeople were going about their own business, he read the short missive.

RUMORS CRIMINAL IS HOLING UP SOMEWHERE OUTSIDE TOPEKA. ADVISE WHEN YOU'RE ON YOUR WAY.

Finally.

His heart ratcheted up a notch or two.

Maybe he could borrow a horse instead of waiting on the blacksmith.

The sound of thudding feet smacking against the dirt drew Caleb's attention.

Sam.

The boy's hair stood on end. His scrawny arms pumped as he ran.

Caleb smiled.

Sam jerked to a stop when he spotted Caleb. "Mr. Dawson." A grin spread across the boy's face. "Didn't think I'd see you yet. Let me turn in this money, and I'll be right back."

He tapped his fingers along the hitching post as he waited. Every minute passing put Lou in danger longer.

The door flew open before slamming shut.

The panes in the glass rattled.

"Sorry." Sam yelled.

Caleb bit back a chuckle. The boy was like trying to tame the wind blowing a tumbleweed across the barren prairie with nothing to stop it.

The boy whipped a pad of paper from his pocket and handed it to Caleb. "I've been doing just like you said." He lowered his voice and leaned closer, whispering, "I've kept my eye on the sheriff." He shifted through the pages. Reading various notes. 'Ate supper. Went to collect mail.' Nothing really of importance. "I haven't noticed anything sus…" His brow furrowed.

"Suspicious?" Caleb studied the boy.

"That's it." He smiled. "Couldn't remember the word. He's been just doing normal things. But I wrote them all down." He jabbed at the tablet with a dirty finger. "Maybe he's not sus-picious after all."

"Perhaps." Caleb continued reading through the several pages of notes. So maybe the sheriff wasn't caught up in anything nefarious, but simply inexperienced. Caleb would rather have that than trying to deal with Klaude, and a lawman walking on the wrong side of the law.

He flipped a couple coins to the boy. "You've done good, Sam. Thank you."

The boy's face lit up as he pocketed the money. "Do you want me to keep watching and taking notes?"

"No. I think you did a fine job. Although I'll get word to you if I need your services again."

The boy beamed and stood a little taller. "Oh, I almost forgot something." He dug into his other pocket. "Right after you left and I started watching the sheriff, some fella came up to me. Said I should give you this note." He withdrew a wrinkled piece of paper. "He was kind of scary looking. Told me I'd be sorry if I didn't follow through."

Could it have been Klaude?

36

Ellie Lou lay sprawled in the dirt, drifting in and out of consciousness. She had to hold it together to protect herself from Klaude's advances. *Please distract him from doing what he plans, Lord. Foil the schemes of the enemy. Somehow. Some way.*

"Stop your laying around." Klaude jerked her to her feet.

She wobbled, trying to stay upright.

"You're a useless piece of trash." He slung her over his shoulder like a sack of flour. She cried as her ribs pinched, struggling to get air into her lungs without searing pain.

"Stop your whining."

She bit her lip to keep from making a sound again. From the feel of it, she had several broken ribs. She prayed they hadn't punctured her lung.

"Need to get you to the hideout before he gets there." Klaude dumped her across the saddle.

Lightning pierced through her as she righted herself, clinging with all her might to the saddle horn. Her vision blurred. She blinked her eyes underneath the feed sack, willing herself not to black out again.

"We'll have fun together later. Maybe in front of your lawman before I kill him." Klaude cackled.

The scent of body odor and something putrid washed over her as he strapped her hands to the pommel.

The decaying smell was familiar.

She struggled to recall why, but her memory was foggy with Klaude's beatings.

The fugitive moaned as the leather of a saddle creaked beside her.

Wait. Hadn't he mentioned something about her shooting him?

That had been weeks ago.

And the stench.

Think, Ellie Lou, think.

Caleb.

When he'd been shot, his wound festered.

So much so Josh had feared he wouldn't be able to save the limb and possibly Caleb too. Until Josh had tried the potato poultice. Well, that and many prayers were what saved Caleb. The Lord had intervened on his behalf.

Did the smell mean the place where Ellie Lou had shot Klaude had gone bad? She'd have to keep it in mind if Caleb didn't make it to her in time. Maybe she could somehow use the knowledge to her advantage.

~*~

Caleb sent a telegram to Clint Peters saying he was on his way to the Topeka area. When he finally collected Chestnut from the blacksmith, more than an hour had passed. There was no way he'd get that far before dark fell. At least Peters should be able to make his way there and scope things out before Caleb arrived. Through several messages sent back and forth, they'd agreed to wait until both were in place before they'd take on Klaude unless there was no other option than rushing in to save Lou.

The words from Klaude's note were burned in Caleb's brain.

GOT YOUR WOMAN. IF YOU WANT HER BACK MEET ME AT YOUR LOVE NEST.

Somehow Klaude had learned about the soddy they'd holed up in through the blizzards. How, Caleb had no idea. He had to get there and save her.

He wasn't fooled in thinking Klaude planned to exchange Lou for Caleb. The deranged criminal wanted to kill them both. Caleb and Peters would be walking into a trap but somehow, they'd have to come up with a plan to save Lou. Failing wasn't an option.

What was the likelihood of Lou having a rope with her? He knew from experience how handy she was with one.

He prayed the outlaw hadn't taken advantage of her. *Protect her from that, Lord. Distract Klaude so he can't do anything evil against her virtue.*

Caleb tried to distract himself from thinking more about the topic. He studied the prairie. Most of the snow had melted. Only small pockets of white dotted the area. Even with the sun reaching the horizon and soon setting, warmth filled the air. Not that a sudden snowstorm couldn't crop up, but it wouldn't be long before spring spread across the area and flowers bloomed on the prairie. Maybe Lou would weave flowers through her hair on their wedding day.

"Don't get the cart before the horse, Dawson. I've got to save her before I can ask her to marry me."

Chestnut shook her head.

Apparently, his mare agreed with him.

"Besides, she doesn't even know I care about her. Not with pushing her away these past couple months." He rubbed his hand along his stubbly jaw. "Looks as if this is the first time not to intentionally shave this evening, Lord. Just as I've given up on my trying to control the situation with getting her back, I'm also giving up the specifics with trying to work out our relationship. You know it's what I want, Lord." He brushed a hand across his tired eyes. "I pray it's something she's interested in too despite all the mixed signals I've given her. I pray she realizes that when she threw her lasso around me, she also lassoed my heart." Caleb snorted. "Boy, wouldn't Josh give me a hard time to see the lovesick cowboy I've turned into."

Darkness settled, and he was forced to slow Chestnut's pace until stars started to twinkle in the night sky, followed by the sliver of moonlight appearing in the western sky. It provided only a faint light to find his bearings in the dark.

He pressed his mare forward. "We've got to find the soddy again, girl. Remember the place where we sheltered, and we found the old barrel of grain?" Caleb must be going loco to talk to his horse as though she understood him. Either that or he was desperate to get to Lou.

Desperate to protect her.

Desperate to get her from Klaude's clutches.

Desperate to tell her how much he loved her.

He sighed. The night air had grown colder. Moisture puffed from his mouth and nostrils.

The shape of something large dotted the horizon ahead of them. He'd found the soddy after all.

~*~

With the feed sack still on Ellie Lou's head, she had no way of discerning what time it was or even how long they'd ridden. They'd entered a building, but she didn't know how long they'd been inside. It had to be something primitive because the floor was uneven, and it smelled like dirt. The scent reminded her of the time she'd spent with Caleb in the soddy waiting for the blizzards to die down. The smell brought back a surge of happy memories, something she could grasp onto instead of intense fear.

Klaude had half-carried her, dropping her hard on the floor. Ropes had squeaked when he'd eased onto something. A bed perhaps?

A chill settled in the room. Ellie Lou shivered. Every fiber of her being complained.

The stench from Klaude's wound filtered through the feed bag. She wrinkled her nose. He'd be in real danger if he didn't deal with it soon. Not that she could tell him anything with the gag still in her mouth.

Her stomach rumbled. Klaude hadn't offered her anything to eat or drink all day. *As much as I long to quench my thirst, Lord, help my soul to long for You and Your presence even more than desiring water. I realize I can't get away from this situation without You intervening. My strength is failing, and I don't know if help is coming from Caleb or anyone else.*

Tears pricked her eyes, streaming down her cheeks and soaking into the dirty cloth wrapped around her mouth and head. *I've been dwelling a lot on the what ifs, if onlys, and why trouble has been brought into my life these past couple years. I guess I've been thinking that just because You're in my life, I shouldn't expect trouble or suffering. Kind of silly when Jesus paid the ultimate price of suffering by dying on the cross for my sins. My pain pales in comparison to Your Son. I'm so thankful You brought Jesus back to life, so I have an opportunity to one day be with both of You in heaven.*

Snoring sounded.

Ellie Lou's shoulders relaxed a bit with the sound.

Even though I don't see a way to escape without risking my life, or dying, or… She swallowed. *I give my life to You, Lord. I trust You to work even when I can't see it. Help me to be like Noah. Having enough faith to trust and obey You in the unseen. In the waiting. To give up trying to control the situation and railing against You when things don't go the way I think they should. Remind me that You know way more than I do because You see everything, where I only see a tiny speck of the picture.*

I don't know what You'll have for me if I get away from Klaude, but I want to be in the center of Your will. Doing what You want me to do. I would've liked to have stayed on the ranch and lived near my friends, but if it's not Your plan, then I'm game to see what You have in store for me. Ellie Lou blinked away the tears. *I trust You, Lord. I trust You. Peace settled upon her in a way she hadn't ever experienced before. Thank You, Lord.*

Another snore cut through the silence followed by a snort.

Ellie Lou leaned against the wall of the structure. The words to the song 'Trusting Jesus' Pastor Drew had taught his congregation filtered back through her memory. 'Trusting as the moments fly, Trusting as the days go by; Trusting Him whate'er befall, Trusting Jesus, that is all.'

You're here with me, aren't You, Lord? I have nothing to fear. You'll be with me no matter what happens. The most important thing is trusting You. Oh, God. Why has it taken me so long to get back to fully trusting in You and walking in the path You have for me instead of plodding along on the road I think is the best. Forgive me for my arrogance, Lord. I've been like a temperamental child, throwing tantrums and demanding my own way. Thinking I knew what was better than You. Ellie Lou bowed her head and the tears flowed again. *Forgive my sinful heart, Lord, which desires to control and be the one in charge of my decisions. Thank You for Your patience with me. Make me clean, purify me.* The words she'd memorized as a child filtered through her memory. *'Behold, thou desirest truth in the inward parts: and in the hidden part thou shalt make me to know wisdom. Purge me with hyssop, and I shall be clean: wash me, and I shall be whiter than snow.'*

I want to be clean, Lord. Wash me. Make me whiter than the snow we had in the blizzards. Make me to hear joy and gladness; that the bones which thou hast broken may rejoice.

Joy surged through her, God's joy and peace that had been missing as she'd tried to control things and hadn't gotten anywhere. She bit back a chuckle. How could she have been so foolish?

Ellie Lou couldn't remember the last time she'd bared her soul before her Lord and Savior. Much too long. She'd make a point of meeting with Him throughout each day, giving each detail of her life for Him to see over. *Help me not to forget how You've spoken to me here, Lord. I don't want to ever go back to doubting as I have these past couple years.*

A peace settled on the room, and all the fear she'd been feeling disappeared, as if her Heavenly Father was sitting beside her, wrapping her in His arms and protecting her. She had a confidence down to her toes that no matter what happened, God would be there to watch over her. To protect her. She could trust Him.

Ellie Lou drifted off to sleep with the knowledge that God was trustworthy.

37

Caleb dismounted, tugging on the reins as he crept towards the back side of the soddy. At least the structure didn't have any windows built into any of the dirt walls, and the thick sod would make it difficult to hear any sounds coming from outside.

"Psst."

His hand rested over his six-shooter as he peered through the darkness.

There.

Movement beside the dilapidated barn.

"Dawson. It's Clint."

His breathing eased up a bit. He pulled on the reins, guiding Chestnut behind the barn where his fellow lawman hunched behind. "Any movement?" Caleb kept his voice low, slanting a glance at the soddy.

All appeared quiet.

"Haven't seen him although there are two horses in the barn. Hadn't decided where to tie up my mount yet." Peters studied the prairie. "Not any place to hide them out here."

"And the barn won't hold both of our horses too. I remember how small it is."

Peters nodded.

"You sure Klaude's in there?" Caleb's heartbeat stalled. *Please let Lou be safe, Lord.*

The U.S. Marshal shrugged. "Can't tell for sure. Any thoughts on the best way to draw him outside without causing harm to the hostage?"

Lou was far more than a hostage, but Caleb didn't have time to consider his emotions right now. He studied the night sky. From his calculations, they had several hours to wait before the sun crested the horizon. "Waiting until morning seems the best option unless we hear something before then."

"One of us should probably position ourselves at the corner of the house so it's easier to hear."

He nodded his agreement. "Have they lit a fire at all?"

Peters shook his head. "No. I imagine it's getting cold in there. Maybe come morning they'll light it for coffee or something."

Somehow, he didn't think the outlaw would be thinking about breakfast. From what Caleb had witnessed of the man, he only cared about killing and getting rid of the only witnesses he'd left alive. It made for one dangerous scoundrel.

They debated back and forth trying to determine the best way to lure Klaude from the soddy without injuring Lou in the process. They still hadn't agreed on the best course of action when the sound of hooves could be heard. They crouched down.

The moon slipped behind a cloud making it difficult to see. A minute later, the cloud moved on, and a glimmer of moonlight filtered through the night.

The horses looked vaguely familiar.

Caleb gave a low whistle.

It was returned.

"Don't shoot." He motioned to Peters. "That's some friends coming to help." He shoved forward and waved a hand in greeting.

The two on horseback angled towards him.

"Sorry we're late to the party." Josh swung down from his horse.

Enoch tipped his Stetson in greeting.

"Didn't know if you two would make it. Was hoping the blacksmith in Hutchinson found you both in time." Caleb shook their hands. "This here is Clint Peters, the fella who took my place as U.S. Marshal. Clint, meet Josh Walker, my former deputy, and Enoch Valentine, the sheriff of Burrton Springs."

"Heard a lot about you, Josh." Peters nodded. "Heard you're a great tracker."

He grinned. "Don't let my sister hear you say that. She's convinced she's better at it than I am."

Enoch's gaze travelled to the soddy. "They held up in there?"

Caleb nodded. "As far as we can tell. It's where Klaude mentioned in his note. Peters says their horses are in the barn."

"We've been talking about waiting until sun up to get him to show his mangy hide or whether we should make a move now. What do you suggest, Walker?" Clint tugged on his mustache.

Josh didn't answer right away as he glanced between them and the soddy. "We'll position a man at each corner of the barn there and there." He pointed. "Another fella at the corner of the soddy in the front, and one of us on the roof."

Caleb envisioned the sod-covered roof from when he and Lou were holed up there for a couple weeks. Dirt had rained down on them daily. "I don't know. You really think it'll support the weight of a man?"

Josh nodded. "I think if it's only for a short time, he crawls on his belly, and sticks close to the edge of the walls, it should be the strongest there. He can be right above the doorway and drop down on Klaude if he comes outside, while the other fella rushes in to get Ellie Lou to safety."

He'd do whatever it took to be the one to oversee Lou's security.

"I think it's best if we set our plan in motion right before sun up, while it's still mostly dark. I don't think Klaude would be figuring on you showing up, Caleb, until sometime tomorrow midday or so."

Enoch dismounted. "How do you plan on getting Klaude's attention?"

Josh grinned. "Thought we could just knock on the door."

Caleb sucked in a breath. "Well. I guess he wouldn't rightly be expecting that, would he?"

"In my experience, sometimes the element of surprise can ward off trouble." Josh smiled. "I'm sure you've all had other ideas too."

Between them, they had many years of law keeping. But in all those years, Caleb had rarely used the element of surprise other than when he fought in the war. The question was, could they pull it off now and succeed in rounding up Klaude without injuring Lou in the process?

"Enoch, keep watch while we say a quick prayer." Caleb clapped the sheriff on the shoulder. "I don't know about you fellas, but I feel we need to cover this rescue and roundup in prayer."

The men nodded and pulled hats from their heads. All of them kept their eyes open.

"God, we need Your help here to keep Lou safe. We have a plan, but we know we can only accomplish it if You're a part of it. Go before us, Lord."

~*~

A sound awakened Ellie Lou. There it was again. She cocked her head, trying to hear despite the feed bag hindering her senses. Another plop. It sounded so familiar. She just couldn't place it.

A light snore followed by a snort came from across the room.

Surely Klaude would be awakened by the noise too.

She shifted into the corner of the house, her fingers grazing the wall. It felt like layers of dirt. Like a soddy. That's what the sound was! Dirt falling from the ceiling. She recognized it from when she and Caleb had been stranded in the abandoned sod house. From the feel of it, she could be in the same one again.

"W-what-t's th-at?" Klaude's words slurred, almost as if he'd been drinking.

She didn't dare make a peep.

A wave of putrid washed toward her, turning her stomach. She shifted her bound hands to her mouth, willing the bile to not erupt.

Another plop.

Klaude growled. "Leave m-me alone."

What was he talking about? Was he dreaming or had someone else entered the room?

If only Ellie Lou could see.

A sharp knock sounded on the wooden door.

Her heart stalled.

Oh, no, Lord. Don't let anyone else get in harm's way.

She scooted even deeper into the corner, hoping to make herself as invisible as possible. Not an easy task when she had no clue if she was accomplishing it.

The knock sounded again.

The thud of boots stumbling across the dirt floor made Lou swallow and hold her breath.

Klaude cursed as he banged against something.

"We know you're in there, Klaude."

She didn't recognize the voice. Ellie Lou tried to swallow past the lump clogging her throat.

Did Klaude have other men he was working with?

The sound of a gun being cocked filled the room.

He wouldn't turn on his own men, would he? Maybe the local lawman had learned where Klaude was hiding.

She struggled against the gag. If only she could call to the man and warn whoever was on the other side of the door. *Dear God, keep them safe.*

A gun fired.

Ellie Lou jumped; her heart galloped.

The door slammed open.

Cold air rushed in.

Scuffling noises came from the center of the room followed by a string of curses.

Hands wrapped around Ellie Lou's arms, pulling her to her feet.

She was cradled in someone's arms and taken outside. She struggled against her captor.

The feed bag was tugged from her head. Her hair fell across her face, blocking her vision.

A man's hand tucked her hair behind her ear.

Caleb's hand.

He loosened the gag. His eyes filled with tears. "Aww, sweetheart. What did he do to you?" He gently set her on her feet, untying her bound hands.

She sagged against him and sobbed.

He gathered her back in his arms and just held her while she cried.

~*~

Caleb's heart felt as though it was torn from his body, thrown on the ground, and stampeded by a herd of buffalo. How could someone have treated a woman so terribly? He held Lou close, letting her cry all her tears even though he wanted to go back in the soddy and beat Klaude to a pulp. *Forgive me, Lord. I know You're the one who hands out justice, but I surely would like to give some to Klaude for hurting Lou like this. Help me to control my anger.* He stroked her back until her tears were spent.

"She all right?" Peters and Enoch stood a couple feet away watching them.

Shouldn't they be helping to guard Klaude? What if he got the drop on Josh?

He frowned.

"Doc says he probably won't make it." Enoch stepped closer. "I guess when you got shot, he must've been injured too. The wound is putrid."

Lou sniffed. "He said I did it."

"Well, I'll be." Peters grinned. "Looks like you've got yourself a fine little lady there, Dawson."

Her brow furrowed. "What's he talking about?"

Caleb didn't want to talk, he wanted to hold her close and never let go. He dipped his head, lightly touching her lips with his.

Her eyes widened, but she didn't pull back.

He took it as permission to proceed. Bending his head lower, he claimed her lips with a sense of urgency. His heart hammered in his chest like a native beating a drum. When he loosened his grasp just a smidgen, his pulse hummed.

A smile spread across her face.

He set her down on her feet.

Pain flickered across her features, and she moaned.

Had his kiss somehow hurt her?

She gasped and held her side. "I think I have some broken ribs."

"Josh. Get out here." Caleb gathered Lou in his arms again.

Her face paled.

The doctor poked his head from the soddy. "What's going on?"

"It's Lou. Something's wrong."

~*~

As much as Ellie Lou wanted to rest in Caleb's arms and profess she was fine, her side prevented her from giving in to the daydream.

The thud of running footsteps sounded as her vision started to darken.

"She said she has some broken ribs." Caleb ran a finger along her jaw.

"Best get her inside. Hopefully the ribs haven't punctured a lung. I don't like how pale she looks. Be careful with her. That's it." Josh kept up the steady line of instructions as Caleb carried her into the building.

Her vision blurred. She shook her head, trying to stay conscious.

The soddy?

How had she gotten to the soddy she and Caleb had shared so many months ago? It made no sense.

"What about him?" Another man stood over Klaude, lying on the floor.

"He didn't make it." Josh's voice was low.

Had they shot Klaude? She hadn't heard any additional gunfire after the door opened.

She shook her head, trying to make sense of what was happening around her.

"Stay with me, Ellie Lou."

Caleb gripped her hand. "Come on, Lou, fight. I haven't come all this way just to lose you now. You stay with me, you hear?"

She blinked her eyes trying to stay awake, but the darkness crowded in.

38

March 13, 1878

"I still say it's too soon to head back." Caleb frowned at Lou. He'd nearly lost her. Why couldn't she understand he was only trying to do what was best for her?

"I'll be fine. Josh said as long as we take it easy, I shouldn't have any trouble."

Caleb still remembered her lying on the bed, her lips so pale.

Josh had said it'd been a miracle the broken ribs hadn't poked her lung.

They'd holed up at the soddy for a few days while Lou had lingered in and out of consciousness. Josh had assured him her time sleeping helped her body to heal from all the beating Klaude had instilled. Even now, the coloring on her face was turning yellow from the outlaw's fist.

Clint hadn't lingered with the rest of them, instead taking Klaude's body back to Topeka. He'd stopped back a day later, handing Caleb the reward money, and bringing along an extra mare and gear he'd requested the U.S. Marshal purchase for him.

"You about ready to mount up?" Enoch poked his head in the doorway. "We've got the horses saddled."

Lou stood, holding onto the bedpost.

She was as stubborn as an eagle grasping its talons in a large fish and not letting go.

He shoved to his feet with a sigh. Like it or not, they were heading back to Burrton Springs. He held out his arm for her.

She smiled and took it.

They hadn't been able to get any time alone with Josh and Enoch underfoot in the small soddy. A light snow had fallen for a few days, and they hadn't wanted to leave until the weather warmed some.

Outside, the other men were already mounted.

Caleb led Lou to the mare he'd purchased.

"She's sweet." Lou patted the mare's muzzle. "What's her name?"

"I thought you might like to name her." He glanced at his friends.

They grinned and kicked their horses into motion.

"What do you mean?" Lou's brown eyes drew together.

He withdrew the bills from his pocket and pressed them into her hand. "Here's the reward money for the capture of Klaude. I know it took longer than we expected, but you were a big part of rounding him up."

Her mouth gaped open for a second before she snapped it shut, just staring at the bills in her hand. "But where did the horse come from?"

He handed her the reins. "I asked Clint to purchase her for me. Saw her when I was still in Topeka. Thought she'd make a great brood mare for the ranch."

She frowned.

This conversation was not going at all the way he'd anticipated it would.

Tears streamed down her cheeks.

Were they happy tears or sad tears?

How could a fella tell?

She blinked, flicking them away. "I'm sure she'll give you a fine start to your ranch. Although you'll want a stallion too." Her cheeks flared with color, and she shifted away, putting her foot in the stirrup.

He stopped her by placing his hand on her boot. "Wait, darling."

Her brows rose.

"The horse is for you. To have on your ranch."

The tears came again.

"Except I don't have it anymore." She thrust herself onto the saddle and kicked the mare's side.

The horse sprang into action.

She what?

How had she lost the ranch?

~*~

Mr. Browning's comment made perfect sense now. Tears streamed down Ellie Lou's cheeks as she urged the horse forward, ignoring the pain from her wrapped ribs. When the bank owner had mentioned a wedding, he'd assumed she and Caleb were together somehow. But why? Was the ranch empty because Caleb had purchased it out from under her?

Hurt seared through her.

How could he?

The sound of thundering hooves thudded behind her.

She kicked the mare, not wanting to face Caleb ever again.

How could he have betrayed her? Buying her ranch when she couldn't pay off her debt and trying to appease her with a horse instead. No wonder the ranch had been abandoned when she was last there. Because its new owner had been off trying to capture Klaude.

Oh, God, why?

Trust Me.

The words echoed in her heart.

But how, Lord?

Quiet followed by the same words.

Trust Me.

"Lou, please wait." He brought Chestnut up alongside her mare, matching stride for stride as the horses galloped.

She started to bend over the horse's neck to increase their speed, but her wrapped ribs prevented her from doing the motion.

Caleb reached across the divide and grabbed the reins. "Whoa, girl."

The mare slowed her pace, coming to a halt.

Traitor.

"How could you when you knew how much it meant to me?" She hurled the words at him as if she were throwing rocks.

"I don't know what all you're thinking, but I paid off the note so you wouldn't lose your home."

Wait. He what? So, he didn't intend to take it away from her? "But Mr. Browning said something about marriage…" Heat sprang up her neck.

Caleb reached for her hand. "There are no strings attached, Lou. I wanted you to have the home that meant so much to you. Wanted to provide for you."

She let his words soak in for a minute. "But why?"

He didn't answer right away. A sad expression flickered across his face before it was gone. "I kind of thought it was obvious, Lou."

She racked her brain recalling all their conversations. He'd mentioned wanting a ranch of his own as well. Did he think they could come together and… Ellie Lou dared not voice her dreams. What if he said no? Or didn't have the same type of feeling for her? Maybe he only cared for her like a big brother. What she felt for him was not the kind of relationship she'd have with a family member. She wanted more. Much more than that. But how could she tell him? What if he said no and didn't care about her?

~*~

Caleb studied the emotions warring on Lou's face. What could he do to convince her of his love for her? He got off his horse, came over to her, and lifted her from her horse. Her startled squeak warmed his heart as he set her on her feet. He squeezed her hand and knelt on one knee. "I love you, Lou. I want to spend the rest of our lives together."

Her cheeks pinked.

"I paid off the note on your property so you wouldn't have to worry about losing it. I wanted you to feel safe. Provided for. Taken care of. I didn't want Browning to tell you about me covering the debt, because I wanted you to know there aren't any strings attached. But I hope you'll consider marrying me, Lou. Not because of the property, but because I've come to care for you deeply. I love you. You've lassoed my heart, darling. What do you say, will you marry me?"

A smile spread across her face.

He tucked her hair behind her ear, lightly touching the yellowing bruise on her cheek. He dipped his head towards her to do some more convincing of his love.

She drew back and tugged her hand free. "I'm sorry. But I can't."

His heart dropped to his toes.

Tears filled her eyes. She wrapped her arms around her middle. Had she reinjured her ribs?

He took a step towards her.

She held a hand up, halting him. "T-there's something I've never told you about my marriage to Charles."

He stilled. What did she mean?

Lou ran her upper teeth along her lower lip. Something she only did when she was nervous.

"You can tell me anything, Lou." He inched closer.

She didn't balk this time.

"W-we were married for ten years."

She'd already told him that before. What did it have to do with anything? He stayed quiet, allowing her time to settle her battling emotions. Whatever she had to say, they'd deal with it.

Lou licked her lips. "In all our time together, we, uh…" Her face turned bright red.

He stepped beside her, reaching for her hand. "Whatever happened, Lou, it's over now."

She shook her head, tears soaking her cheeks.

He wiped them gently away with a fingertip. "It's all right, darling."

"But it's not." She turned her face away. "We tried for years to conceive a child…"

Caleb stroked her back.

"We never were able to…" Her words were so quiet he had to lean closer to hear them.

"It doesn't matter, Lou. Whether the Lord sees fit to give us a child, we trust Him. I don't want to marry you just so we can have a child. I want to marry you because I love you with my whole heart."

"B-but one day when the babies don't come, you'll grow to resent me. To regret your decision to marry me." She covered her face with her hands, softly crying.

He drew her into his arms. *Lord, give me the words to get through to her. To let her understand the depth of my love.*

~*~

Ellie Lou's heart was breaking. To have found love again only to have to let it go. Her shoulders shook with sobs.

Caleb drew her into his arms and stroked her shoulders.

It's not fair, Lord. Why would You do this?

"I've learned a lot over the years and especially these past few months with knowing you, Lou." Caleb's soft words murmured against her hair.

She sniffed and shifted so she could see his face. "W-what do you mean?"

"It's been hard to trust God through the years. With losing my parents before I left for the war." The muscle in his jaw flickered.

She rested her hand on it.

He placed his hand over top of hers. "Then fighting in the war. Seeing all the sorrow and heartbreak. Getting injured." He rubbed his hand on his left shoulder, over the scar she'd seen after he'd been shot. "Then when I met up with you, I started to see God working in my life again. For so long I wandered. I didn't learn to fully trust again until Klaude shot me." He flexed his right arm.

She didn't move, not wanting to break his train of thought.

"I pushed you away because I was afraid of losing my arm. Saw the results of how it tore apart relationships during the war. I didn't want that for you. Us. I failed to trust God with you. With my life. I see how wrong I was. God spoke to my heart, urging me back to Him. To trust Him in all areas of my life. No matter what I went through." He glanced at her, his blue eyes softening. "I was really put to the test when you were taken captive by Klaude. Especially after all he'd done to everyone else." He swallowed, not continuing.

Ellie Lou squeezed his hand, praying he'd have the words to complete his thoughts.

"I had to place you in God's hands and trust Him to work when I couldn't. It was one of the hardest things I've ever had to do." He tugged her close, tipped her chin, and stared into her eyes.

Her heart quickened.

"Through it all, I've learned God worked all things together for good. My good. Our good. He saved you from Klaude…"

Caleb didn't need to verbalize the different ways God had protected her from the outlaw. Ellie Lou was very aware of the provisions God had bestowed on her.

"So even if the Lord never sees fit to give us a child, provided you agree to marry me..." He grinned and waggled his eyebrows, "…I know we can trust Him to work things for our good. Even if He brings heartache and suffering into our lives, He's trustworthy. He's there even in the midst of our pain."

Hadn't God gotten her through every difficulty she'd faced in the past year? It hadn't always looked the way she wanted it to, but God had continued to stay by her side. He'd never left her. A shiver ran down the length of her body.

"I feel He's brought us together for a reason, and I'd like to explore that together with you. I can't promise things will always be easy or we won't experience struggles. But I can promise, we'll work together to trust God no matter what we face. What do you say, Lou? Are you willing to have faith like Noah? To trust and obey the Lord by serving Him with me by your side, for the rest of our lives?"

How can I say no when he puts it like that? I'd be showing a lack of faith and trust in God if I decline Caleb's proposal because I'm afraid he might eventually regret marrying me if I don't provide a child. Am I again trying to control the situation instead of placing it in God's hands?

She bent her head. *I thought my life was over when Charles died. And then again when I lost the ranch only to find out I never did. You've provided for me every step along the way. Even through my grief, You were there. When I was trying to figure things out on my own, You were patiently waiting for me to come to You. Waiting for me to turn to You instead of floundering in all the unknowns. Forgive me, Lord, for not seeing it sooner. I trust You with my future, Lord. Even if it means I don't ever have any children. Thank You for sending Caleb to convince me, too.* Ellie Lou lifted her head and smiled. *I give my life to You, Lord. I trust you to work in every aspect of it.*

Caleb grew restless beside her, and his brow furrowed.

"Yes." She smiled at him.

"What did you say?" He cocked his head.

She ran her finger along the side of his whiskery face. "Yes, I'll marry you."

"Whoo hoo!" He whipped off his Stetson and threw it into the air. Tugging her closer, he gathered her in his arms, his lips touching hers.

Softly, gently at first.

Her heart raced, and her pulse thudded as she met him kiss for kiss. Their hearts intertwined as one, lassoing an invisible rope of trust and love.

EPILOGUE

December 7, 1878

The first wave of pain hit Ellie Lou in the middle of the night. She shouldn't have had that second helping of pie before bed. Ignoring the momentary discomfort, she rolled to her side, snuggling against Caleb's wide chest. His arms circled around her in his sleep. She tugged the blanket to her chin, relaxing in his warmth.

Nine months since she'd married him, and they'd taken up residence on the ranch. Every day she thanked the Lord for bringing Caleb into her life. For taking her on the journey to trust Him with her future because in the process she'd received a story she never would've been able to envision.

Her eyes fluttered shut only to be awakened by another pain. She placed a hand on her side as the pain radiated from her back to the front. Maybe this was more than indigestion.

She forced her errant pulse to calm. Josh had said the first stage could take a long time. No need to awaken Caleb yet. She shifted, trying to get comfortable as another pain tightened her bulging stomach. At what point had Josh said to have Caleb ride for town? Ellie Lou couldn't remember. All the details the doctor had gone over at her last appointment were a blur. She probably should've taken notes.

"Darling?" Caleb's sleep-filled voice whispered in her ear.

Another pain kept her from responding to him as she tried to breathe through the contraction.

"Lou? What's wrong?" Her husband was fully awake now.

Moonlight streamed through the window, bathing their bed in light.

She squeezed his hand, to keep from crying out.

"Is it time?" Caleb pushed back the blanket, reaching for his pants draped across the edge of the bed. He'd insisted on keeping them there so he could get ready at a moment's notice.

She'd teased him, saying first babies took long to come. That they'd have plenty of time for him to ride to town to get Josh and return. Ellie Lou panted. "Think so."

He tugged on the britches, tucking his nightshirt into them.

"The p-pains are…" She held her breath when another sharp pain hit. "C-close together."

His blue eyes widened.

She panted her way through another contraction, reaching for his hand and squeezing it tight. "D-don't leave me."

"I'd feel better if Josh were here to deliver the baby."

Ellie Lou bit her lip and shook her head. "No time."

"But I've never delivered a baby before." He crouched beside her.

She rested against the pillow, trying to catch her breath but she could feel pressure and felt the need to push. "You were there…"

Another sharp pain.

"… for Blaze's birth."

"I know sweetheart, but I didn't have to do anything. What if something goes wrong?" His face paled. "Especially when this baby is a miracle."

They'd both been surprised to learn she'd been with child just weeks after they were married. Caleb had called it a gift from God in honor of their trusting Him.

"N-need to push." She shifted her back against the headboard of the bed.

Caleb hesitated for a minute before he nodded. "Let me check first. Don't bear down yet." He shifted the covers. "I can see the head." Tears filled his eyes as he lightly rested his hand on her extended abdomen. "The next time a pain comes on, bear down as hard as you can."

She nodded, not having the energy to respond.

"That's it. Good job, sweetheart. You've got this." He grabbed a clean towel draped on the washstand beside the bed, positioning it underneath her.

Ellie Lou moaned as another contraction flared. She pushed with all her might.

"You're doing great, darling. One more push." Caleb's gaze intertwined with hers.

She gathered what little energy she had left and gave one more thrust. Something slippery brushed against her legs.

"It's a girl." Tears filled Caleb's eyes.

"Is she all right?" Her shoulders bunched. *Please, Lord, let her be healthy and strong.*

The baby let out a loud cry.

Ellie Lou's breathing eased. What a blessed sound. *Thank You, Lord.*

"She's beautiful. Just like her mama." He gathered the infant in the towel, placing her on Ellie Lou's chest.

Her arms trembled as she gathered their daughter in her arms. Tears pricked and streamed down Ellie Lou's cheeks. "Welcome, little one." She ran her finger along the tiny jaw, so much like Caleb's.

The infant scrunched her eyes as she cried.

Ellie Lou jiggled her. "There's no need to cry, sweetheart. Mama's here." She smiled at her husband. "Papa is too." Her heart surged with love. For their new baby. For Caleb. For her Heavenly Father who taught them how to have faith like Noah.

~*~

Caleb eased on the bed a while later, careful not to awaken the baby. He wrapped his arms around Lou, kissing her on the forehead. "You did a great job, little mama."

His wife snuggled close to him, leaning over, and kissing his lips.

Emotions surged through him. The Lord had blessed them in so many ways. His throat tightened.

"What should we call her?" Lou shifted the baby into his arms.

He gathered the bundle close to him, staring at his daughter's big brown eyes. Just like her mother's. Both of their features could be seen in the infant's little face. Caleb smiled as his daughter watched him. "I think we should call her Faith. God has taught us a lot this past year." He caught Lou's gaze.

She smiled and yawned, leaning hard against his shoulder. "I like it."

"Someday we'll tell her the story about how we learned to walk by faith and not by sight. How we learned to trust and obey our Heavenly Father." He traced his finger along the infant's tiny mouth.

"And we'll teach her the importance of having faith like Noah. Trusting God to write the story of her life instead of trying to write her own." She kissed Caleb's cheek. "I can't think of a finer name than Faith."

Note from the Author

On January 1-3 and January 6-8, 1886, a set of blizzards swept across the plains in what would become known as "The Great Blizzard of 1886." Temperatures dropped to 30 degrees below zero with negative wind chills. Drifts as high as twelve feet or more were common throughout the state of Kansas. It's estimated over seventy-five percent of the livestock were decimated during this storm. While I adjusted the year for the blizzard to suit my story, I tried to stick as close to the details of the historical event as much as I possibly could.

Thank you for journeying with me to Burrton Springs. I pray the Lord has touched your heart and encouraged you through Jules', Annie's, Gertrude's, and Ellie Lou's stories. God bless.

A Devotional Moment

Trust in the Lord with all thine heart; and lean not unto thine own understanding. In all thy ways acknowledge him, and he shall direct thy paths. ~ Proverbs 3:5-6

Trust is not readily given these days; we tend not to believe the trustworthiness of others until they've proven themselves. Unfortunately, this wariness to trust can carry over into our faith in God. Because people so often let us down, we become stingy with our trust in anyone. But with God, we need to open our hearts and allow Him in so that we can receive the solace and promises He's already promised, including the salvation that brings eternal life.

In **Convincing Lou**, the protagonists have fallen upon hard times. Almost everyone around them, and circumstances outside their control have made them lose their trust in every aspect of their lives. They are defeated at every turn, with poor decisions compounding their troubles. When disaster strikes, they must dig deep in their hearts to find God, and to trust that He will guide their steps to shape their lives into a better and brighter future.

Have you ever felt as if nothing you did went right? People betrayed you, Job offers fell through, you failed tests that were supposed to be easy to pass? Perhaps you've made some poor decisions that landed you in a bad place, relationship, or situation. When "everything" goes wrong, it's easy to lose hope and to give up and resign yourself to living a sad life. It's during these low times that it's even more important to lean on God. Remember that even if no one else in the world is willing to help you, He will…even if that help comes as the strength to endure your current situation so that you can learn and grow and experience a happier, brighter tomorrow.

HEAVENLY FATHER, HELP ME TO STEP BACK FROM POOR CHOICES AND TAKE THE TIME TO PRAY AND FELLOWSHIP WITH YOU SO THAT I MAY SEEK THE RIGHT PATH, THE ONE WHERE YOU HOLD ME UP, SUSTAIN ME, AND MAKE A BETTER FUTURE FOR ME. IN JESUS' NAME I PRAY, AMEN.

Thank you

We appreciate you reading this White Rose Publishing title. For other inspirational stories, please visit our on-line bookstore at www.pelicanbookgroup.com.

For questions or more information, contact us at customer@pelicanbookgroup.com.

White Rose Publishing
Where Faith is the Cornerstone of Love™
an imprint of Pelican Book Group
www.PelicanBookGroup.com

Connect with Us
www.facebook.com/Pelicanbookgroup
www.twitter.com/pelicanbookgrp

To receive news and specials, subscribe to our bulletin
http://pelink.us/bulletin

May God's glory shine through
this inspirational work of fiction.

AMDG

You Can Help!

At Pelican Book Group it is our mission to entertain readers with fiction that uplifts the Gospel. It is our privilege to spend time with you awhile as you read our stories.

We believe you can help us to bring Christ into the lives of people across the globe. And you don't have to open your wallet or even leave your house!

Here are 3 simple things you can do to help us bring illuminating fiction™ to people everywhere.

1) If you enjoyed this book, write a positive review. Post it at online retailers and websites where readers gather. And share your review with us at reviews@pelicanbookgroup.com (this does give us permission to reprint your review in whole or in part.)

2) If you enjoyed this book, recommend it to a friend in person, at a book club or on social media.

3) If you have suggestions on how we can improve or expand our selection, let us know. We value your opinion. Use the contact form on our web site or e-mail us at customer@pelicanbookgroup.com

God Can Help!

Are you in need? The Almighty can do great things for you. Holy is His Name! He has mercy in every generation. He can lift up the lowly and accomplish all things. Reach out today.

Do not fear: I am with you; do not be anxious: I am your God. I will strengthen you, I will help you, I will uphold you with my victorious right hand.

~Isaiah 41:10 (NAB)

We pray daily, and we especially pray for everyone connected to Pelican Book Group—that includes you! If you have a specific need, we welcome the opportunity to pray for you. Share your needs or praise reports at http://pelink.us/pray4us

Free eBook Offer

We're looking for booklovers like you to partner with us! Join our team of influencers today and periodically receive free eBooks!

For more information
Visit http://pelicanbookgroup.com/booklovers

www.ingramcontent.com/pod-product-compliance
Lightning Source LLC
Chambersburg PA
CBHW030357310726
48979CB00001B/337

* 9 7 8 1 5 2 2 3 0 4 8 6 9 *